The Sweet Hereafter

Also by Russell Banks

Affliction
Success Stories
Continental Drift
The Relation of My Imprisonment
Trailerpark
The Book of Jamaica
The New World
Hamilton Stark
Family Life
Searching for Survivors

The Sweet Hereafter

A Novel by

Russell Banks

HarperCollins*Publishers*

Portions of this novel have appeared in *Adirondack Life, North American Review,* and the *Ontario Review.*

FIRST EDITION

Designed by Cassandra J. Pappas

Library of Congress Cataloging-in-Publication Data

Banks, Russell, 1940–
    The sweet hereafter / Russell Banks.—1st ed.
      p. cm.
    ISBN 0-06-016703-3 (cloth)
    I. Title.
PS3552.A49S94   1991
813'.54—dc20   90-56404

91 92 93 94 95 CC/RRD 10 9 8 7 6 5 4 3 2 1

for Chase

By homely gift and hindered Words
The human heart is told
Of Nothing—
"Nothing" is the force
That renovates the World—

Emily Dickinson (#1563)

The Sweet Hereafter

Dolores Driscoll

A dog—it was a dog I saw for certain. Or thought I saw. It was snowing pretty hard by then, and you can see things in the snow that aren't there, or aren't exactly there, but you also can't see some of the things that are there, so that by God when you do see something, you react anyhow, erring on the distaff side, if you get my drift. That's my training as a driver, but it's also my temperament as a mother of two grown sons and wife to an invalid, and that way when I'm wrong at least I'm wrong on the side of the angels.

It was like the ghost of a dog I saw, a reddish-brown blur, much smaller than a deer—which is what you'd expect to see out there that early—although the same gingerbread color as a deer it was, moving fast behind the cloud of snow falling between us, then slow, and then stopped altogether in the middle of the road, like it was trying to make up its mind whether to go on or go back.

1

I couldn't see *it* clearly, so can't say what it was for sure, but I saw the *blur* clearly, that's what I mean to say, and that's what I reacted to. These things have to happen faster than you can think about them, because if they don't, you're going to be locked in place just like that dog or deer or whatever the hell it was, and you'll get smacked head-on the same as that dog would have if I hadn't hit the brake and pulled the wheel without thinking.

But there's no point now to lingering over the dog, whether it *was* a dog or a tiny deer, or even an optical illusion, which, to be absolutely truthful, now seems likeliest. All that matters is that I saw something I didn't expect out there and didn't particularly identify at the time, there being no time for that—so let's just say it was *like* a dog, one of those small red spaniels, smaller than a setter, the size of a kid in a rust-colored snowsuit, and I did what anyone with half a brain would have done: I tried to avoid hitting it.

It was in first light and, as I said, blowing snow by then, but when I started my route that morning, when I left the house, it was still dark, of course, and no snow falling. You could sniff the air, though, and smell it coming, but despite that, I had thought at first that it was too cold to snow. Which is what I said to Abbott, who is my husband and doesn't get out of the house very much because of his being in a wheelchair, so I have this habit of reporting the weather to him, more or less, every morning when I first step out of the kitchen onto the back porch.

"I smell snow," I said, and leaned down and checked

the thermometer by the door. It's posted low on the frame of the storm door, so Abbott can scoot over and open the inside door and check the temperature anytime he wants. "Seventeen below," I told him. "Too cold to snow."

Abbott was at one time an excellent carpenter, but in 1984 he had a stroke, and although he has recovered somewhat, he's still pretty much housebound and has trouble talking normally and according to some people is incomprehensible, yet I myself understand him perfectly. No doubt it's because I know that his mind is clear. The way Abbott has handled the consequences of his stroke is sufficient evidence that he is a very courageous man, but he was always a logical person with a lively interest in the world around him, so I make an effort to bring him as much information about the world as I can. It's the least I can do.

"Never . . . that . . . cold," he said. He's worked out a way of talking with just the left side of his mouth, but he stammers some and spits a bit and makes a grimace that some people would find embarrassing and so would look away and as a result not fully understand him. I myself find his way of talking very interesting, actually, and even charming. And not just because I'm used to it. To tell the truth, I don't think I'll ever get used to it, which is why it's so interesting and attractive to me. Me, I'm a talker, and consequently like a lot of talkers tend to say things I don't mean. But Abbott, more than anyone else I know, has to make his words count, almost like a poet, and because he's passed so close to death he has a clarity about life that most of us can't even imagine.

"North . . . Pole's . . . under . . . snow," he said.

No arguing with that. I grabbed my coffee thermos, pecked him with a kiss and waved him goodbye as usual, shut the door and went out to the barn and got my bus started. I kept an extra battery and jumper cables in the kitchen, just in case, but the old girl was fine that morning and cranked right up. By nature I'm a careful person and not overly optimistic, especially when it comes to machinery and tools; I keep everything in tiptop condition, with plenty of backup. Batteries, tires, oil, antifreeze, the whole bit. I treated that bus like it was my own, maybe even better, for obvious reasons, but also because that's my temperament. I'm the kind of person who always follows the manual. No shortcuts.

Weather, meaning snow or ice, stopped me numerous times a year—of course, those were days that Gary Dillinger, the principal, called school off anyhow, so it didn't count—but in twenty-two years I did not miss a single morning or afternoon pickup because of a mechanical breakdown, and although I went through three buses in that time, it was only to have each bus replaced with a larger one, as the town grew. I started back in 1968, as a courtesy and convenience, with my own brand-new Dodge station wagon, carting my two boys, who were then in Sam Dent School, and scooping up with them the six or eight other children who lived on the Bartlett Hill Road side of town. Then the district made my route official, enlarging it somewhat, and gave me a salary and purchased me a GMC that had twenty-four seats. Finally, in 1987, to handle the baby boomers' babies, I'd guess you'd call them, the district had to get me the International fifty-seater. My old Dodge wagon finally gave out at 168,000 miles, and I drove it behind the barn, drained it, and put it up on blocks, and now for my personal vehicle and for running Abbott over to Lake Placid for his therapy I drive an almost new Plymouth Voyager van. It's got a lift for his chair, and he can lock the chair into the passenger's side and sit next to me up front, which gives him a distinct pleasure. The old GMC they use for hauling the high school kids over to Placid.

Luckily, our barn being plenty large enough and standing empty, I was always able to park the bus at home overnight, where I could look after it in a proper way. Not that I didn't trust Billy Ansel and his Vietnam vets at the Sunoco, where the district's two other buses were kept and serviced, to take good care of my bus; I did—they are intelligent mechanics and thoughtful men, especially Billy himself, and anything more complicated than a tune-up I happily turned over to them. But when it came to daily maintenance, I was like the pilot of an airplane—no one was going to treat my vehicle as carefully as I did myself.

That morning was typical, as I said, and the bus started up instantly, even though it was minus seventeen out, and I took off from our place halfway up the hill to commence my day. The bus I had given the name Shoe to, which is just something I do, because the kids seemed to like it when they could personalize the thing. I think it made going to school a little more pleasurable for them, especially the younger children, some of whose home lives were not exactly sweetness and light, if you know what I mean.

My old Dodge wagon, which was a masculine-type

car, had been nicknamed Boomer by my own kids during a period when the springs were bad. Since the district was not then paying for repairs, I couldn't afford to get them replaced right away, causing the vehicle to make a booming sound when it bottomed out on the washboard ruts on Bartlett Hill Road, which at that time had not yet been paved. I noted how fast the other children seized on the use of the name, asking me, "How's ol' Boomer today?" and suchlike when I picked them up, as if the vehicle was a horse they felt affectionate toward. So later, when my sons were in high school and I got the GMC, I made a little act of introducing it to the children as Rufus, Boomer's larger, dumber cousin, which is how it seemed to me and to the children as well. The International got named Shoe because when I drove it with a load of thirty, thirty-five kids I felt like the old woman who lived in a shoe who had so many children she didn't know what to do, and it tickled the kids to hear me tell it, and in no time they were slapping old Shoe on the side as they lined up at their stop to climb aboard, saying things like "Shoe sleep good last night?" "Shoe eat a good breakfast this morning?" That sort of remark. By staying away from the cutesy names, sticking with names that were slightly humorous, I was able to get the older kids, especially the boys, who could be curt, to go along with the game, making the ride more cheerful for everyone that way. It was something we could all participate in together, which was a value I tried to promote among young people.

My first stop that morning was at the top of Bartlett

Hill Road, where it branches into Avalanche Road and McNeil. I pulled over and made my turnaround so the bus was facing east and waited for the Lamston kids to come down the hill on McNeil. The three of them, since the day the oldest, Harold, started school, always got to the stop late, no matter how often I threatened to leave them if they weren't there waiting for me, so eventually I just made it a habit to come a little early and pour myself a cup of coffee and wait. It's like when they were born their clocks were set permanently five minutes behind everybody else's, so the only way you could meet them on time was to set your own clock five minutes early.

I didn't mind. It gave me a chance to enjoy my second cup of coffee in solitude in the bus with the heater running. It was peaceful, way up there on top of Bartlett Hill looking east toward Giant and Noonmark and Wolf Jaw, watching the sky lighten, with the mountains outlined in black against this milky stripe of light widening from the horizon. Made you appreciate living here, instead of some milder place, where I suppose life comes somewhat easier. Down in the valley, you could see the house lights of Sam Dent coming on one by one, and along Routes 9 and 73 the headlights of a few cars flashed like fireflies as people headed out to work.

I've spent my whole life in this town, and I can safely say I know everyone in it, even the newcomers, even the summer people. Well, not all the summer people; just the regulars, who own their own houses and arrive early and leave late. Them I know because when school's out I work part time sorting their mail in the post office and helping Eden Schraft deliver it. That is, I used to, before the accident. Now I work in Lake Placid, driving for the hotels.

That morning, while I waited for the Lamstons, I was thinking about my sons. Reginald and William. We always called them that, never Reggie or Billy; I think it helped them grow up faster. Not that I was in a hurry for them to grow up. I just didn't want them to become the kind of men who think of themselves as little boys and then tend to act that way when you need them to act like adults. No, thanks. William, who is the younger, is in the army in Virginia and was just back from Panama then, and although he had not been wounded or anything, he was sounding a little strange and distant to me, which is understandable, I suppose. He hadn't been shipped out to Arabia yet. Reginald was having some marital problems, you might say, in that his wife, Tracy, was bored with her job at the Plattsburgh Marriott, where she worked as a receptionist, and wanted to get pregnant. As he was still in night school at Plattsburgh State and wasn't making much as a draftsman, he preferred to wait a few years before having a child. I told him why didn't he tell Tracy to find a job that wasn't boring. That irritated him. We were talking on the phone; I guess she was out somewhere. "Ma, it's not that *simple*," he said, as if he thought I was simpleminded. Well, I knew it was complicated—I've been married twenty-eight years—but what else could I say? Anyhow, I was feeling cut off from my sons, which is unusual and gives me an empty feeling in the stomach when it happens, almost like hunger, and I wanted to do something to change it, but nothing would come to my mind.

Then suddenly there they were, the Lamstons, the two older boys, Harold and Jesse, banging on the door, and the little girl, Sheila, who was barely six, running along behind. I flipped open the door, and they marched in, silent, sober-faced, as always, wearing their hand-me-down snow-suits, lugging lunchboxes and schoolbooks, all three plumping down next to one another halfway back. They had their choice of seats, but they always put themselves behind me precisely in the middle of the bus, between the boys, most of whom preferred to sit way in the back, and the girls, who tended to cluster in the front near me, while whoever was last to get picked up took whatever seats were left, usually those nearest the Lamstons.

I never exactly liked the Lamston kids; they made it hard. But I felt sorry for them, so instead I acted as if I was very fond of them. They were what you call uncommunicative, all three, although they certainly communicated fine with one another, always whispering back and forth in a way that made you think they were criticizing you. I think they felt different from the other kids. Due to their father, Kyle Lamston, a sometime housepainter who was a drinker and was known in town for his propensity to commit acts of public violence. Their mother, Doreen, had the hangdog look of a woman who has to comfort such a man. The Lamstons were field-mouse poor and lived until recently in a trailer on a lot a half mile in on McNeil Road. Poverty and house trailers are not uncommon in Sam Dent, however.

No, I'm sure it was the violence that made those children act like they were different from the others. They had secrets.

Little, pinch-faced kids, a solemn trio they were, commiserating with one another in whispers behind my back while I drove and every now and then tried to chat them up. "How're you this morning? All ready to read 'n' write 'n' 'rithmetic?" That sort of thing. Make myself sick. "Pretty damned cold this morning coming down the hill, I bet." Nothing. Silence.

"Harold, you planning to play little league this summer?" I asked him. Still nothing, like I was talking to myself or was on the radio.

Most days I just ignored them, left them to themselves, since that's clearly what they wanted, and whistled my way down the hill to the second stop, treating it in my mind like it was my first stop coming up and not the second and I was still alone in the bus. But that day for some reason I wanted to get a rise out of at least one of the three. Maybe because I felt so cut off from my own children; maybe out of some pure perversity. Who knows now? Fixing motives is like fixing blame—the further away from the act you get, the harder it is to single out one thing as having caused it.

Their father, Kyle Lamston, was a man I'd known since he was a boy in town; his family had come from over the border, Ontario someplace, and settled here in the early 1950s, when there were still a few dairy farms left in the area that kept unskilled people working year round. The only Canadians you see nowadays are tourists. Kyle was a promising youth, athletic, good-looking, smart enough, but he got into alcohol early, when he was still going through the turbulence and anger of a male teenager, and like a lot of unruly boys, he seemed to get stuck there.

Doreen was a Pomeroy from Lake Placid, a sweet little ding-a-ling of a girl, and she fell for Kyle and before she knew it was pregnant and situated in a trailer up on McNeil Road on a woodlot Kyle's father had once owned, with Kyle coming home later and later every night from the Spread Eagle or the Rendez-Vous, drunk and feeling trapped by life and blaming her, no doubt, for that, and taking it out on her.

Now he was in his thirties and already gone to fat, and after half a dozen DWI convictions, permanently without a driver's license, making it difficult for him to get off that hill and go to work, of course. What little money Kyle did earn housepainting, he spent most of it on booze at the Spread or the Rendez-Vous. Food stamps, welfare, and local and church charity kept them more or less fed, clothed, and sheltered, but the Lamstons were a family that, after a good start, had come to be characterized by permanent overall failure, and people generally shunned them for it. In return, they withheld themselves. It was their only point of pride, I suppose. Which is why the children behaved so sadly aloof, even to me. And who could begrudge them?

"Harold!" I said. "You hear me ask you a question?" I turned around and cut him a look.

"Leave us alone!" he said, coming right back at me with those cold blue eyes of his. His brother, Jesse, sat by the window, looking out as if he could see into the dark.

Harold was trying to wipe his baby sister's red face with the end of his scarf. She had been crying in that silent way of a very sad and frightened person, and I suddenly felt terrible and wished I had kept my big mouth shut.

"I'm sorry," I said in a low voice, and turned back to my driving.

From the Lamstons' stop at McNeil and Avalanche, the route ran west along the ridge into the dark, with the black heights of Big and Little Hawk on your right and the valley and town of Sam Dent on your left, out to the crest of the hill, where I picked up a kid I actually liked personally a whole lot and was always pleased to see. Bear Otto. He was an energetic, oversized, eleven-year-old Abenaki Indian boy adopted by Hartley and Wanda Otto. For years they had tried and failed to conceive a child of their own, until finally they gave up and somehow found Bear in an orphanage over in Vermont, and I guess because Hartley was quarter Indian himself, a Western-type Indian, Shawnee or Sioux or something, they were able to adopt him right off. Now, three years later—which is how it often happens, as if the arrival of an adopted child somehow loosens up the new parents—Wanda was suddenly pregnant.

Bear was ready and waiting for me, and the second I swung open the door he jumped straight into the bus from the ground, as if he had been planning it, and grinned in triumph and held out the flat of his hand for a high five, like a black kid from the city. I slapped it, and he said, "Yo, Dolores!" and bounced back down the aisle and sat in the middle of the last seat with his legs stretched out, raiding his lunchbox and waiting for the other boys. He had a round burnt-orange baby face with a perpetual peaceful smile on it, as if someone had just told him a terrific joke and he was telling it over again to himself. His hair, which was straight and coal black and long in back, hung in bangs across his broad forehead. Bear was supposed to be only eleven, but because of his size he looked thirteen or fourteen. A stocky boy, but not fat, he was built like one of those sumo wrestlers. Numerous times, in the quick bristly quarrels that boys like to get into, I had seen him play the calm, good-natured peacemaker, and I admired him and imagined that he would turn into a wonderful man. He was one of those rare children who bring out the best in people instead of the worst.

The Ottos were what you might call hippies, if you considered only their hair and clothing, mannerisms, politics, house, et cetera—their general life-style, let us say, which was extreme and somewhat innovative. But in fact they were model citizens. Regular at the town meetings, where they offered sound opinions in a respectful way, and members of the voluntary fire brigade. They even took the CPR training and the emergency first aid courses offered at the school, and they always helped out at the various fund-raising bazaars and carnivals in town, although they were not themselves churchgoers. They both were tall and thin and moved and talked slowly. Vegetarians, they were.

Hartley, who was a furniture-maker for a company up in Keeseville, had a thick, unkempt beard and wore his hair in a long ponytail, which to me was a little pathetic-looking, now that he was turning gray. Wanda, who made pots with sticks and straw stuck into holes in the clay and baskets with

13

tubes of clay in the straw—very original items, which she sold at fairs around the state—wore old-fashioned spectacles and had hair like that woman Morticia, the mother on *The Addams Family* TV show. Their house was a dome, half buried in the side of Little Hawk. They had built it themselves, a peculiar-looking structure, although people who have been inside tell me it is quite large and comfortable, if dark. Like the inside of an army field tent, I'm told. The Ottos had a special interest in protecting the environment, as you might expect, and were from someplace downstate and I believe were college educated. There were persistent rumors that they grew and smoked marijuana, which, as far as I'm concerned, was their business, since nobody else got hurt by it.

I keep saying "was," as if they are no longer with us, like the Lamstons, who have moved to Plattsburgh. But in fact the Ottos are still here in Sam Dent, living in their dome, Hartley making his Adirondack porch chairs up in Keeseville and Wanda her straw pots and clay baskets at home. She has delivered her baby safely, thank God, a healthy little boy (whose name I don't know, since I don't see them much anymore and don't keep track of those things as much as I used to). But I'm telling about life in Sam Dent before the accident, and so much has changed since then that it's difficult for me to describe people or things concerned with the accident, except in terms that put them into the past.

Beyond the Ottos' and over the crest of Bartlett Hill, the road drops fairly fast, and I made three stops in short order, so I barely got the bus out of first gear before having to hit the brakes and pull over again. These were the Hamilton kids, the Prescotts, and the Walkers, seven in all, little kids, first, second, and third graders, mostly, the children of young couples living in small houses that they built piecemeal themselves on lots cut out of a tract of land that had once belonged to my father and grandfather.

The acreage, along with the old family house and barn, passed to me and Abbott when my dad died back in 1974 (my ma died early, when I was nineteen), and then in '84, when Abbott had his stroke, we sold off most of the uphill land that fronted on the road. Sold too cheaply, it turned out, as it was a few years too soon to take advantage of what they call the second-home land boom. But we needed the money right then and there, for Abbott's hospital bills and so on, since his insurance had run out so fast, and those young couples needed land to build their homes to raise their children in.

I've never especially regretted it. I'd rather watch the little tatty Capes and ranches of local folks, people I've known since they were children themselves, going up on that land than the high-tech summer houses and A-frame ski lodges with decks and hot tubs and so on built by rich yuppies from New York City who don't give a damn for this town or the people in it.

I've got nothing against outsiders per se, you understand. It's just that you have to love a town before you can live in it right, and you have to live in it before you can love it right. Otherwise, you're a parasite of sorts. I know that

the tourists, the summer people, bring a load of season-
al cash to town, but as Abbott likes to say, "Short . . .
term . . . profits . . . make . . . long . . . term . . . losses."
Which is true about a lot of things.

With the Hamilton, Prescott, and Walker kids safely
aboard, I drove slowly past my own house, where I could
see from the light in the kitchen window that Abbott was
on his second cup of coffee and listening to the radio
news—he likes the National Public Radio news from Burlington, which is one of his sources of unusual facts. He
listens to the radio the way some people read the newspaper—he looks right at it, his brow furrowed, as if commit-
ting what he hears to memory. He hates television. Which
is unusual in an invalid, I understand, but may account for
the fact that he is rarely depressed by his condition. He
always had more of a radio personality than a television
personality anyhow. I gave him a blast of the horn, as I
always do, and rolled past the house.

By now there was some noise in the bus, the early
morning sounds of children practicing at being adults, making themselves known to one another and to themselves in
their small voices (some of them not so small)—asking
questions, arguing, making exchanges, gossiping, bragging,
pleading, courting, threatening, testing—doing everything
we ourselves do, the way puppies and kittens at play mimic
grown dogs and cats at work. It's not altogether peaceful or
sweet, any more than the noises adults make are peaceful
and sweet, but it doesn't do any serious harm. And because
you can listen to children without fear, the way you can

watch puppies tumble and bite and kittens sneak up on one another and spring without worrying that they'll be hurt by it, the talk of children can be very instructive. I guess it's because they play openly at what we grownups do seriously and in secret.

There was enough light, a predawn grayness, so that I could by this time see the lowered sky, and I knew that it was going to snow. The roads were dry and ice-free—it had stayed cold and hadn't snowed for over a week—and because the temperature was so low, I figured that the new snow would be dry and hard, so was not concerned that I had not put chains on the tires that morning. I knew I'd be needing them for the afternoon run, though, and groaned silently to myself—putting on chains in the cold is tedious and hard on the hands. You have to remove your gloves to snap the damned things together, at least I do, and the circulation in my fingers—due to cigarettes, Abbott tells me, although I quit fifteen years ago—is not good anymore.

But for now I was not worried. You drive these roads for forty-five years in every season and all kinds of weather, there's not much can surprise you. Which is one of the reasons I was given this job in 1968 and rehired every year since—the others being my considerable ability as a driver, pure and simple, and my reliability and punctuality. And, of course, my affection for children and ease with them. This is not bragging; it's simple fact. No two ways about it—I was the most qualified school bus driver in the district.

By the time I reached the bottom of Bartlett Hill Road, where it enters Route 73 by the old mill, I had half my load, over twenty kids, on board. They had walked to their places on Bartlett Hill Road from the smaller roads and lanes that run off it, bright little knots of three and four children gathered by a cluster of mailboxes to wait there for me—like berries waiting to be plucked, I sometimes thought as I made my descent, clearing the hillside of its children. I always enjoyed watching the older children, the seventh and eighth graders, play their music on their Walkmans and portable radios and dance around each other, flirting and jostling for position in their numerous and mysterious pecking orders, impossible for me or any adult to understand, while the younger boys and girls soberly studied and evaluated the older kids' moves for their own later use. I liked the way the older boys slicked their hair back in precise dips and waves, and the way the girls dolled themselves up with lipstick and eyeliner, as if they weren't already as beautiful as they would ever be again.

When they climbed onto the bus, they had to shut their radios off. It was one of the three rules I laid down every year the first day of school. Rule one: No tape players or radios playing inside the bus. Headsets, Walkmans, were permissible, of course, but I could not abide half a dozen tiny radio speakers squawking three kinds of rock 'n' roll behind me. Not with all the other noises those kids made. Rule number two: No fighting. Anyone fights, he by God walks. And no matter who starts it, both parties walk. Girls the same as boys. They could argue and holler at one another all they wanted, but let one of them strike another, and both of them were on the road in seconds. I usually had to enforce this rule no more than once a year, and after that the kids enforced it themselves. Or if they did hit each other, they did it silently, since the victim knew that he or she would have to walk too. I was well aware that I couldn't ever stop them altogether from striking each other, but at least I could make them conscious of it, which is a start. Rule number three: No throwing things. Not food, not paper airplanes, not hats or mittens—nothing. That rule was basically so I could drive without sudden undue distraction. For safety's sake.

I'm a fairly large woman, taller and heavier than even the biggest eighth-grade boy (although Bear Otto was soon going to be bigger than I am), and my voice is sharp, so it was not especially difficult, with only these few rules, to maintain order and establish tranquillity. Also, I made no attempt to teach them manners, no moves to curb or restrain their language—I figured they heard enough of that from their teachers and parents—and I think this kept them loose enough that they did not feel particularly restricted. Besides, I have always liked listening to the way kids talk when they're not trying to please or deceive an adult. I just perched up there in the driver's seat and drove, letting them forget all about me, while I listened to their jumble of words, songs, and shouts and cries, and it was almost as if I were not present, or were invisible, or as if I were a child again myself, a child blessed or cursed (I'm not sure which) with foresight, with the ability to see the closing off that adulthood would bring, the pleasures, the shame, the secrets, the fearfulness. The eventual silence; that too.

At Route 73 by the old mill, I banged a left and headed north along the Ausable River, picking up the valley kids. There was always a fair amount of vehicular traffic on 73 at this hour, mostly local people driving to work, which never presented a problem, but sometimes there were downstate skiers up early on their way to a long weekend at Lake Placid and Whiteface. Them I had to watch out for, especially today, this being a Friday—they were generally young urban-type drivers and were not used to coming up suddenly on a school bus stopped at the side of the road to pick up children, and the flashing red lights on the bus didn't seem to register somehow, as if they thought all they had to do was slow down a little and then pass me by. They thought they were up in the mountains and no people lived here. To let them know, I kept a notebook and pen next to my seat, and whenever one of those turkeys blew past me in his Porsche or BMW, I took his number and later phoned it in to Wyatt Pitney at state police headquarters in Marlowe. Wyatt usually managed to get their attention.

Anyhow, this morning I was stopped across from the Bide-a-Wile Motel, which is owned and operated by Risa and Wendell Walker, and Risa was walking their little boy, Sean, across Route 73, as is customary. Sean had some kind of learning disability—he was close to ten but seemed more like a very nervous, frightened five or six, an unusually runtish boy and delicate, with a sickly pale complexion and huge dark eyes. He was a strange little fellow, but you couldn't help liking him and feeling protective toward him. Apparently, although he was way behind all the other kids his age in school and was too fragile and nervous to play at sports, he was expert at playing video games and much admired for it by the other children. A wizard, they say, with fabulous eye-hand coordination, and when sitting in front of a video game, he was supposed to be capable of scary concentration. It was probably the only time he felt competent and was not lonely.

It had started to snow, light windblown flecks falling like bits of wood ash. Risa had her down parka over her nightgown and bathrobe and was wearing slippers, and she held Sean by the hand and carefully walked him from the motel office, where they had an apartment in back, to the road, which, although it's only two lanes, is actually a state highway along there, the main truck route connecting Placid and the Saranac region to the Northway.

There were no cars or trucks in sight as Risa brought her son across to the bus. He was Risa's and Wendell's only child and the frail object of all their attention. Wendell was a pleasantly withdrawn sort of man who seemed to have given up on life, but Risa, I knew, still had dreams. In warm weather, she'd be out there roofing the motel or repainting the signs, while Wendell stayed inside and watched baseball on TV. They had a lot of financial problems—the motel had about a dozen units and was old and in shabby condition; they had bought it in a foreclosure sale eight or ten years before, and I don't think they'd put up the No Vacancy sign once in that time. (Sam Dent is one of those towns that's on the way to somewhere else, and people get this far, they usually keep going.) Also, I think that the Walkers' marriage was shaky. Judging from what happened to them after the accident, it was probably just that motel and their love for the boy, Sean, that had bound them.

I flung open the door, and the child, because he was

so small, stepped up with difficulty, and when he got to the landing he turned and did an unusual thing. Like a scared baby who wanted his mother to lift him up and hug him, he held his arms out to Risa and said, "I want to stay with you."

Risa had large dark circles under her eyes, as if she hadn't slept well, or at all, for that matter, and her hair was tangled and matted, and for a second I wondered if she had a drinking problem. "Go on now," she said to the boy in a weary voice. "Go on."

The kids sitting near the door were watching Sean, surprised and puzzled by his behavior, maybe embarrassed by it, since he was doing what so many of them would sometimes like to do but did not dare, certainly not in public like this. One of the eighth-grade girls, Nichole Burnell, who was sitting next to the door and has a wonderful maternal streak, squinched over a few inches and patted the seat next to her and said, "C'mon, Sean, sit next to me."

With his large eyes fixed on Risa's face, the boy edged sideways toward Nichole and finally sat, but still he watched his mother, as if he was frightened. Not for himself but for her. "Is he okay?" I asked Risa. Normally he just marched on board and found himself a seat and stared out the window for the whole trip. A very private boy enjoying his thoughts and fancies, thinking maybe about his video games.

"I don't know. He's fine, I mean. Not sick or anything. It's just one of those mornings, I guess. We all have them, Dolores, don't we?" She made a wistful smile.

"By Jesus, I sure do!" I said, trying to cheer the woman

up, although in fact I almost never had those mornings myself, so long as I had the school bus to drive. It's almost impossible to say how important and pleasurable that job was to me. Though I liked being at home with Abbott and had the post office and mail carrier job to get me through the summers, I could hardly wait till school started again in September and I could get back out there in the early morning light and start up my bus and commence to gather the children of the town and carry them to school. I have what you call a sanguine personality. That's what Abbott calls it.

"Are *you* okay, Risa?" I asked.

She looked at me and sighed. Woman to woman. "You want to buy a good used motel?" she said. She looked across the road at the row of empty units. Not a car in the lot, except their Wagoneer. It's the Holiday Inns and the Marriotts that keep folks like the Walkers from making a living.

"Winter's been tough, eh?"

"No more than usual, I guess. The usual just gets harder and harder, though."

"I guess it does," I said. A big Grand Union sixteen-wheeler had come up behind me and stopped. "But I got enough problems of my own, honey," I said. "Last thing I need is a motel." We were talking finances, not husbands— or at least I was. I suspected she was talking husband, however. "I got to get moving," I said, "before the snow blows."

"Yes. It will snow some today. Six to eight inches by nightfall."

I thought about the chains again. Sean was still watching his mother with that strange grief-stricken expression on his small, bony face, and she waved limply at him, like she was dismissing him, and stepped away. Shutting the door with one hand, I released the brake with the other, waited a second for Risa to cross in front of the bus, and pulled slowly out. I heard the air brakes of the sixteen-wheeler hiss as the driver chunked into gear and, checking the side mirror, saw him move into line behind me.

Then suddenly Sean shrieked, *"Mommy!"* and he was all over me, scrambling across my lap to the window, and I glimpsed Risa off to my left, leaping out of the way of a red Saab that seemed to have bolted out of nowhere. It had come around the bend in front of me and the truck and hadn't slowed a bit as I drew back onto the road, and the driver must have felt squeezed and had accelerated and had just missed clipping Risa as she crossed to the other side. I hit the brakes, and thank God the driver of the truck behind me did too, managing to pull up an inch or two from my rear.

"Sean! Sit the hell down!" I yelled. "She's okay! Now sit down," I said, and he obeyed.

I slid my window open and called to Risa. "You get his number?" All I'd caught was that the car was a tomato-red Saab with a ski rack on top.

She was shaken, standing there white-faced in the motel lot with her arms wrapped around herself. She shook her head no, turned away, and walked slowly back to the office. I drew a couple of deep breaths and checked Sean, who was seated now but still craning and peering wide-eyed after his mother. Nichole had him on her lap, with her arms around his narrow shoulders.

"There's a lot of damn fool idiots out there, Sean," I said. "I guess you got a right to worry." I smiled at him, but he only glared back at me, as if I was to blame.

Again, I put the bus into first gear and started moving cautiously down the road, with the Grand Union truck rumbling along behind. I said, "I'm sorry, Sean. I'm really sorry." That was all I could think of to say.

There were half a dozen more stops along the valley, and then I turned right onto Staples Mill Road and made my way uphill to the ridge, where you get a terrific view east and south toward Limekiln and Avalanche mountains. It's mostly state forest up there, not many houses, and the few you see are old, built back before the Adirondack Park was created.

The snow was falling lightly now, hard dry flakes floating on the breeze. There was enough daylight that I could have shut off my headlights, but I didn't, even though they weren't helping me see the road any better. In fact, it was the time of day when headlights make no difference, on or off, but they let the bus itself be seen sooner and more clearly by oncoming cars. Not that there was any traffic up on Staples Mill Road, especially this early. But when you drive a school bus you have to think of these things. You have to anticipate the worst.

Obviously, you can't control everything, but you are obliged to take care of the few things you can. I'm an optimist, basically, who acts like a pessimist. On principle. Just in case.

Abbott says, "Biggest . . . difference . . . between . . .
people . . . is . . . quality . . . of . . . attention." And since a
person's quality of attention is one of the few things about
her that a human *can* control, then she damn well better do
it, say I. Put that together with the Golden Rule in a
nutshell, and you've got my philosophy of life. Abbott's
too. And you don't need religion for it.

Oh, like most people, we go to church—First Meth-
odist—but irregularly and mostly for social reasons, so as
not to stand out too much in the community. But we're not
religious persons, Abbott and I. Although, since the accident, there have been numerous times when I have wished
that I was. Religion being the main way the unexplainable
gets explained. God's will and all.

The first house you come to up there on the ridge is
Billy Ansel's old cut-stone colonial. I always liked stopping
at Billy's. For one thing, he used me as an alarm clock, not
leaving for work himself until I arrived to pick up his
children, Jessica and Mason, nine-year-old identical twins. I
liked it when the parents were aware of my arrival, and he
was always looking out the kitchen window when I pulled
up, waiting for his kids to climb into the bus. Then as I
pulled away I'd see the house lights go out, and a mile or
two down the road, I'd look into my side mirror, and there
he'd be, coming along behind in his pickup, on his way into
town to open up his Sunoco station.

Normally he followed me the whole distance over the
ridge to the Marlowe road, then south all the way into
town, keeping a slow and distant sort of company with the
bus, never bothering to pass on the straightaways, until

finally, just before I got to the school, he turned off at the garage. Once I asked him why he didn't pass me by, so he wouldn't have to stop and wait every time I pulled over to make a pickup. He just laughed. "Well," he said, "then I'd get to work before eight, wouldn't I, and I'd have to stand around the garage waiting for the help to show up. There's no point to that," he said.

Truth is, I don't think he wanted to move through that big empty house alone, once his kids were gone to school, and I believe it particularly pleased and comforted him, as he drove into town, to catch glimpses of his son and daughter in the school bus, waving back at him. Their mother, Lydia, a fairy princess of a woman, died of cancer some four years ago, and Billy took over raising the children by himself—although believe me, there are plenty of young women who would have been happy to help him out, as he is one fine-looking man. Smart and charming. And a successful businessman too. Even I found him sexy, and normally I don't give a younger man a second look.

But it was more than sexy; there was always something noble about Billy Ansel. In high school, he was the boy other boys imitated and followed, quarterback and captain of the football team, president of his senior class, et cetera. After graduation, like a lot of boys from Sam Dent back then, he went into the service. The Marines. In Vietnam, he was field commissioned as a lieutenant, and when he came back to Sam Dent in the mid-seventies, he married his high school sweetheart, Lydia Storrow, and borrowed a lot of money from the bank and bought Creppitt's old Sunoco station, where he had worked summers, and turned it into a regular automotive repair shop, with three bays and all kinds of electronic troubleshooting equipment. Lydia, who had gone to Plattsburgh State and knew accounting, kept the books, and Billy ran the garage. The stone house up on Staples Mill they bought a few years later, when the twins were born, and then renovated top to bottom, which it sorely needed. They were an ideal couple. An ideal family.

Billy Ansel, though, was always a man with a mission. Nothing discouraged him or made him bitter. When he came back to Sam Dent, right away he joined the VFW post in Placid, and soon he became an officer and went to work making the boys who had served in Vietnam respectable there, at a time when, most places, people still thought of them as drug addicts and murderers. He got them out marching proudly with the other vets every Fourth of July and Veterans Day. In fact, until recently, to work for him at the garage, you yourself had to be a Vietnam vet. He hired young men from all over the region, surly boys with long hair and hurt looks on their faces. At different times he even had a couple of black men working for him—very unusual in Sam Dent. His men were loyal to him and treated him like he was their lieutenant and they were still back in Vietnam. It was strange and in a way thrilling to watch a lost boy get rehabilitated like that. After a year or two, the fellow would have learned a trade, more or less, and he'd brighten up, and soon he'd be gone, replaced a week later by another sad-faced angry young man.

All the way across the back ridge on Staples Mill Road, Billy followed the bus. Whenever I slowed to pick up a waiting child, I'd look into the side mirror, and there he'd be, grinning through his beard at the kids in the back seat, who liked to turn and make V-for-victory signs at him. Especially Bear Otto, who regarded Billy Ansel as a hero, and of course the twins, who, because of Bear's protection, were allowed by the older boys to sit in the back seat of the bus. Bear dreamed of going into the Marines himself someday and working afterwards in Billy's garage. "Can't go to no Vietnam no more," he once told me. "But there's always someplace where they need the U.S. Marines, right?" I nodded and hoped he was wrong. I have a son in the military, after all. But I understood Bear Otto's desire to become a noble man, a man like Billy Ansel, and I respected that, naturally. I just wished the boy had more ways of imagining the thing than by becoming a good soldier. But that's boys, I guess.

Out there on the far side of Irish Hill, just before Staples Mill Road ties onto the old Marlowe road and makes a beeline for Sam Dent, three miles away, there's a stretch of tableland called Wilmot Flats. Supposedly, in ancient times it was the bottom of a glacial river or lake, but now it's mostly poor sandy soil and scrub brush and jack pine, with no open views of the mountains or valleys, at least not from the road. The town dump takes up half the Flats, with the other half parceled into odd lots with trailers on them and a couple of hand-built houses that are little more than shanties, tarpaper-covered clusters of tiny rooms heated by kerosene and wood. The folks who live in them are mostly named Atwater, with a few Bilodeaus thrown in. Every winter there's a bad fire up on the Flats, and at town

meeting for a spell everyone talks about instituting regula-
tions to govern the ways houses are heated, as if the state
legislature hadn't already tried to regulate them from down
in Albany. But nothing ever comes of it—there's too many
of us who heat with kerosene or wood to change things.
They're dangerous, of course, but what isn't?

Anyhow, I was making my stops up along the Flats,
picking up the last of my load—nine kids up there, except
when there's a virus going around—boys and girls of various ages who are the poorest children in town, generally.
Their parents are young, little more than teenaged kids
themselves, and half of them are cousins or actual siblings.
There's intermarriage up there and all sorts of mingling that
it's better not to know about, and between that and alcohol
and ignorance, the children have little chance of doing more
with their lives than imitating their parents' lives. With
them, says Abbott, you have to sympathize. Regardless of
what you think of their parents and the rest of the adults up
there. It's like all those poor children are born banished and
spend their lives trying to get back to where they belong.
And only a few of them manage it. The occasional plucky
one, who happens also to be lucky and gifted with intelligence, good looks, and charm, he might get back, before he
dies, to his native town. But the rest stay banished, permanently exiled, if not up there on Wilmot Flats, then someplace just like it.

That's when I saw the dog. The actual dog, I mean—
not the one I thought I saw on the Marlowe road a few
minutes later. It's probably irrelevant, but I offer it as a
possible explanation for my seeing what I thought was a

dog later, since both were the same dull red color. The dog
on Wilmot Flats was a garbage hound, one of those wan-
dering strays you see hanging around the dump. They are
often sick and vicious and are known to chase deer, so the
boys in town shoot them whenever they come across one
in the woods. Over the years I've come up on four or five
of their rotting corpses in the woods behind our house, and
it always gives me a painful chill and then a protracted sad
feeling. I don't like the dogs one bit, but I hate to see them
dead.

As I was saying, I had picked up the kids on the Flats
and was passing by the open chain-link entrance to the
dump, when this raggedy old mutt shot out the gate and
ran across the road in front of me, and it scared the bejesus
out of me, although I could not for the life of me tell you
why, as he was ordinary-looking and there was no danger
of my hitting him.

My mind must have been locked onto something
contrasted—my sons Reginald and William, probably, since
I felt that morning particularly estranged from them, and
you tend to embrace with thought what you're forbidden
to embrace in fact. For when that dog entered my field of
vision, it somehow astonished and then frightened me. The
dog was skinny and torn-looking, a yellow-eyed young
male with a long pointed head and large ears laid flat
against his skull as he darted across the road, leapt over the
snowbank, and disappeared into the darkness of the scrub
pine woods there.

Although the snow was blowing in feathery waves by
then, the road was still dry and black, easy to see, and I

gripped the wheel and drove straight on, as if nothing had happened. For nothing *had* happened! Yet I wanted intensely to pull the bus over and stop, to sit there for a moment and try to gather my fragmented thoughts and calm my clanging nerves.

I glanced into the side mirror at Billy Ansel's face smiling through the windshield of his pickup, an innocent and diligent man waving to children at play, and I felt a wave of pity for him come over me, although I did not know what I pitied him for. I turned back from the mirror and stared straight ahead at the road and clamped my hands onto the steering wheel and drove on toward the intersection at the Marlowe road, where I slowed, and when I saw that there was no traffic coming or even going, I turned right and headed down the long slope toward town.

The road was recently rebuilt and is wide and straight, with a passing lane and narrow shoulders and a bed of gravel and guardrails, before it drops off a ways on the right-hand side to Jones Brook, which is mostly boulders up there and not much water. Eventually, as the brook descends it fills, and by the time it joins the Ausable River down in the valley it's a significant fast-running stream. There's an old town sandpit down there dug into the ancient lakebed, and a closed-off road in from the Flats, near the dump. On the left-hand side, the land is wooded and rises slowly toward Knob Lock Mountain and Giant in the southeast.

Coming down from the Flats on the Marlowe road toward town, the greatest danger was that I would be going too slow and a lumber truck or some idiot in a car would come barreling along at seventy-five or eighty, which you can easily do up there, once you've made the crest from the other side, and would come up on me fast and not be able to slow or pass and would run smack into me, or, more likely, first would hit Billy Ansel's pickup truck lollygagging along behind and then the bus. As a result, since I didn't have any more stops to make once I'd gathered the kids from the Flats, I tended to drive that stretch of road at a pretty good clip. Nothing reckless, you understand. Nothing illegal. Fifty, fifty-five is all. Also, if I happened to be running a few minutes late, that was the only time when I could make up for it.

After passing through the gloom and closed-in feeling of Wilmot Flats, when you turn onto the Marlowe road and start the drive toward town, you tend to feel uplifted, released. Or I should say, I always did. The road is straight and there is more sky than land for the first time, and the valley opens up below you and on your right, like Montana or Wyoming—a large snow-covered bowl with a range of distant mountains surrounding it, and beyond the mountains there are still more mountains shouldering toward the sky, as if the surface of the planet were the same everywhere as here. This was always the most pleasurable part of my journey—with the bus in high gear and running smooth, enough pale daylight now, despite the thin gauzy snow falling, to see the entire landscape stretched out before me, and the busload of children peaceful behind me as they contentedly conversed with one another or silently prepared themselves for the next segment of their long day.

And, yes, it was then that I saw the dog, the second

dog, the one I maybe only thought I saw. It emerged from the blowing snow on the right side of the road, popped up from the ditch there, or so it seemed, and crossed to the center of the road, where it appeared to stop, as if unsure whether to continue or go back. No, I am almost sure now that it was an optical illusion or a mirage, a sort of afterimage, maybe, of the dog that I had seen on the Flats and that had frightened and moved me so. But at the time I could not tell the difference.

And as I have always done when I've had two bad choices and nothing else available to me, I arranged it so that if I erred I'd come out on the side of the angels. Which is to say, I acted as though it was a real dog I saw or a small deer or possibly even a lost child from the Flats, barely a half mile away.

For the rest of my life I will remember that red-brown blur, like a stain of dried blood, standing against the road with a thin screen of blown snow suspended between it and me, the full weight of the vehicle and the thirty-four children in it bearing down on me like a wall of water. And I will remember the formal clarity of my mind, beyond thinking or choosing now, for I had made my choice, as I wrenched the steering wheel to the right and slapped my foot against the brake pedal, and I wasn't the driver anymore, so I hunched my shoulders and ducked my head, as if the bus were a huge wave about to break over me. There was Bear Otto, and the Lamston kids, and the Walkers, the Hamiltons, and the Prescotts and the teenaged boys and girls from Bartlett Hill, and Risa and Wendell Walker's sad little boy, Sean, and sweet Nichole Burnell, and all the kids from the valley, and the children from Wilmot Flats, and Billy Ansel's twins, Jessica and Mason—the children of my town—their wide-eyed faces and fragile bodies swirling and tumbling in a tangled mass as the bus went over and the sky tipped and veered away and the ground lurched brutally forward.

Billy Ansel

Just to show you how far I was from predicting the accident or suspecting that it could occur—even though, except for Dolores Driscoll, who drove the bus, I was surely the person in town closest to the event, the only eyewitness, you might say—at the moment it occurred I was thinking about fucking Risa Walker. My truck was right behind the bus when it went over, and my body was driving my truck, and one hand was on the steering wheel and the other was waving at Jessica and Mason, who were aboard the bus and waving back at me from the rear window—but my eyes were looking at Risa Walker's breasts and belly and hips cast in a hazy neon glow through the slats of the venetian blind in Room 11 of the Bide-a-Wile.

So I don't know anything of what immediately preceded the accident, although once it happened, of course, I saw it all, every last mind-numbing detail. And still do, every time I close my eyes. The swerve off the road to the right, the skid, the smashing of the guardrail and the snowbank; and then the tilted angled plummet down the embankment to the sandpit, where, moving fast and somehow still upright, the bus slid across the ice to the far side; and then the ice letting go and the rear half of the yellow bus being swallowed at once by the freezing blue-green water.

I don't close my eyes a whole lot now. Unless I'm drunk and can't help it—therefore, a frequently desired state, you might say.

Many of the folks in Sam Dent have come out since the accident and claimed that they knew it was going to happen someday, oh yes, they just *knew* it: because of Dolores's driving, which, to be fair, is not reckless but casual; or because of the condition of the bus itself, which Dolores serviced at home in her barn, and as a consequence it did not get the same supervision by me as the other school buses got; or because of that downhill stretch of road and the fact that there's almost no shoulder to it on either side of the guardrail; or because of the sandpit below the highway there, which the town had opened up a few years before and then abandoned when it filled with water, thinking no one could get to it except by the old blocked-off access road on the other side of the Flats.

It's a way of living with a tragedy, I guess, to claim after it happens that you saw it coming, as if somehow you had already made the necessary adjustments beforehand. I could understand that. But it irritated me to hear it, especially with so many journalists poking microphones in people's faces and with all the downstate lawyers crawling around looking for someone to blame, so I want to say right out front that I was the person closest to the accident and I never saw it coming.

I knew that stretch of road as well as anyone in town, and I knew the bus inside and out, and I knew better than anyone what Dolores's driving habits were, because one of my habits was to follow her into town every morning; and believe me, I was not in the slightest afraid of an accident. I would be now, of course, because the accident has changed everything, but back then, even though I expected death in a general way as much as the next person—probably even more so, since I am a widower and a Vietnam vet and had already learned a few things about the precariousness of daily life—I was able that morning, while I drove along behind the school bus, to let my mind fix on the image of the woman I happened to be sleeping with, a woman I was having an illicit affair with. Illicit because she was married to a friend of mine.

I feel guilty for it, of course—for conducting the affair, I mean, not for having a fantasy about sex with her at that awful moment in my life, in her life, in the life of everybody in this town, practically. I could as easily have been thinking about money, which I did not have much of, as sex with Risa, which at that time I had quite a lot of, owing, I suppose, to my freedom of movement and to her unhappiness with her husband, Wendell, and her financial problems—although we liked to believe then that we were in love with each other, and often said it: "I love you, I love you, oh God, how I love you." That sort of thing; playing a role. We did talk that way then. We don't anymore.

But it was a lie, and I think we both knew it. I surely did. I still loved my wife, Lydia, and I don't think Risa loved anyone except her son, Sean. Nevertheless, we were both lonely and both burdened with strong sexual natures. But neither of us had the ability to say that to the other in a way that would not be hurtful. So, instead, we said, "I love you," and let it go at that. I have the benefit of hindsight now, of course, and at the time maybe I half believed the tender words I whispered in her ear after we had made love and I was still inside and surrounding her, covering her body with mine in the darkness of the motel room.

We used to meet like that, in Room 11 at the Bide-a-Wile, after Wendell had gone early to bed alone, which he had been doing for several years, except when there was a Montreal Expos ball game on TV—Wendell adored the Expos; probably still does. I would leave my kids with a baby-sitter, usually Nichole Burnell, who took care of the house and kids from after school two days a week until eleven at night, when her father, Sam, drove over from Bartlett Hill and picked her up. The drill was for me to kiss the twins good night, tell Nichole that I was going down to the Rendez-Vous or the Spread Eagle for a few beers or to Placid for a movie, and a few minutes later, with the key that Risa had given me, to let myself into Room 11 and sit in the darkness and wait for Risa to arrive.

It sounds sordid, I know, but it didn't feel cheap or low. It was too often too lonely, too solitary, for that. Many nights Risa could not get away to Room 11, and I sat there by myself in the wicker chair beside the bed for an hour or so, smoking cigarettes and thinking and remembering my life before Lydia died, until finally, when it was clear that Risa could not get away from Wendell, I would leave the room and walk across the road to the lot next to the Rendez-Vous where I had parked my truck and drive home.

On those nights when Risa did arrive, we spent our time together entirely in darkness, for we couldn't turn on the room light, and we barely saw each other, except for what we could make out in the dim light from the motel sign outside falling through the blinds: rose-colored profiles, the curve of a thigh or shoulder, a breast, a knee. It was melancholy and sweet and reflective, and of course very sexual, straightforwardly sexual, for both of us.

Our meetings were respites from our real and very troubled lives, and we knew that. Whenever I saw Risa in daylight, in public, it was as if she were a wholly different person, her sister, maybe, or a cousin, who only resembled in vague ways the woman I was having an affair with. I'm not sure that's how I appeared to her—men and women see each other differently. For instance, a man generally doesn't even know how small a woman really is until he holds an article of her clothing up in front of him, one of her nightgowns, say, and sees how small and flimsy it is and how like a child's and unlike his own, and how thick and heavy his hands seem. Women almost always appear larger to us than they actually are, and we don't have much opportunity to observe how small and delicate their bodies are in comparison to ours.

They know our size, of course, know it thoroughly, for they have felt our weight on top of them—smaller people always know the size of people who are larger than they. But we men have usually taken the physical measure of the women in our lives only with our eyes, and because we are secretly afraid of them, we tend to see women as having bodies that are at least as large as our own. I think that's one reason why a man is so often surprised by how easily he can injure a woman with his hands. Although I myself have never hurt a woman with my hands. But you know how men talk to one another. Surprise is one of our main motifs. We like to pretend we're surprised by common knowledge.

I remember one night shortly after my wife, Lydia, went into the hospital to stay, I gathered up all her clothing and spread it across our bed—dresses, blouses and skirts, jeans and shirts, nightgowns, her underwear, even—and folded everything neatly and boxed it and carried the boxes out to the garage, where we have a storage room in back. I don't know why I did that; she hadn't died yet, although I knew of course that in a few weeks at most she would be dead from the cancer. But I could not bear to look at her clothes hanging in our closet or see them whenever I opened a dresser drawer; I could not bear even to walk past the closet or dresser and know that her clothes were inside, hanging or neatly folded in darkness like some foolish hope for her eventual return.

That night, without planning it, I made myself a double-sized drink of Scotch and water (the twins had finally fallen off to sleep), and I walked back to our bedroom and simply started to pack her clothing, and at once it seemed deeply correct somehow, and so I went on doing it until the job was done. I must have known this was a task that I would have to do soon anyhow, and I must have sensed that it would be much more painful for me later, with her dead, so I did it now, while she was still alive, while I could keep myself from weeping with self-pity.

It was not so bad, it was almost a kindness, as if she were about to leave me and the children for a long journey, and as I held up her thin blouses and nightgowns one by one and studied them, I was amazed at how small they were, what bare scraps of cloth they were, seen like that, without her body inside to fill them out and give them weight.

I remember that night and standing there beside our bed and holding up my wife's articles of clothing as clearly as if it were last night; it was a discovery of an aspect of her deepest reality and, through it, a discovery of a part of my own. Mourning can be very selfish. When someone you love has died, you tend to recall best those few moments and incidents that helped to clarify your sense, not of the person who has died, but of your own self. And if you loved the person a great deal, as I loved Lydia and my children, your sense of who you are will have been clarified many times, and so you will have many such moments to remember. I have learned that.

Nights now I can sit in my living room alone, looking at the glass of the picture window, with the reflection of my body and the drink in my hand and the chair and lamp beside me glaring flat and white back at me, and I am in no way as real in that room as I am in my memories of my wife and children. Sometimes it's not as if they have died so much as that I myself have died and have become a ghost.

You might think that remembering those moments is a way of keeping my family alive, but it's not; it's a way of keeping myself alive. Just as you might think my drinking is a way to numb the pain; it's not; it's a way to feel the pain.

Four years ago—well, four years before the accident, the year before Lydia died—she and I and the twins spent two weeks on the island of Jamaica. It was late in the winter, early March, which is when if you're going to get out of Sam Dent at all, you get out then. I don't care how much you think you like the snow and ice and darkness of upstate New York; after four or five months of it, nobody in this region manages to keep from being depressed that late in the winter. And unless you drive a snowplow or run a ski lift, you're not making any money here anyhow, so if you can afford it, you leave for anywhere south of Albany. That March, for the first time in my life I could afford it, the garage was finally running in the black, and Lydia was feeling bad for the first time, although we did not yet know why. By May they'd remove her thyroid; by the following May she'd be dead. We merely thought we deserved a vacation, so to speak.

We rented a house, a "villa" the travel agent called it, but it was a house, a modest three-bedroom cinder-block affair surrounded by a chain-link fence. It was a compound, more or less, situated up on a hill in an inland village a dozen miles west of Montego Bay. There was a small swimming pool and a terrace and a yard stuffed with flowers, and we had a part-time gardener and a cook, as advertised, local folks whose relation to us was the same as the one most folks back home in Sam Dent bore to summer people. In Jamaica we were winter people, which was a little unsettling at first, but in a day or two we got used to it (it's amazing how fast you can accommodate yourself to luxuries like domestic help and swimming pools), which gave me some insight into the Adirondack summer people.

We weren't big drinkers, Lydia and I, but we were smoking a lot of dope. Both of us. Not so much back at home, because after all we both had to work every day and take care of the kids and couldn't very well walk around stoned all day and night, and unless you were a teenager, marijuana was somewhat difficult to acquire in Sam Dent. Even so, by the time we went to Jamaica, marijuana had become our recreational drug of choice, you might say, which meant that three or four times a week, usually late at night in our bedroom at home, we got high. In Jamaica, though, there was an abundance of very strong dope, which they called ganja and sold cheap. There was cocaine too, but we bought ganja. Every other kid on the street sold it; you could smell it in the marketplace, on the crowded streets of Montego Bay, even in the yard of our house.

I would rise early, and feeling wicked and weirdly dislocated, would walk out onto the terrace and look over the hills to a silvery wedge of sea glistening in the morning sun, and the breeze would carry the smell of the natives' wood-burning cook fires and marijuana smoke across the tops of the trees straight into my face, and just like in Vietnam, I would think, What a damned good idea, to get stoned early and stay stoned all day long and go to sleep stoned. So I'd roll a joint and take off. It made the dream and the threat of travel and being surrounded by permanently poor black people whose language was incomprehensible to me both safe and real—it woke me up without scaring me.

With marijuana, your inner life and outer life merge and comfort each other. With alcohol, too, they merge, but they tend to beat up on you instead, and I didn't particularly like getting beat up on. Which is why I have never had a problem with alcohol. Until now, I mean. Since the accident. I admit it; what do I lose by admitting it? I do have a problem with alcohol, and I'll probably continue that way until something terrible happens and brings me up short, something I can't or won't imagine now. It could be the collapse of my business; although frankly I don't think that would do it. It could be my own death.

But back then I had a problem with marijuana, and I did not know it. I thought it was just me taking unnecessary chances, and I was still young and undamaged enough, despite Vietnam, to think you could get away with taking unnecessary chances without admitting that you had a problem. I believed that it was an interesting way to live. Lydia too—although she was more cautious than I and followed a ways behind me, just in case I stumbled and fell, which was her habit and temperament in most things. We were a powerful couple, and I cannot think of her without feeling my heart instantly harden against the thought, because when I remember her and how powerful and happy we were and why I loved her so, I think at once of her death. Just as with the twins, Jessica and Mason. I can barely say their names without feeling the flesh of my heart turn into iron. This is not bitterness; it's what happens when you have eaten your bitterness.

We had rented a car for the entire two weeks, a beat-up yellow Ford Escort, and every day we left the house on a family outing of some kind—the beach at Doctor's Cave, Rose Hall, the straw market, river rafting, whatever took our fancy—and usually on our way home in the afternoon we stopped at a pathetic shabby little shopping center in Montego Bay called Westgate, to pick up a few household supplies, like toilet paper or paper towels, and snacks for the kids, who were always tired and fussy by then. They loved those things called coco-pops, clear plastic tubes of flavored ice hawked by kids in the parking lot, sticky disgusting things that melted as soon as you bought them, and while Lydia and I scurried up and down the aisles of the store, the twins sucked their coco-pops and waited outside in the car.

One afternoon late in our stay, we drove back from what I think was the beach at Doctor's Cave—I don't recall exactly where we were coming from, but I do remember feeling sunburned and sandy, which certainly suggests the beach—and stopped at Westgate. The last time we had come here, Jessica and Mason had been hassled in the parking lot by a bunch of local kids attracted to them by their whiteness and the fact that they were twins, which seemed to have an unusual fascination for people down there, even though they were not identical twins. It was harmless enough, but because there hadn't been any adults to control the Jamaican kids, the episode had scared Jessica and Mason. They were only four years old and did not have much interest in other cultures.

Anyhow, this time, instead of waiting out in the lot in the car, they followed us into the store, a cavernous supermarket with no air-conditioning and smelling of sour milk, bad meat, and pickles. It was like every food store on the island that we happened to enter during those two weeks: half-empty shelves stocked more with paper goods and bottles of rum for tourists than with food for the natives—a generally depressing place, which I wanted to avoid, and but for the kids, who seemed to need a few familiar things to eat and drink, potato chips, cereal, packaged cookies, that sort of thing, I would have. Those items comforted the children somehow. They were lonely in Jamaica, and being the only white children in the village, or so it must have seemed to them, they were always a little tense and frightened. All their routines were broken, and they were not used to being without TV, and they were not accustomed to receiving so much daytime attention from us. The twins were at a very cautious age that spring, and, too, they may have sensed, even before I or she herself did, that their mother was sick. Also, they weren't able, as Lydia and I were, to get stoned every day and night.

Looking back, I feel very sorry for them. Then, I thought that we were all having the time of our lives, which made it easier for me to accept the high level of anxiety that the time of our life extracted as payment. We were surrounded by black people, people who carried machetes and sold drugs openly and talked a foreign-sounding English in loud voices, who pointed at us because of our skin color and made ugly noises with their lips at my wife or smiled and lied and tried to take our money. But here we are, on vacation in Jamaica, I thought. Isn't that just the greatest thing an American dad can do for his family? I think I'll celebrate and reward myself by getting blasted on this terrific ganja I bought today for only ten bucks while getting the car filled with gas.

You think that way down there.

While we paid for our groceries at the register— always a slow and sullen process interrupted by several arguments and exchanges between the Jamaican clerks and customers—Mason went on ahead of us to the car, so that when we arrived there he was already seated in back, slurping at his second coco-pop. I put the bag of groceries into the trunk, got in and backed away from the front of the store and drove quickly out of the lot, sweating in the car, which distracted me somewhat. I again regretted not having rented an air-conditioned car.

I remember that they were burning off the sugarcane fields at that time of year. West of Montego Bay there were broad fields of smoldering cane stubble, and the air was filled with a sugary haze that smelled like burnt molasses. It looked like after a firefight, with patches of grass flaming in the distance and the air filled with a spooky haze that filtered out the sunlight but did not dull the bright green foliage or the tall yellow grass. There was a kind of false breeze, caused by the distant and immense heat of the fires, so that the air blew warmly against your face, pushing toward the fires that burned behind you.

When we had crossed the plain, we entered a neigh-

borhood of seaside houses owned by foreigners and rich
Jamaicans, where high concrete walls topped with razor
wire ran alongside the narrow winding coastal road. Then,
after a few miles, we turned left and started the three-mile
climb into the hills to our village. Halfway up the first long
hill, I turned to smile at the twins in back. They had been
silent since Westgate, and I expected them to be asleep,
curled up in each other's arms like litter mates, like puppies
or kittens, which was their inclination then, so that you
couldn't tell whose blond head belonged to which set of
arms and legs, or whether they were two separate children
at all and not one strange creature with two heads and eight
limbs, which I am sure is how they themselves sometimes
felt.

But they were not sleeping. Mason stared absently
out the window; he was alone in the back seat. Jessica was
gone.

Had she somehow climbed over to the front, to sit in
her mother's lap, and I hadn't noticed? I looked over at
Lydia, whose eyes were half closed, approaching sleep,
trusting me to get us all safely, smoothly back to the house.
She wore shorts and halter, her pale hair tied back with a
pink scarf, her tanned arms and legs glittering with dried sea
salt. There was no child on her lap. Our daughter was gone.

I said nothing, kept driving the overheated Escort up
the curving narrow road, and with a sideways glance
checked the rear doors, for perhaps one had opened and—
too horrible to believe, maybe, but not too horrible to
imagine, not for me—she had fallen from the car without a
cry and, amazingly, no one had seen it, not even her twin

brother, seated next to her. Both doors were shut tight.

We were almost at the top of the hill, approaching the turnoff to the potholed lane that led along the narrow tree-covered ridge to our house. Pale green sunlight fell at oblique angles through the trees and speckled the roadway and the packed dirt yards of the tiny tin-roofed houses. I remember that. Barefoot children walked along the edges of the rain gullies, lugging water home from the village stand-pipe in buckets that they balanced on their heads. It was almost evening, time to begin cooking supper. Where was our daughter? How had she been taken from us?

I kept driving straight on toward what we called home and could not say aloud the words that were thrashing me, as if somehow by remaining silent I could keep the terrible thing from having occurred. Finally, when we passed through the gate and drew up in front of the house, I said, without turning back to him, "Mason, is Jessica asleep?"

I was afraid, terrified, and did not yet believe that such a thing could happen to you in America or even while on vacation from America. My wife had not yet died, and my two children had not yet been taken from me in the accident, so all I had to go on was what had happened to me in Vietnam when I was a nineteen-year-old kid, and by some necessary logic, I believed that because terrible things had happened to me then and there, it was impossible for them to happen here and now. I did not want to give up that logic; it was like my childhood: if I admitted that my daughter had been kidnapped or had fallen from the car or had simply been lost in a foreign country, then the whole world for the rest of my life would be Vietnam. I knew that.

Mason's response was very strange—or at least that's how I remember it. Of course, you have to keep in mind that Lydia and I were pretty much stoned most of the time, so that when we were coming down we were thinking about having been high, and when we finally were down, like now, we were thinking about getting high again. Our perspective on things was tilted, and foreground kept getting confused with background, and vice versa. Mason answered, "You left her at the store." Straight out, as if he were slightly pleased by my having abandoned his twin sister and somewhat annoyed by his having to remind me.

But twins are like that. They behave in ways, especially regarding each other, that can seem very strange to someone who is not a twin himself. They have a morality that is different from ours—at least when they are young they do—because, unlike other children, they are not inclined to imitate adults until much later. To children who are twins, even when they are not identical, the other twin is both more and less real than everyone else in the family, and they deal with each other the way we deal with ourselves alone. Which means that it's like twins are permanently stoned. I don't think that's an exaggeration.

I started to holler. "Jesus, Mason! I left her at the *store*? Why the hell didn't you *say* something?"

"My God! How could we do that?" Lydia cried. "How could we have left her there?"

"I thought she was sleeping!" I shouted at her. By now I had the car turned around and headed back up the drive toward the gate. "I thought she was sleeping in back!"

"Hurry," she said. "And shut up. Please."

"What the hell did I do? I didn't do anything wrong, it was a goddamn *accident*," I said.

"No one's to blame, we're both to blame, we're all to blame, even she is, so let's just get back there and pray that she's all right. That no one—"

"She'll be fine," I said. "No one'll hurt her. These people, they love children." I said it, but I didn't believe it. How could my four-year-old daughter be safe among people I myself felt frightened of? The image of flaxen-haired Jessica searching the aisles of the store for us, wide-eyed, fighting tears, lower lip trembling as she starts to call for us, "Mommy? Daddy? Where are you?"—the thought made me tremble with rage, and because I could not blame my wife or son for what Jessica was enduring, I had to blame myself alone, and because, as Lydia had said, I could not blame myself alone, I blamed love.

This was the beginning of what I have come to think of as the permanent end of my childhood and adolescence. The Vietnamization of my domestic life. Which is why I am telling you this. What had been an exception was now possibly the rule. That headlong terrified drive back down the hill and across the smoking cane fields to Westgate in Montego Bay, Jamaica—there began the secret hardening of my heart, a process that today, as I guess is obvious, is nearly complete.

Jessica was not in the parking lot. A scattering of skinny shirtless boys in bare feet kicked a bundled rag in loopy overhead arcs. I drew the car up in front of the grocery store, leapt out, and made for the door; then remembered Mason and came running back. But Lydia already had him out of the car and was hurrying along behind, holding his hand. He was oddly calm and watched the older boys enviously, as if he did not understand what was happening to our family, although of course he did.

There was a single strange thought leading me into the store: I will make this one last try to save her, and then I will give it up. I must have known that if my child was indeed to be lost to me, then I would need all my strength just to survive that fact, so I had decided ahead of time not to waste any of my strength trying to save what was already lost.

You are probably astonished that I gave her up so easily. And although you could say that it was only a minor event in my life, a scare is all, that broke me, you'd be wrong; I think I was broken long before that afternoon in Jamaica, possibly in Vietnam but more likely not. Maybe in the womb, or even earlier. If not broken, I was weakened. Which is not all bad, you understand. The way we deal with death depends on how it's imagined for us beforehand, by our parents and the people who surround them, and what happens to us early on. And if we believed properly in death—the way we actually do believe in taxes, for instance—and did not insist on thinking that we had it beat, we might never even have had a Vietnam war. Or any war. Instead, we believe the lie, that death, unlike taxes, can be postponed indefinitely, and we spend our lives defending that belief. Some people are very good at it, and they become our nation's heroes. Some, like me, for obscure reasons, see the lie early for what it is, fake it for a while and grow bitter, and then go beyond bitterness to . . . to what? To this, I suppose. Cowardice. Adulthood.

We entered the store frantic, wild-eyed, looking ridiculous, I'm sure, and the three women at the registers saw us and smiled knowingly and pointed, together in a single gesture, as in a chorus line, to the counter at the end, where Jessica was seated cross-legged like a little blond yogi, sucking on an orange coco-pop and studying the pages of a Jamaican romance comic book. She hadn't seen us, or if she had, she had decided to ignore us.

Lydia got to her first and swept her up in her arms. Mason and I hung back a bit—emotions in dignified check. When Lydia put her down, Jessica marched quickly past me and out the door, haughty, empowered by neglect, with Mason falling in line behind her, and the two of them got into the back seat of the car and began together to study the drawings of the black men and women in love. A tall, broad-shouldered cashier asked me for two dollars for the comic book and the coco-pops Jessica had consumed, and I paid her, and Lydia and I left the store.

We never returned to that store; we couldn't face the cashiers, I think. Also, we stopped smoking marijuana. It was one of those episodes that clarify things, that shape and control your future behavior. We never went back to Jamaica, of course: a year later, Lydia was dead. Four years later, the twins were dead. And now, here am I.

I could say that I saw it all coming, like most people in town do, but unlike them, I'd almost be lying. It's just that after Jamaica, while I expected death, I did not anticipate it.

That's how Risa thinks, however, and she believes it, poor woman—she actually believes that she saw it all coming. Before the accident, for several years, mainly due to her collapsed marriage and numerous financial problems, she was merely a woman depressed and troubled; but that's what she thinks of now as prescience. Which is like writing history backward, if you ask me, fixing the past to fit the present. Hindsight made over into foresight.

"Oh, I knew it, Billy," she told me after the accident, when finally we could speak of it to each other. "I knew for the longest time, I knew that something terrible was coming down. When I heard the sirens and the alarm from the firehouse, nobody had to tell me that something terrible had happened, that something unimaginably awful had been visited on me and Wendell, and on you, too, and on the entire town. I knew it instantly, because I had known for months that it was coming. That was why all those months, all the time we were meeting each other, in fact, I was so unhappy and turbulent in my emotions."

Risa actually said that to me. And when she did, it turned me off, but there was a time when that particular cast to her mind, the superstitious part of it, you might say, made her appear wonderfully attractive to me. After the accident, however, it made her seem stupid and weak, and it embarrassed me to find myself talking so intimately with her.

She had always been essentially the same person, of course, just as I had been, but the Bide-a-Wile Motel, which she and Wendell bought from the bank at auction and which anyone who'd ever tracked the economy of this town could have predicted would be nothing but a sinkhole for their little bit of money (that's the sort of thing you *can* predict), was probably the start of her decline, the ending of her dream, the end of *her* youth. Some people, when their dreams collapse, turn superstitious in order to explain it, and Risa is one of them. The motel, in addition to the insurmountable financial difficulties it created for them, made Wendell, who'd always worked behind the counter of someone else's business, never his own, look lazy and a little dumb and pessimistic to her, which of course he was anyhow and had been from the day they married. But she hadn't seen it before, and now she believed that his character was getting in front of her realizing a very important dream. That got her angry at him in a profound way, which drove him further into himself, and although they both loved their boy Sean dearly, they soon began to love each other less. That's when he started going to bed early and alone, and Risa started meeting me in Room 11.

By that time, which was about three years before the accident, their marriage was essentially dead, except for their love of Sean, of course. I suppose I want to believe that; anyone who's an interloper in a marriage wants to think the marriage was dead before he pulled up and parked; but in this case I'm sure it's the truth.

It started innocently enough—that is, without my knowing anything had been started. I've known Risa and Wendell most of my life; we more or less grew up together here in Sam Dent, although Risa is a few years younger than Wendell and I. When I was in Vietnam, Wendell, who was bagging groceries at Valley Grocery in Keene Valley, started dating Risa, who was then barely out of the eighth grade. They stuck together, though, and the year she graduated high school, he got a job as a Tru-Value cashier in Marlowe, and they got married. I always liked Wendell, even though he was indeed, as Risa eventually discovered, lazy and pretty dumb and pessimistic. That's a hard combination for a wife to like, and frankly I never would have hired him to work for me, even if he had been one of the Vietnam vets who for a long time were the only people I hired at the garage. But Wendell made it relatively simple, by being good-looking and passive, for a man to call him a friend. (Some folks might regard him as low-key or easygoing, but I have to say passive.)

What it came down to was that in an important sense, Wendell didn't really give a damn about much. He liked sports—TV sports, that is; he was a little heavy in the gut to play any himself—and he was very fond of his son. Not like Risa was, of course, for she was much more intense about everything than he, but sufficiently fond to have his heart broken by the boy's death.

Wendell is like the rest of us, a person whose life has two meanings, one before the accident and one after. I doubt, however, that he worries much about connecting the two meanings, as the rest of us do, but that's Wendell Walker. That was always Wendell Walker. Even so, I felt guilty because, before his life became a tragedy, he was basically a likable fellow. Just as, before her life became a tragedy, Risa's superstitious nature was an aspect of her character that was downright attractive. At least to me it was.

I was a widower and a relatively young man still, with two small children in a big house and a business that was making money but was top-heavy with debt. Those were the facts that filled my head night and day—the death of my wife, the needs of my children, and cash flow at the garage. For a year or so after Lydia died, and even for most of the year before she died, it was as if I had no sexual nature. From the time she went to the hospital to stay, I woke alone in that huge king-sized bed of ours every morning in darkness and never once had an erection or even thought about the pleasures Lydia and I had taken from each other in that bed at exactly that time of day so many hundreds of times; I couldn't permit such a thought. I had work to do, children to wash and dress and feed and get off to school so I could get to the garage by eight, and at the garage I'd work like two men until the kids got out of school, so I'd be free then to drive them to Cub Scouts and Brownies, to their friends', to the dentist in Placid, to Ames in Saranac for winter boots, stopping off at the Grand Union for groceries that I'd cook for supper and popcorn for after supper while watching TV together, and when they had gone to bed, I'd stay up late drinking and doing the garage account books that Lydia used to take care of. I had started drinking pretty heavily by then; but nothing like now.

For a long time, though, that was my whole life. There was no way I could let myself think about anything that did not lie directly before me—the death of my wife, the physical and emotional needs of my children, and my business. It was as if during that period I were crossing a crevasse on a high wire, and if I once looked down at the ground or off to the side or even ahead of me or behind, I'd fall, and I'd take down with me anyone holding on to me, meaning my children.

Then I started to change. First in erotic dreams and after a while in fantasy—little pornographic movies in which I was both actor and audience: my sexual nature had begun to reassert itself. It was only chromosomal and glandular, but even so, whenever it happened I felt oddly disloyal to Lydia. While she was alive I had been able to wake from my dream or fantasy and immediately cast her in the leading female role and let reality take over; but with her gone, if I tried casting her, the dream turned instantly to grief and sorrow. It was specifically to avoid that pain that I auditioned for the sex scenes numerous women I knew personally and believed I could be attracted to—the wives and daughters of the town of Sam Dent. And to my surprise, my number one sex goddess turned out to be Risa Walker.

I say surprise because Risa was by no stretch of the imagination the sexiest woman in town. That title went by male consensus to Wanda Otto, whom the boys in the garage called The Beatnik Queen, because of her long straight hair and her eye makeup and the low-cut knit dresses she wore. It was probably the image of 1960s hippie sex that she evoked—most of my mechanics suffered from a kind of time warp anyhow. Also, Wanda behaved in what you might call a provocative way—at least it provoked the boys in the garage, who scrambled to fill her Peugeot with gas whenever she drove in. Normally, when someone pulled up to the pump, Bud or Jimbo or whoever was on duty only crawled further into the vehicle he was working on and pretended not to see or hear it. Selling gas was strictly a necessary frill at the station, and whoever happened to be on duty was supposed to look after it; there was no regular attendant, and I myself spent most of my time in the office, with Lydia when she was alive and alone afterwards, or supervising the more delicate and difficult jobs out in the garage. No one wanted to pump gas. But Wanda Otto never to my knowledge wore a bra, and so long as she was without her husband, Hartley, or her son, the Indian boy Bear, she had a habit of driving into the station with her dress pulled halfway up her very attractive thighs. Wanda could get a mechanic out from under the hood and beside her open window faster than any other customer. She laughed easily and flirted and used expressions like "Shit!" and "Fuck!" if you told her she was down a quart, and that turned men on. Although it probably scared them too, because I don't know of anyone who ever made a direct pass at Wanda, at least not when he was sober. They just talked about it with one another.

Risa, by contrast, though she is an intense person and when present fills your entire screen, drawing all your attention, is unadorned, shy, and private. Her manner, until the accident, was upbeat and warm, but her smile was undercut by a look of permanent sadness that she seemed to be trying to hide, as if she were struggling to protect you from it. Everyone liked Risa, but when she pulled in with her Wagoneer, no one rushed out to fill her tank, and like most people, she often had to fill it herself. She is tall, broad-shouldered, with ample breasts and a nice large female butt that she covers with somewhat mannish clothes, flannel shirts and loose jeans, that sort of thing. Typical for up here. She is the kind of woman who makes a man think of his favorite sister, if he has one, or his best friend's sister, if he doesn't. Not a likely candidate for erotic fantasy.

But lying half drunk in the darkness in that king-sized bed in my house on the hill, the twins sleeping soundly in their room at the end of the hall, I'd imagine Risa Walker naked and ecstatic, and it positively thrilled me. Took me straight out of the misery of my daily life and let my hormones run things for a while. Risa released me sexually when no other woman could. Women like Wanda Otto are already so close to naked and ecstatic in public, it's not much of a thrill to take them one more step alone and in private. In fact, what you imagine is a woman you can't satisfy—an image that is well known for dousing the fire in a man. But picturing Risa—calm, reticent, controlled, decent, and modest Risa Walker—picturing her wild with passion, sweating and naked, long legs akimbo, hands digging into your back, mouth grunting and licking into your ear . . . well, that's a picture a man can cook with.

In time, the fantasies were insufficient. That's how it is—the more vivid the imagined sex, the less satisfying it is as sex. You have to keep upping the ante, just like they do in pornographic movies, until finally you have to either replace it with the real thing or else rent a different movie. I didn't want a different movie; by then all I wanted was Risa Walker. Any other woman was a diminishment, and even a slight diminishment was a total loss. I wanted, I needed, Risa.

The trouble was, Risa was thoroughly married to a friend of mine, and in all the years I had known her, she had not once shown the slightest interest in going to bed with anyone other than her husband. Especially not with me. To be fair, I had not given her much opportunity. I am known as a self-contained man and am probably not very approachable, which has always been my choice of character anyhow, insofar as a person can choose his character.

I like to be the strong, silent man in charge, the boss, the point man, the lieutenant, the head of the household, et cetera, a preference that may come from my having been the oldest of five children, with a more or less incompetent mother and a father who took off for Alaska when I was twelve and was never heard from again. Looking back, it seems I spent most of my youth cleaning up my father's mess and the rest of my life making sure that no one mistook me for him. He was an impractical man, not quite honest, a fellow of grand beginnings and no follow-through, one of those men who present their children and wives with dreams instead of skills, charm in place of discipline, and constant seduction for love and loyalty. When he took off to make a fortune in the oil fields, he left behind a huge hole in the yard that was going to be a swimming pool, a pile of cinder blocks that was going to be a restaurant, a hundred old casement windows that were going to be a greenhouse, a stack of IOUs written to half the people in town, and a promise to

Russell Banks

return by fall, which no one in town wanted him to keep.

Anyhow, when I began trying to seduce Risa Walker, I found myself behaving like my father, which embarrassed me and made me feel incompetent as well. I felt his phony smile on my face, heard his glib words coming from my mouth, and it made me cringe. I'd be pumping gas into her Wagoneer and mouthing lines like "Gee, Risa, you're looking swell these days! Life must agree with you, or you must agree with life, or something like that anyhow. . . ." I'd smile and smile and yammer on, playing a part. Then suddenly I'd switch roles. I'd have somehow become a member of the audience, and I'd hear myself yammering on, and it would be my father, and I'd see myself wink and grin and see my father, so I'd break off in the middle and freeze Risa out completely, leaving her somewhat confused, I'm sure. Other times I'd call her on the phone, and if Wendell answered, I'd gab about the Expos and the weather and local politics, like we were close buddies, which we were not; if Risa answered, I'd just ask for Wendell. Passing by the motel in my truck, if I happened to see her outside, I'd slow almost to a stop, wave like a long-lost friend, and when she made a move toward me, I'd speed up and take off, as if I were heading to a fire.

I have never been good with women, that is, skilled at the games that most men play—flirting, cajoling, soliciting their attention and favors—and until Risa, had never especially wanted to be. After all, I had always been able to count on Lydia. Who needed to flirt? Lydia and I in a sense spent our whole lives together: we were childhood friends and then high school sweethearts, and when I came back from Vietnam we discovered that we still loved each other, and so we got married. Technically, I was faithful to Lydia from beginning to end. There were a couple of occasions while we were married when, drunk or stoned or just inattentive, I slipped into what might be called compromising positions with a few local women, who shall remain nameless, but I got out before any damage was done and was even able to come home feeling virtuous. And there were a few sexual encounters with bar girls and prostitutes when I was in the service, Stateside and in Vietnam and once in Honolulu. Sowing wild oats, as they say. But in fact, for my age, I was unusually inexperienced in sexual matters.

The night Risa and I finally got together, it happened not because of anything I did but because Risa simply came up and put it to me at the bar at the Rendez-Vous, where I was sitting over a beer watching an NBA playoff on TV with three or four other men. She'd come through the door and stood there a minute as if looking for someone in particular. Then she walked straight to me, slipped her arm through mine and leaned in close and whispered in my ear, "Listen, Billy, when you're through here, why don't you come over and visit me? Room 11," she added, and patted my forearm and departed. As simple as that.

I left at halftime. Los Angeles was beating the hell out of Utah, and I just said I was going home. It was a cold, clear spring night with a sky full of stars, and my breath puffed out in front of me in little clouds as I walked past my pickup in the parking lot, crossed the road, and practically jogged the hundred or so yards along the road to the motel and went straight to Room 11.

I don't know how much in fact I had controlled or arranged it, how much I actually had seduced her with my awkward embarrassed onslaughts of alternating attention and withdrawal—probably a lot (sometimes you act a part and don't realize that the role is of a man who doesn't know how to act). But that night it appeared to me that Risa alone had made it possible for me to be, once again, not my father but myself, the strong, silent type of man I admired and had grown used to being, and I was deeply relieved and immensely grateful to her.

From then on, I guess you could say we were in love. At least we called it that. From start to finish, though, it was a secret affair. Risa has always assured me that no one knew we were in love; she insists that during the nearly three years we were involved she confided in no one. Consequently, she had her private version of the love affair, and I had mine, and there was no third version to correct them. None that I know of, anyhow.

As a result, until the morning of the accident, Risa Walker and I behaved toward each other as if we could go on like that forever—meeting and making love a couple of times a week in a darkened room late at night for an hour or two, and acting like mere acquaintances the rest of the time. Our love affair seemed to be permanently suspended halfway between fantasy and reality. Our sense of time and sequence was open-ended; it was like a movie with no beginning and no ending, and it remained that way because we did nothing to make our relationship public, to involve other people, a process that would have been started if Risa had ever confided in someone or if I had revealed it to someone. That would have objectified it somehow, taken it outside our heads, and no doubt would have led Risa to choose between me and Wendell, or would have led me to demand it. She would have chosen me, I believe that, and we would have married soon after. And then, by the time of the accident, when we lost our children, we would have had each other to turn to, instead of away from, which is what we did.

Out there on the Marlowe road that snowy morning, I remember at last climbing back up the embankment from the sandpit to the road and seeing her in the crowd. It was by then a large mixed stunned gathering along the shoulder of the road, of parents and local folks trying to calm and comfort one another, and cold exhausted state troopers, firemen, and rescue workers, and a pack of ravenous photographers and journalists. There was even a TV camera crew from the NBC affiliate in Plattsburgh on the scene, headed by a blond woman in tights and leg warmers and a leather miniskirt who kept shoving her microphone at people's gray faces, asking them what they were feeling. As if they could say.

Of course, I thought of Vietnam, but nothing I had seen or felt in Vietnam had prepared me for this. There was no fire and smoke or explosive noise, no wild shouts and frightened screams; instead, there was silence, broken ice, snow, and men and women moving with abject slowness: there was death, and it was everywhere on the planet and it was natural and forever; not just dying, perversely here and merely now.

And when I saw Risa Walker standing among the

others up there by the road, it was as if I were seeing her for the first time in my life—as if seeing her on newsreel footage, a woman from the village who had lost her son, a mother who had lost her only child. She was like a stranger to me then, a stranger whose life had just been made utterly meaningless. I know this because I felt the same way. Meaning had gone wholly and in one clot right out of my life too, and as a result I'm sure I was like a stranger to her as well. Our individual pain was so great that we could not recognize any other.

The bus had not been hauled out—you could see the front end of the vehicle up on the ice-cluttered far bank of the pit, like some huge dying yellow beast caught struggling to clamber out and frozen in the midst of the attempt, with the rest of the thing underwater. The snow and the cold made everyone down there—the rescue workers, the wet-suited divers from Burlington, the state troopers—move slowly, hunched in on their bodies as if with fear and permanent resentment, like lifetime prisoners in a Siberian gulag.

On the near bank, covered with dark green wool blankets, were the bodies of the last of the children removed from the bus by the divers, the kids who had been seated near the back. They had been laid out in the trampled snow but had not been brought up to the road yet. And among these were the bodies of Risa's son, Sean, who had been in front but whose body had got jammed under a seat, and the Ottos' boy, Bear, and my twins, Mason and Jessica.

I had seen them myself, I looked straight down into their peaceful ice-blue faces, and then quickly drew the blankets back over them again, turned and walked away alone, numb and solid as stone, and climbed slowly, on legs that weighed like lead, the steep side of the frozen embankment to the road. Photographs of them alive and smiling would have made me cry and fall down and beat the earth with my fists; their actual dead faces only sealed me off from myself.

I don't know where I was going, whom I was looking for. Yes, I do know. Lydia. I was looking for Lydia—to tell her that our children were dead, and that I had not been able to save them, and that finally we were all four of us together again.

The last of the ambulances had left for the medical center in Marlowe, where they were taking the survivors before dispatching the most seriously injured children to Lake Placid and Plattsburgh, and the firehouse in Sam Dent, where they had set up a temporary morgue, and there was a break while the workers waited for them to return for the rest. The wrecker from my garage, driven by Jimbo Gagne, was being brought around by the dump road from Wilmot Flats, preceded by a huge town snowplow, for that road had not been used since fall and was under six or eight feet of snow.

Except for Dolores Driscoll, who was uninjured and had remained down by the sandpit, lost and mumbling in a kind of shock but refusing stubbornly to leave the scene, there were no more survivors. Everyone knew that now. Those of us who had not left with the ambulances knew what we were waiting for—the removal of the last of the bodies of our children. Some people sobbed and wailed into the arms of friends and strangers, whoever would hold them; a few had been placed in the back seats of friends' cars; a few others, like Risa, just stood among friends and relatives and stared silently at the ground, their minds emptied of thought or feeling.

I guess I was one of these, although at first I had tried to keep on working down below alongside the other men, as if my own children had not been on the bus, as if this had happened to someone else and not me. At first, a few people—Jimbo and Bud from the garage, who had raced out at once with the wrecker when they heard on the CB that there'd been an accident (a message that in fact I myself had called in, although I don't know how I managed that; I don't even remember it), and Wyatt Pitney, the state trooper, and a couple of guys on the rescue squad—had tried to get me the hell out of there, but like Dolores, I wouldn't leave.

Later, I learned that people thought I was being courageous. Not so. There were selfish reasons for my behavior. I shoved everyone away and kept more or less to myself, silent, stone-faced, although continuing nonetheless to help the other men, as we received one child after another from the divers and wrapped them in blankets and dispatched them in stretchers up the steep slope to the road and the waiting ambulances, as if by doing that I could somehow prolong this part of the nightmare and postpone waking up to what I knew would be the inescapable and endless reality of it. No one spoke. Somehow, at bottom, I did not want this awful work to end. That's not courage.

It was still snowing pretty hard; close to half a foot of

it had fallen since the bus had gone over. There was no horizon. The sky was ash gray and hung low over the mountains. Within a few hundred yards the spruce trees and pines in the wide valley below the road and the thick birch trees and the road itself quickly dimmed and then simply faded into sheets of falling snow and disappeared entirely from view. There was a long disorderly line of cars, pickups, snowmobiles, and police cruisers parked on the shoulder, while several troopers wearing fluorescent orange jackets stood out in the middle of the road directing traffic, hurrying onlookers—skiers mostly, up for the weekend, delighted by the new snow, slowed suddenly and properly sobered by the sight of our town's disaster, memorizing as much of it as they could, so as to confirm it to their friends later, when it appeared in the newspapers and on television—past the scene and on to their weekend.

When I reached the top of the embankment, I stepped over the orange plastic ribbon the state troopers had hung along the roadway to keep people from scrambling down to the crash site. One of the troopers, a man I knew vaguely, came toward me, as if to escort me, and when I looked straight through him and waved him off, he backed quickly away, as if I had cursed him. That's when I saw Risa, standing a few feet in front of Wendell, who looked as though someone had punched him in the chest: all the force had gone out of him, and his face was twisted with the pain of the blow. By comparison, Risa was solid and resolved, already mourning, and slowly she looked up and then saw me when I passed near her. We could no longer pretend to love each other or even pretend to be hiding our love. Our eyes locked for a fraction of a second, and then we both looked away, and I moved on.

After that it was as if no one dared to talk to me or come forward in any way; I walked straight down the line of parents and other townspeople, the onlookers, cops, and reporters, until finally I was alone, plodding along the side of the road, moving uphill, back the way barely two hours earlier the school bus had come and then right behind it I had come in my pickup, idly daydreaming of sleeping with Risa Walker.

The snow continued to fall, and from the perspective of Risa and the others back at the accident site, I must have disappeared into it, just walked straight out of their reality into my own. In a few moments I was utterly alone in the cold snowy world, walking steadily away from everyone else, moving as fast as I could, toward my children and my wife.

For a long time that's how it was for me; perhaps it still is. The only way I could go on living was to believe that I was not living. I can't explain it; I can only tell you how it felt. I think it felt that way for a lot of people in town. Death permanently entered our lives with that accident. And while some people simply denied it, as poor Dolores Driscoll seems to have done, or moved to another part of the state and attempted to start their lives over, like the Lamstons, or tried to believe that death had been there all along, like Risa, claiming no difference between then and now, which is a way of denying it too—for me, and perhaps for some of the children who survived the accident, like Nichole Burnell and the Bigelows and Baptistes and the several sad little Bilodeau kids whose older brothers and sisters had been killed, for us there was life, true life, real life, no matter how bad it had seemed, before the accident, and nothing that came after the accident resembled it in any important way. So for us, it was as if we, too, had died when the bus went over the embankment and tumbled down into the frozen water-filled sandpit, and now we were lodged temporarily in a kind of purgatory, waiting to be moved to wherever the other dead ones had gone.

We didn't have available to us the various means that many of our neighbors and relatives had for easing the blow. At least I didn't. The Christians' talk about God's will and all—that only made me angry, although I suppose I am glad that they were able to comfort themselves with such talk. But I could not bring myself to attend any of the memorial services that the various churches in Sam Dent and the neighboring towns invited me to. It was enough to have to listen to Reverend Dreiser at the twins' funeral. He wanted us all to believe that God was like a father who had taken our children for himself. Some father.

The only father I had known was the one who had abandoned his children to others.

And then there were those folks who wanted to believe that the accident was not really an accident, that it was somehow *caused,* and that, therefore, someone was to *blame.* Was it Dolores's fault? A lot of people thought so. Or was it the fault of the State of New York for not replacing the guardrail out there on the Marlowe road? Was it the fault of the town highway department for having dug a sandpit and let it fill with water? What about the seat belts that had tied so many of the children into their seats while the rear half of the bus filled with icy water? Was it the governor's fault, then, for having generated legislation that required seat belts? Who *caused* this accident anyhow? Who can we *blame?*

Naturally, the lawyers fed off this need and cultivated it among people who should have known better. They swam north like sharks from Albany and New York City, advertising their skills and intentions in the local papers, and a few even showed up at the funerals, slipping their cards into the pockets of mourners as they departed from the graveyard, and before long that segment of the story had begun—the lawsuits and all the anger and nastiness and greed that people at their worst are capable of.

At first, however, people behaved well, which is to say, they behaved as you would expect: they decently gathered around one another and tried to provide comfort and aid. That's when you could be glad that you lived in a small town, relieved that you had family and friends, whether they could help you or not. The attempt was dignified and praiseworthy.

Most of my own family, at first, did exactly that, and I was appropriately grateful. We are not an unusual family—that is, we are not much of one. My mother, because of Alzheimer's, had been in a nursing home in Potsdam for over two years then, and she no longer even remembered the bare fact of my existence, let alone my children's; but my three sisters, who are married and have children of their own, called me as soon as they heard about the accident on the evening news. They and I are not personally close, we are in no sense confidants, but they are conscientious women and live in the area, you could say—the nearest, Sally, in Saratoga Springs, with her husband, who is an accountant for the racetrack commission, the other two in western New York, Rochester and Buffalo, where their husbands work, one as a machinist, the other as some kind of technician for Eastman Kodak. My brother, Darryl, the youngest, is out of the loop altogether. Years ago, he followed our father to Alaska but only got as far as Washington State and didn't quite disappear; once every eighteen months or so, he gets drunk and calls me late at night. I never heard from Darryl when the twins were killed, although I am sure he learned about it right away from my sisters, and when a year or so later he did call me, drunk as usual, very late at night, neither of us mentioned it, me for my reasons, and he no doubt for his. I was probably as drunk that night as he was. Of course, I never called him, either, to tell him what had happened; that would have been impossible for me, almost unthinkable—in fact, it took me until this very instant to think of it.

But it didn't matter, because, regardless, I was unable to take the comfort offered me. Something metallic in me refused to yield, and when one by one my sisters phoned and offered to come up to Sam Dent, an old compulsion took over; the same thing happened when various local people—Reverend Dreiser, Dorothy Coburn, even the men from the garage—called or came by to see how I was or to ask if there was anything they could do for me. It's something I have done since childhood, practically. When a person tries to comfort me, I respond by reassuring him or her—it's usually a her—and in that way I shut her down, smothering all her good intentions by denying my need.

I can't help it, and I'm not sorry for it; I'm even a little proud. People think I'm cold and unfeeling, but that's a price I've always been willing to pay. The truth is that I'm beyond help; most people are; and it only angers me to see my sisters or my friends here in town wasting their time. To forestall or cover my anger, I jump in front of them, and suddenly I myself have turned into the person come to provide comfort, reassurance, help, whatever it is they originally desired to provide me with. I take their occasion and make it my own. I never know this at the time, of course; only afterwards, when I'm alone again, sitting in my living room with a glass of whiskey in my hand, brooding over my solitude, trying to generate a little feeling, even if it's only self-pity.

When my youngest sister, Sally, called on the night of the accident, she was the first in the family to reach me, but it was maybe the fifteenth telephone call I'd received since hiking through the snow all the way home from the site. I had walked in whited out like a snowman, shucked my soaked clothes and put on a bathrobe, sat down at the kitchen table, opened a bottle of Scotch, and started to drink. I knew what it looked like and was glad no one could see me, although I was not ashamed. I knew why I was drinking, and it wasn't to numb the pain. Gary Dillinger, the school principal, called, and Wyatt Pitney, and Eden Schraft; and I reassured them all that there was nothing they could do for me. I'm okay, I'll be fine. They believed me: not that I was fine; they believed that there was nothing they could do for me. I was like a wounded animal gone to ground: better leave him to heal alone, or you might get bit trying to help. A couple of reporters called, and I simply hung up on them.

Jimbo Gagne called from the garage, and as usual, it was like we were both in Vietnam again—I was playing the lieutenant and he the corporal. We were all logistics. What did I want him to do with my truck? Leave it at the garage; I'd drive my car in tomorrow. Where should he put the wrecked bus? Out of sight behind the garage, and keep people away from it, because there was sure to be an investigation. Was there anything I needed? No, but if people came into the garage and asked, tell them I might be taking a few days off from work, so there'll probably be a delay for a couple of jobs.

"Are you okay, Billy?" He finally came right out and asked it. "How're you doing up there on the hill? You got somebody at the house with you?"

"Are *you* okay, Jimbo?" I returned. "It must have been rough on *you* out there."

"Yeah, sure," he said. "I'm all right, I guess. It was rough . . . ," he began, but then realized where that would lead and swerved away. "But, yeah, Billy, I'm okay."

By eight that night, when my sister Sally called, I was thoroughly drunk and was responding automatically, as if my mouth were a telephone answering machine: You have reached the home of Billy Ansel, he has suffered an irretrievable loss, has discovered that he is inconsolable, and thus, to save you trouble and him embarrassment, has removed himself from normal human contact. He will probably not return, but if you wish to leave a message anyhow, do so at the sound of the ice cubes tinkling in his glass, and if someday he does return, he will try to respond to your message.

But don't count on it.

Before you lose your children, you can talk about it—as a possibility, I mean. You can imagine it, like I did that time in Jamaica, years ago, and then later you can remember the moment when you first imagined it, and you can describe that moment coherently to people and with ease. But when the thing that you only imagined actually happens, you quickly discover that you can barely speak of it. Your story is jumbled and mumbled, out of sync and unfocused. At least that's how it has been for me.

People who have lost their children—and I'm talking here about the people of Sam Dent and am including myself—twist themselves into all kinds of weird shapes in order to deny what has happened. Not just because of the pain of losing a person they have loved—we lose parents and mates and friends, and no matter how painful, it's not the same—but because what has happened is so wickedly unnatural, so profoundly against the necessary order of things, that we cannot accept it. It's almost beyond belief or comprehension that the children should die before the adults. It flies in the face of biology, it contradicts history, it denies cause and effect, it violates basic physics, even. It's the final contrary. A town that loses its children loses its meaning.

Desperately, we struggled to arrange the event in our minds so that it made sense. Each of us in his own way went to the bottom and top of his understanding in search of a believable explanation, trying to escape this huge black nothingness that threatened to swallow our world whole. I guess the Christians in town, and there are a lot of them, got there first, at least the adults did, and I'm glad for them, but I myself could not rest there, and I believe that secretly most of them could not, either. To me, the religious explanation was just another sly denial of the facts. Not as sly, maybe, as insisting that the accident was actually *not* an accident, that someone—Dolores, the town, the state, *someone*—had caused it; but a denial nevertheless. Biology doesn't matter, the Christians argued, because this body we live in is not ultimately real; history doesn't matter, they said, because God's time is different and superior to man's anyhow; and forget cause and effect, forget what you've been told about the physical world, because there is heaven and there is hell and there is this green earth in between, and you are always alive in one of the three places.

I was raised, like most folks in Sam Dent, with a Christian perspective, and I remember it well: they made no bones about it. Billy, they said, there is no such thing as death. Just everlasting life. Isn't that great? That was the bottom line, whether you were Protestant like me and Lydia or Catholic like half the other folks in town. But when I was nineteen and went to Vietnam, I was still young enough to learn something new, and the new thing was all this dying that I saw going on around me. Consequently, when I came home from Vietnam, I couldn't take the Christian line seriously enough even to bother arguing with it. To please Lydia and the kids, I went to church a couple of times a year, but the rest of the time I stayed home and read the Sunday paper. Then Lydia died, and the Christian perspective came to seem downright cruel to me, because I had learned that death touched everyone. Even me. I stopped going to church altogether.

I still believed in life, however—that it goes on, in spite of death. I had my children, after all. And Risa. But four years later, when my son and daughter and so many other children of this town were killed in the accident, I could no longer believe even in life. Which meant that I had come to be the reverse, the opposite, of a Christian. For me, now, the only reality was death.

I went to the funeral service, of course; there was no way to avoid it without hurting and bewildering innocent people. And not to go, to stay holed up in my house like I had been doing, would have drawn too much attention to me, the last thing that I wanted. But the night before the funeral, late, I ventured out of my house for the first time and drove down the hill to town. I had been drinking pretty steadily for four days, but at that particular hour was sober—or at least sober enough to drive. It was a clear, starry night. A nearly full moon was circled by a ring of pale blue haze. There were no other vehicles on the road, and no lights on in the town. Sam Dent was a ghost town surrounded by fields of glistening snow under moonlight, with the hulking shades of the mountains blocking out half the sky.

I pulled in at the garage and drove around to the back, where the bus had been hauled by the wrecker and dropped, and for a few moments I sat in my truck with the motor running and looked at the thing—a huge dead fish, one of those leviathans drawn up from the deepest bottom of the sea, the ice-encrusted carcass of a creature from another age. Most of the windows had been smashed by the force of the accident and by the divers, the headlights and grille were gone, the sides and roof were bent and dented, and the tires were flattened and torn. It was dead, permanently stilled, silent, harmless.

I don't know why I was there, staring with strange loathing and awe at this wrecked yellow vehicle, as if it were a beast that had killed our children and then in turn been slain by the villagers and dragged here to a place where we could all come, one by one, and verify that it was safely dead. But I did want to see it, to touch it with my hands, maybe, in a primitive way to be sure finally that we had indeed killed it.

I got out of my truck, leaving the motor running and the headlights on, and walked slowly toward the bus. It was very cold; my shoes squeaked against the hard-packed snow on the ground, and my breath glided out in front of me in pale thin strips. There were several other vehicles parked in the darkness in the back lot—customers' cars scheduled to be repaired but crowded out of the garage and a couple of wrecks stashed there for parts or being rebuilt for the demolition derby. The orange plastic tape that the state police had wrapped around the bus to warn people away from it looked like tangled lines from the harpoons we had stuck it with.

For a moment I stood at the side of the bus, looking up at the windows; and then I heard the children inside.

Their voices were faint, but I could hear them clearly. They were alive and happy, going to school, and Dolores was moving through the gears, driving the bus up hill and down, cheerfully doing her duty; and I longed to join them, felt a deep aching desire to be with them, the first clear emotion I had felt since the accident; I wanted simply to pull the door open and walk inside and smell the wet wool and rubber boots and the lunches carried in paper sacks and tin boxes, hear their songs and gossip and teasing; I wanted to be with them in death, with my own children, yes, but with all of them, for they seemed at that moment so much more believable than I myself was, so much more alive.

But it was not the voices of the children that I heard, of course; it was the hiss of the wind in the pines at the edge of the lot, where the forest begins, the cold wind that blows down along the valley from the north. And it was not the sound of Dolores driving up hill and down; it was the engine of my own vehicle idling a few yards behind me, illuminating me and the bus with its headlights. For a long moment I stood there, listening to the wind and the low thrum of the truck, and slowly returned to reality.

And then, as I stepped away and turned back toward my truck, I heard the unmistakable thump of a car door open and close, and the crackle of leather footsteps on the hard dry snow of the lot. A tall man emerged from the darkness next to the truck and entered the circle of light between us. He wore a tan wool topcoat and was hatless, a middle-aged man with a bulbous tangle of curly gray hair that made his head appear much too large for his tall thin angular body. His hands were jammed deep in his coat pockets, and he hunched over slightly against the chilling wind that blew from behind him. Now, in the shadows at the far end of the lot, I saw the car he had been sitting in, a light-colored Mercedes sedan, silver or gray. The head-lights were off, but the engine was running; doubtless I had not heard it over the sound of my own vehicle and the wind, the engine of the bus and the voices of the children.

The man came up to within a few feet of me and made a strange little smile, almost wistful. "You work for Ansel?" he said.

"I am Ansel."

"Yes, I thought so." He had bright blue wide-open eyes that were impossible to read and sharp small features. He was clean-shaven, and his skin was pink and taut. It was a likable face, but the face of a smooth talker, self-confident and intelligent, and pleased, even eager, to let you look directly at him. "I'm sorry about your children, Mr. Ansel," he said, lowering his voice.

"You are, eh?"

"Yes."

For a few seconds neither of us spoke; we just looked straight into each other's eyes. He was good at it, he didn't get nervous or scared or even glance away; he held his ground and waited for me to break the silence or the stare, whichever I preferred.

"I take you to be a lawyer," I said, holding on to the stare.

"Yes, I am an attorney. My name is—"

"Mister, I don't want to *know* your name."

He hesitated a second. Then in a soft voice he said, "I understand."

"No. No, you don't understand."

"I can help you." He went on looking right into my eyes, as if he knew something I didn't.

"No, you can't help me. Not unless you can raise the dead." I was sorry at once for having said it, a cliché, a boy's smart remark, not a man's sad one. I had revealed to him, and to myself, a desire that I did not want to permit myself and that I was instantly ashamed of.

Pushing past him, I made quickly for my truck, but when I pulled the door open and started to get in, he came up beside me and held out a business card. "Here," he said. "You may change your mind."

I took the card and lifted it up and read it in the moonlight: *Mitchell Stephens, Esq.*, of a four-named firm, one of them Stephens, in New York City. Then I passed it back to him. "Mr. Stephens," I said to him, "if right now I was to beat you with my hands and feet so bad that you pissed blood and couldn't walk right for a month, would you sue me? Because that is what I'm about to do, you understand."

"No, Mr. Ansel," he said in a weary voice. "No, I wouldn't sue you. And I don't think there's anyone in this county who would even arrest you for it. But you're not about to beat me up, are you?"

I looked over at the bus. The children waved back at me, bright knots of apparition. The lawyer was right; I was no danger to him. I was a ghost.

"No, I'm not going to beat you up. Just don't talk to

me again," I said to him. "Don't come around my garage, and don't come to my house or call me on the telephone."

"You may change your mind. I can help you," he said again.

"Leave me alone, Stephens. Leave the people of this town alone. You can't help any of us. No one can."

"You can help each other," he said. "Several people have agreed to let me represent them in a negligence suit, and your case as an individual will be stronger if I'm allowed to represent you together as a group."

"My 'case'? I have no case. None of us has a case."

"You're wrong about that. Very wrong. Your friends the Walkers have agreed, and Mr. and Mrs. Otto, and I'm talking with some other folks. It's important to initiate proceedings right away. Things get covered up fast. People lie. You know that. People lie about these things. We have to begin our own investigation quickly, before the evidence disappears. That's why I'm out here tonight," he added, and he drew a small black automatic camera from his coat pocket.

"Our children aren't even buried yet," I told him. "It's you—you're the liar. Risa and Wendell Walker, I know them, you're right, but they wouldn't hire a goddamned lawyer. And the Ottos, they wouldn't deal with *you*, for Christ's sake. You're lying to me about them, and probably to them about me. We're not fools, you know, country bumpkins you can put the big-city hustle on. You're just trying to use us," I told him. "You want us to pull each other in."

He was not lying, though, and I knew it, and at

bottom I didn't give a damn what the others were doing, even Risa. It was almost funny to me at that moment, in a cruel and slightly superior way. Ghosts don't enter into class action lawsuits. I calmly smiled at the lawyer, and I think I even wished him luck, and got into my truck and closed the door on him. Slowly I backed the truck away from him and drove out of the lot, turned left, and headed down the valley toward the Rendez-Vous.

As I had so many times over the last couple of years, I parked my truck in the deserted parking lot outside the Rendez-Vous, which, like everything else in town, was closed, and walked across the road to Room 11 at the Bide-a-Wile. I don't know if I expected Risa to be there, but surely I hoped she would be—I had no other reason to go there this late.

She was sitting by the window in the wicker chair, and when I let myself into the darkened room, she said simply, without expression, "I knew you'd come."

"Well, I can't say I did." I sat down opposite her, on the edge of the bed, and put my hands on my knees. "Habit, I guess."

"Me, too," she said. "Thank God for habits."

We tried for a few moments to talk the way we used to, the way people who love each other are supposed to talk—intimately, more or less honestly, about their feelings for one another and for other people as well. We tried to talk not as if nothing had happened, of course, but with the accident and the loss of our children as a context. It was useless. I couldn't say anything true about how I felt, and neither could she.

"This is the first time I've been able to leave the house," I said.

"People keep calling on the phone and coming by to see if they can help out."

"No one can help."

"No. Not really. But they try."

"Yes, they try."

"You'll go to the funeral, though, won't you?"

"Yes," I said, "I'll be there. But I'd rather stay at home alone."

"There'll be a lot of people there."

"I expect so."

"I wish it was just going to be the families, you know, like us. They're the only ones who really understand."

"I guess so."

"But people have been very thoughtful and sympathetic."

"Yes. They have."

We sounded like strangers sitting in a dentist's waiting room. Finally, though, we gave it up and were silent for a while. Then she told me how she had known all along that something like this was going to happen. She had felt it in her bones, she said. As if she wanted me to be amazed and praise her for it.

I decided that she was stupid to think that and even stupider to say it, although I did not tell her so. Instead, I told her about my unexpected meeting with the lawyer, Stephens. Without saying why, I said that I'd stopped by the garage and while I was there I'd caught the lawyer taking pictures of the bus with a flash camera, which was more or less the truth. "The sonofabitch tried to get me to hire him for some kind of negligence suit," I said. "He told me he'd already got you and Wendell signed up, you and Wendell and the Ottos, and I told him to shove it. We don't need a lawyer," I added.

"What do we need?"

"Good question." I stood up and took a step toward the door; I still had my coat and wool cap on. "But we don't need a lawyer," I said. "Count me out."

She looked up at me, and in the bands of moonlight falling through the blinds I could see her face clearly, and it was no longer lovely to me. It didn't even look like a woman's face anymore; it was like the face of a male actor who had made himself up as a woman. "Well," she said, "goodbye."

"Goodbye." I pulled my gloves over my hands and opened the door and stepped outside, where I turned and said to her, "I have to go home now."

"You go home, Billy."

I closed the door on her and walked away. We spoke again, of course, on numerous occasions, but always with other people surrounding us; we managed not to meet again in a room alone, however, or to speak face-to-face, and so it was as if we never saw each other after that, never saw the people we had once been, Risa Walker and Billy Ansel. From then on, we were simply different people. Not new people; different.

Mitchell Stephens, Esquire

Angry? Yes, I'm angry; I'd be a lousy lawyer if I weren't. I suppose it's as if I've got this permanent boil on my butt and can't quite sit down. Which is not the same, you understand, as being hounded by greed; although I can see, of course, that it probably sometimes looked like greed to certain individuals who were not lawyers, when they saw a person like me driving all the way up there to the Canadian border, practically, saw me camping out in the middle of winter in a windy dingy little motel room for weeks at a time, bugging the hell out of decent people who were in the depths of despair and just wanted to be left alone. I can understand that.

But it wasn't greed that put me there; it's never been greed that sends me whirling out of orbit like that. It's anger. What the hell, I'm not ashamed of it. It's who I am. I'm not proud of it, either, but it makes me useful, at least. Which is more than you can say for greed.

That's what people don't get about negligence lawyers—good negligence lawyers, I mean, the kind who go after the sloppy fat cats with their corner offices and end up nailing their pelts to the wall. People immediately assume we're greedy, that it's money we're after, people call us ambulance-chasers and so on, like we're the proctologists of the profession, and, yes, there's lots of those. But the truth is, the good ones, we'd make the same moves for a single shekel as for a ten-million-dollar settlement. Because it's anger that drives us and delivers us. It's not any kind of love, either—love for the underdog or the victim, or whatever you want to call them. Some litigators like to claim that. The losers.

No, what it is, we're permanently pissed off, the winners, and practicing law is a way to be socially useful at the same time, that's all. It's like a discipline; it organizes and controls us; probably keeps us from being homicidal. A kind of Zen is what. Some people equally pissed off are able to focus their rage by becoming cops or soldiers or martial arts instructors; those who become lawyers, however, especially litigators like me, are a little too intelligent, or maybe too intellectual is all, to become cops. (I've known some pretty smart cops, but not many intellectual ones.) So instead of learning how to break bricks and two-by-fours with our hands or bust chain-snatchers in subways, we sneak off to law school and put on three-piece suits and come roaring out like banshees, all teeth and claws and fire and smoke.

Certainly we get paid well for it, which is a satisfaction, yes, but not a motivation, because the real satisfaction, the true motivation, is the carnage and the smoldering aftermath and the trophy heads that get hung up on the den wall. I love it.

That's why I spent most of six months up there in Sam Dent, practically becoming a citizen. Not my idea of a winter vacation, believe me. But anytime I hear about a case like that school bus disaster up there, I turn into a heat-seeking missile, homing in on a target that I know in my bones is going to turn out to be some bungling corrupt state agency or some multinational corporation that's cost-accounted the difference between a ten-cent bolt and a million-dollar out-of-court settlement and has decided to sacrifice a few lives for the difference. They do that, work the bottom line; I've seen it play out over and over again, until you start to wonder about the human species. They're like clever monkeys, that's all. They calculate ahead of time what it will cost them to assure safety versus what they're likely to be forced to settle for damages when the missing bolt sends the bus over a cliff, and they simply choose the cheaper option. And it's up to people like me to make it cheaper to build the bus with that extra bolt, or add the extra yard of guardrail, or drain the quarry. That's the only check you've got against them. That's the only way you can ensure moral responsibility in this society. Make it cheaper.

So that winter morning when I picked up the paper and read about this terrible event in a small town upstate, with all those kids lost, I knew instantly what the story was; I knew at once that it wasn't an "accident" at all. There are no accidents. I don't even know what the word means, and I never trust anyone who says he does. I knew that some-body somewhere had made a decision to cut a corner in order to save a few pennies, and now the state or the manufacturer of the bus or the town, somebody, was busy lining up a troop of smoothies to negotiate with a bunch of grief-stricken bumpkins a settlement that wouldn't displease the accountants. I packed a bag and headed north, like I said, pissed off.

Sam Dent is a pretty town, actually. It's not Aspen or Vail, maybe, and it sure isn't Saint Bart's or Mustique, where frankly I'd much rather have been at that time of year, but the landscape was attractive and strangely stirring. I'm not a scenery freak like my ex-wife, Klara, who has orgasms over sunsets and waterfalls and not much else, but once in a great while I go someplace and look up and see where I am, and it's unexpectedly beautiful to me: my stomach tightens, and my pulse races, and this powerful blend of fear and excitement comes over me, like something dangerous is about to happen. It's almost sexual.

Anyhow, the town of Sam Dent and the mountains and forests that surrounded it, they gave me that feeling. I grew up in Oak Park, Illinois, and have spent my entire adult life in New York City. I'm an urban animal, basically; I care more about people than landscape. And although I have sojourned in rural parts quite a bit (I've spent months at a time in Wounded Knee, in eastern Washington, in Alabama, where I won a big asbestosis case, in the coal-mining region of West Virginia, and so on), I can't say the landscape of those places particularly moved me. They were places, that's all. Interchangeable chunks of the planet. Yes, I needed to learn a whole lot about each of them in order to pursue my case effectively, but in those other cases my interest in the landscape was more pragmatic, you might say, than personal. Strictly professional.

Here in Sam Dent, however, it somehow got personal. It's dark up there, closed in by mountains of shadow and a blanketing early nightfall, but at the same time the space is huge, endless, almost like being at sea—you feel like you're reading one of those great long novels by whatsername, Joyce Carol Oates, or Theodore Dreiser, that make you feel simultaneously surrounded by the darkness and released into a world much larger than any you've dealt with before. It's a landscape that controls you, sits you down and says, Shut up, pal, I'm in charge here.

They have these huge trees everywhere, on the mountains, of course, but down in the valleys and in town, too, and surrounding the houses, even outside my motel room; they've got white pine and spruce and hemlock and birches thick as a man, and the wind blows through them constantly. And since there's very little noise of any other kind up there—almost no people, remember, and few cars, no sirens howling, no jackhammers slamming, and so forth— the thing you hear most is the wind blowing in the trees. From September to June, the wind comes roaring out of Ontario all the way from Saskatchewan or someplace weird like that, steady and hard and cold, with nothing to stop or slow it until it hits these mountains and the trees, which, like I say, are everywhere.

What they call the Adirondack Park, you understand, is no small roadside park, no cutesy little campground with public toilets and showers—I mean, we're talking six million acres of woods, mountains, and lakes, we're talking a region the size of the state of Vermont, the biggest damn park in the country—and most of the people who live there year round are scattered in little villages in the valleys, living on food stamps and collecting unemployment, huddling close to their fires and waiting out the winter, until they can go back outdoors and repair the damage the winter caused.

It's a hard place, hard to live in, hard to romanticize. But, surprisingly, not hard to love—because that's what I have to call the feeling it evokes, this strange combination of fear and awe I'm talking about, even in someone like me.

That wasn't what I expected, though. When I first drove up there, the day after the school bus went over, I was astonished by what I saw. Upstate New York, to me, had always been Albany, with maybe a little Rip Van Winkle, Love Canal, and Woodstock tossed in; but this was wilderness, practically. Like Alaska. Suddenly, I'm thinking *Last of the Mohicans.* "Forest primeval," I'm thinking. America before the arrival of the white man.

I'm driving along the Northway above Lake George between these high sheer cliffs with huge sheets of ice on them, and I look off to the side into the woods, and the woods come banging right back at me, a dense tangle of trees and undergrowth that completely resists penetration, and I start hoping my car doesn't break down. This is not Bambi territory. It's goddamn dark in there, with bears and bobcats and moose. Ten thousand coyotes, I read in the *Times.* Sasquatches, probably.

Of course, it was dead of winter then, that first time, and there was five or six feet of snow over everything, and daytime temps that got stuck below zero for weeks in a row, which only made the woods and the mountains more ominous. Trees, rocks, snow, and ice—and, until I turned off the Northway and started down those narrow winding roads into the villages, no houses, no sign of people. It was scary, but it was also very beautiful. No way around it.

Then I began to see the first signs of people—and I mean poor people here. Not like in the city, of course, not like Harlem or Bedford-Stuyvesant, where you feel that the poor are imprisoned, confined by invisible wire fences, life-long prisoners of the rich, who live and work in the high-rises outside. No wonder they call them ghettos. They ought to call them reservations.

Up here, though, the poor are kept out, and it's the rich who stay inside the fence and only in the summer months. It's like Ultima Thule or someplace beyond the pale, and most of the people who live here year round are castoffs, tossed out into the back forty and made to forage in the woods for their sustenance and shelter, grubbing nuts and berries, while the rest of us snooze warmly inside the palisade, feet up on the old hassock, brandy by our side, *Wall Street Journal* unfolded on our lap, good dog Tighe curled up by the fire.

I'm exaggerating, of course, but only slightly, because that is how you feel when you cruise down these roads in your toasty Mercedes and peer out at the patched-together houses with flapping plastic over the windows and sagging porches and woodpiles and rusting pickup trucks and junker cars parked in front, boarded-up roadside diners and dilapi-dated motels that got bypassed by the turnpike that Rockefeller built for the downstate Republican tourists and the ten-wheeler truckers lugging goods between New York City and Montreal. It's amazing how poor people who live in distant beautiful places always think that a six-lane highway or an international airport will bring tourists who will solve all their problems, when inevitably the only ones who get rich from it live elsewhere. The locals end up hating the tourists, outsiders, foreigners—rich folks who employ the locals now as part-time servants, yardmen, waitresses, gamekeepers, fix-it men. Money that comes from out of town always returns to its source. With interest. Ask an African.

Sam Dent. Weird name for a town. So naturally the first thing I ask when I register at a sad little motel in town is "Who the hell was Sam Dent?"

This rather attractive tall doe-eyed woman in a reindeer sweater and baggy jeans was checking me in, Risa Walker, who I did not know at the time was one of those parents who had lost a child in the so-called accident. I might not have been so flippant otherwise. She said, "He once owned most of the land in this town and ran a hotel or something." She had that flat expressionless voice that I should have recognized as the voice of a parent who has lost a child. "Long time ago," she added. Like it was the good old days. (Good for Sam, I'll bet, who probably died peacefully in his sleep in his Fifth Avenue mansion.)

She gave me the key to my room, number 3, and asked would I be staying longer than one night.

"Hard to say." I passed her my credit card, and she took the imprint. I was hoping that tomorrow I'd find a better place in town or nearby, maybe a Holiday Inn or a Marriott. This motel was definitely on the downhill slide and had been for years—no restaurant or bar, a small dark room with scarred furniture and sagging bedsprings, a shower that looked as if it spat rusty lukewarm water for thirty seconds before turning cold.

It turned out there was no other place in town to stay, and as I needed to be close to the scene of the crime, so to speak, I ended up staying at the Walkers' motel throughout those winter and spring months and into the summer, every time I was in Sam Dent, even when things got a little ticklish between me and Risa and her husband, Wendell. It never got that ticklish, but when the divorce started coming on, I was giving her advice and not him. Throughout, I kept the room on reserve, not that there was ever any danger of its being taken, and paid for the entire period, whether I used it or not. It was the least I could do.

The most I could do for the Walkers was represent them in a negligence suit that compensated them financially for the loss of their son, Sean. And that's only part of it, the smaller part. I could also strip and hang the hide of the sonofabitch responsible for the loss of their son—which just might save the life of some other boy riding to school in some other small American town.

That was my intention anyhow. My mission, you might say.

Every year, though, I swear I'm not going to take any more cases involving children. No more dead kids. No more stunned grieving parents who really only want to be left alone to mourn in the darkness of their homes, for God's sake, to sit on their kids' beds with the blinds drawn against the curious world outside and weep in silence as they contemplate their permanent pain. I'm under no delusions—I know that in the end a million-dollar settlement makes no real difference to them, that it probably only serves to sharpen their pain by constricting it with legal language and rewarding it with money, that it complicates the guilt they feel and forces them to question the authenticity of their own suffering. I know all that; I've seen it a hundred times.

It hardly seems worth it, right? Thanks but no thanks, right? And I swear, if that were the whole story, if the settlement were not a fine as well, if it were not a punishment that, though it can never fit the crime, might at least make the crime seem prohibitively expensive to the criminal, then, believe me, I would not pursue these cases. They humiliate me. They make me burn inside with shame. Win or lose, I always come out feeling diminished, like a cinder.

So I'm no Lone Ranger riding into town in my white Mercedes-Benz to save the local sheepherders from the cattle barons in black hats; I'm clear on that. And I don't burn myself out with these awful cases because it somehow makes me a better person. No, I admit it, I'm on a personal vendetta; what the hell, it's obvious. And I don't need a shrink to tell me what motivates me. A shrink would probably tell me it's because I myself have lost a child and now identify with chumps like Risa and Wendell Walker and that poor sap Billy Ansel, and Wanda and Hartley Otto. The victims. Listen, identify with the victims and you become one yourself. Victims make lousy litigators.

Simply, I do it because I'm pissed off, and that's what you get when you mix conviction with rage. It's a very special kind of anger, let's say. So I'm no victim. Victims get depressed and live in the there and then. I live in the here and now.

Besides, the people of Sam Dent are not unique. We've all lost our children. It's like all the children of America are dead to us. Just look at them, for God's sake—violent on the streets, comatose in the malls, narcotized in front of the TV. In my lifetime something terrible happened that took our children away from us. I don't know if it was the Vietnam war, or the sexual colonization of kids by industry, or drugs, or TV, or divorce, or what the hell it was; I don't know which are causes and which are effects; but the children are gone, that I know. So that trying to protect them is little more than an elaborate exercise in denial. Religious fanatics and superpatriots, they try to protect their kids by turning them into schizophrenics; Episcopalians and High Church Jews gratefully abandon their kids to boarding schools and divorce one another so they can get laid with impunity; the middle class grabs what it can buy and passes it on, like poisoned candy on Halloween; and meanwhile the inner-city blacks and poor whites in the boonies sell their souls with longing for what's killing everyone else's kids and wonder why theirs are on crack.

It's too late; they're gone; we're what's left.

And the best we can do for them, and for ourselves, is rage against what took them. Even if we can't know what it'll be like when the smoke clears, we do know that rage, for better or worse, generates a future. The victims are the ones who've given up on the future. Instead, they've joined the dead. And the rest, look at them: unless they're enraged and acting on it, they're useless, unconscious; they're dead themselves and don't even know it.

If you want to know the truth, in my life, in my personal life, that is, though my ex-wife, Klara, is the apparent victim (all you have to do is ask her), the true victim is my daughter, Zoe. Not me, that's for sure. Because, though I may have lost her, Zoe's not literally dead. At least not that I know of. Not yet. The last time I heard from her she was out in L.A., walking around like a tattooed zombie with one of her purple-haired zombie boyfriends.

She's my only child; I loved her more than I thought was humanly possible. Certainly more than I've ever loved anyone else. I've told my story—it's a compulsion, I guess—to friends and strangers and even to shrinks, all of whom feel sorry for me, if you can believe that, which is a way of feeling sorry for themselves, I've learned; I've attended Al-Anon meetings and ToughLove workshops for parents and spouses of addicts, where they promote a kind of spiritual triage ("Mitch, chill out, man, you've got to learn to *separate* from your child," they say, while you watch her drowning before your eyes); and I've spent more time talking to Klara in the last five years than in the entire fifteen years we were married—I've done everything the loving father of a whacked-out drug-addicted child is supposed to do. I've even done a Rambo and kicked a few doors off their jambs and dragged Zoe out of filthy rat-infested apartments, garbage heaps with satanic altars lit by candles in a goat's skull on a TV in a corner; I've locked her up in rehab hospitals, halfway houses, and the Michigan farms of understanding relatives. Two weeks later, she's back on the streets. New York, Pittsburgh, Seattle, L.A. The next time I hear from her, it's a phone call scamming for money, money supposedly for school or a new kind of therapist who specializes in macrobiotic drug treatment or, sobbing with shame and need, a plane ticket home (that's usually the one that gets me). I send the money, hundreds, thousands of dollars; and she's gone again. A month or two later, she's calling from Santa Fe—same scam, same format, different details: an acupuncturist specializing in treating drug addiction, a registration fee for a culinary arts school in Tucson, and if those stories don't work, she breaks back to the old plea to let her come home to New York and let's solve this problem together, Daddy, dear Daddy, once and for all, if I'll just send the plane ticket and money to get her stuff out of hock, etc. By now, of course, I realize that if I don't send money, she'll raise it some other way, dealing drugs or pornography or even hooking. It's like I'm in the position of having to buy her clean needles to protect her against AIDS. Forget protecting her against the drugs. Forget healing her mind.

Five years of this, and what happens? You get pissed off—believe me, enough rage and helplessness, your love turns to steamy piss. Of course, long before Zoe dropped out of boarding school and hit the streets, I was pissed off—it's in my genes, practically—but she's succeeded in providing me with a nice sharp focus for it, so that, except when I'm burning myself out on something like the Sam Dent school bus case, I'm dizzy and incoherent, boiling over, obsessed, useless—mad. I'd rather be a cinder than a madman. But there's no way I'll let myself become a victim.

That guy Wendell Walker, who with his wife, Risa, owned the motel I was staying at, the Bide-a-Wile—he surprised me. At first, I pegged him as a permanent loser, one of those guys who love their own tragedy, who feel ennobled and enlarged by it. But of all the parents in Sam Dent who had lost a child when the bus went over, he turned out to have the least interest in remaining a victim. Except for Wanda Otto, maybe. We're talking about the parents of some fourteen kids here, some of whom, like Billy Ansel, lost more than one child, so actually we're talking about a list of only eight families in all. Of which, in those first few weeks before the case took off, I was able to interview five who had not already signed up with another attorney, which put them off limits to me, or who were not talking to anyone at all, like Billy Ansel, and even him I eventually got to. In a way.

And there was the girl Nichole Burnell, who survived the wreck; she was going to be the linchpin of the case, an all-American teenaged beauty queen whose life was ruined by her injuries and by the trauma of having survived such an ordeal. A living victim is more effective with a jury than a dead one; you can't compensate the dead, they feel. That's how I planned to present her; luckily, it was how her parents viewed the event too. She had been their destiny, their glory: for their future, they had nothing but her future, and since it had been taken from her, it had been taken, as they saw it, from them as well: so now they were out for blood. One way or the other, they were going to continue to use her to get what they thought was their due.

Fine by me. I had my agenda too. In spite of the injuries, Nichole Burnell looked good, she talked good, and she had suffered immeasurably and would for the rest of her life. A beautiful articulate fourteen-year-old girl in a wheel-chair. She was perfect. I could hardly wait to see the other side depose her.

Wendell Walker, on the other hand, when I first met him, seemed utterly defeated, gone, a dark hole in space. Useless, even to himself. I had chucked my stuff in my room and wandered back out to the motel office, to get directions to where the bus had gone over and to check out some of the local response to the event—to start work, in other words—but also to see if there was someplace in town where I could get a decent meal. It seemed unlikely, but you never know about these small towns. I once found a terrific barbecue shack in Daggle, Alabama.

The office was gloomy and dark, cold as a meat locker; behind the counter, a door leading to what I took to be the apartment where the proprietors lived was open a crack, and a skinny band of light fell across the linoleum floor of the room. I thought I was alone, but when I walked up to the counter, looking for a bell or something to signal the woman who had checked me in, I saw a figure there, a large, heavyset man in a straight-backed chair, sitting behind the counter in the darkness as if in bright light, looking at his lap as if reading a magazine. It was a strange position, alert but frozen in place. He looked catatonic to me.

"Sorry, buddy," I said. "I didn't see you there. How's it going?"

No answer; no response whatsoever. He just went on staring down at his lap, as if he didn't hear or see me. One of those country simples, I thought. Inbreeding. Great. First local I get to talk to, and he turns out to be an alien. "The boss around?" I asked.

Nothing. Except that his tongue came out and licked dry lips. Then I recognized it: I've seen it a hundred times, but it still surprises and scares me. It's the opaque black-glass look of a man who has recently learned of the death of his child. It's the face of a person who's gone to the other side of life and is no longer even looking back at us. It always has the same history, that look: at the moment of the child's dying, the man follows his child into darkness, as if he's making a last attempt to save it; then, in panic, to be sure that he himself has not died as well, the man turns momentarily back toward us, maybe he even laughs then or says something weird, for he sees only darkness there too; and now he has returned to where his child first disappeared, fixing onto one of the bright apparitions that linger there. It's downright spooky.

"I'm sorry, bud," I said to him. "I just arrived here."

Still no response. Then he stirred slightly, turned his soft hands over, and placed them on his knees. He was wearing a Montreal Expos sweatshirt and loose khakis, a fat guy, slump-shouldered, not too bright-looking.

Suddenly, he said, "Are you a lawyer?" His voice was low but thin, flattened out, like a piece of tin. He still hadn't turned to face me, but I guess he'd taken my measure already. What the hell, I suppose I looked like a lawyer, especially up here, especially now. Something like this happens, people expect to see lawyers crawling around. Guys in suits and topcoats.

"Yes, I'm a lawyer."

"A good one?"

"Yes, sure. One of the best," I said.

Slowly he turned toward me and in the dim light examined my face. "Well, good. I need a lawyer," he said, and when he stood up, his large soft body tightened, and surprisingly the man looked very tough to me, like a fist, and I said to myself, Well, well, I damned near misread this guy entirely. "Come inside," he said. "My wife and I want to talk to you."

I reached into my pocket, drew out a card, and handed it to him, and he accepted it without a glance, like a bellhop taking a tip, and placed it facedown on the counter. With the other hand, he swung open the door to their quarters, washing the office in domestic light, and walked straight into the living room beyond, where I saw the woman in an easy chair, watching television with the sound off.

I followed him into the small room, and we three sat and talked for several hours, and all the while they watched the soundless television, never once looking at me or each other. Creepy, yes, but at the time it seemed entirely appropriate, even necessary, to our conversation.

This was a happy start for me, a lucky break. The Walkers were classically pissed off. Both of them. They wanted revenge, which was useless to them, of course—they weren't going to get it, but they didn't know that yet.

And as I later learned, they wanted money, not as compensation but because they had been broke for so long and had always wanted it.

I learned from them that first night in town a lot of what the newspapers hadn't yet told me—the names of the other parents whose children had been killed, the usual route of the school bus, the condition of the driver when she picked up their son, Sean, the weather, the exact spot where the bus went off the road, the origin and history of the sandpit it ended up in, and so forth.

It seemed clear that the bus driver, Dolores Driscoll, was a dead end; she was probably only doing exactly what she had done for years, and besides, she herself had no real property or earning power to attach and was a popular woman in town to boot, a nondrinker with a crippled husband she supported. Not the kind of person you want to sue for negligence. The deep pockets, I knew, were going to be found in the pants worn by the state, the town, and the school board, or, more precisely, by their insurance companies. I explained that to them.

I asked them who else might be willing to join in a suit.

"I don't know," Risa said, her eyes still on the flickering screen of the TV. The Cosby show, which I hate. Ozzie and Harriet in blackface. "Nobody's much talked about it yet. Although there's been a lot of lawyers in town, I heard. A couple of them checked in here today. But they seemed—"

"Too young and too old," Wendell said. "One or the other. Too goddamn eager."

I knew the types. I explained that the best people to enter the suit were people who were unlikely to sign on with lawyers such as that. No, I said, what we needed were folks who, like them, were intelligent and articulate, who came across as sensitive, loving parents, people with a solid family life, with no criminal background or history of trouble in town. Good neighbors I wanted, decent hardworking people like themselves, I said, laying it on a little.

"Well, okay, there's Kyle and Doreen," Risa said. "The Lamstons. Up on Bartlett Hill. They lost all three of their kids. After everything they've been through. Especially Doreen." Risa was at that stage where every now and then she didn't believe that she had lost her child; she thought that maybe it had only happened to other people in town.

"Kyle's a drunk, a belligerent drunk," Wendell said. "Nobody likes him. He's trouble."

"Belligerent, you say. Is he a known wife-beater?"

"Yeah, a wife-beater," he said. "I'm afraid so. A 'known' one. He's that all right."

"All right, there's the Hamiltons. Joe and Shelley Hamilton."

Wendell said, "Anybody knows that guy knows he's been stealing antiques from summer houses and reselling them to dealers in Plattsburgh for years."

I was starting to like this man, Wendell Walker. He looked like a pushover, but he had an attitude. In the middle of a wrecked life, drowning in sadness, he was still able to hold his grudges. He'd probably kept them locked up inside himself for years, feeling guilty, and now for the first time in his life he believed he was entitled to lay about him. His wife, though, was more conventionally linked to other people, a good-looking, once sexy woman who still courted her neighbors' good opinions and attention. She was trying to put the best possible construction on things, even if it meant lying to herself.

Wendell, though, he didn't give a damn. Not anymore.

They went on down the list of parents, most of them dismissed by Wendell out of hand, as his resentments and grudges and old injuries, one by one, surfaced and got expressed.

"Sonofabitch owes over fifty thousand bucks in unpaid bills to the bank and half the businesses in town, and he's about to lose his house and cars. . . ."

"She's over to the Rendez-Vous or down to the Spread Eagle every night and has slept with every drunk in town at least twice. . . ."

"The Bilodeaus and the Atwaters are all inbred. They're so dumb they don't know Saturday . . ."

And so on down the line, with Risa reluctantly concurring. Until they got to the Ottos, Wanda and Hartley, who had lost their adopted son, an Indian boy named Bear. Wanda was pregnant, they were smart people apparently, college educated, even, had moved to Sam Dent a dozen or so years ago from the city and had made a respected life here as craftsmen.

"Yeah, well, I bet they're pot-smokers," Wendell grumped.

"You don't know that." Risa lit a cigarette, as if in defiance.

"They ever been busted?" I asked, and lit one myself. "No," Risa said.

"Not to your knowledge is what you mean," Wendell shot back. I wondered if he knew that his wife was probably having an affair with somebody.

I made notes and let them continue. I especially liked the part about the adopted Indian boy and Wanda's pregnancy. It was possible she'd lose the baby over this. That happens. The pot business I'd check out later. (It turned out to be nothing, of course. At least no record. Local suspicion was all.)

It was Wendell who mentioned Billy Ansel. Risa kept silent, and I figured he was the guy she was having her affair with. That could be trouble, so I put an asterisk next to his name; but otherwise he was almost too good to be true. Ansel was a widower, much admired in town, a Vietnam vet, a war hero, practically. And he had lost his two children, who were twins. Also, he had actually witnessed the event; he'd been following the bus in his truck on his way to work that morning and had helped remove the victims. He'd know, by God, that his kids were dead. No denial there.

The bus, Wendell said, had been hauled back to Ansel's garage. "I went to school with him," Wendell added. "I guess he's maybe the most liked man in this town. And he knows it. And likes it. But what the hell, that's all right, I guess. He drinks," he added. "But mostly at home. Otherwise, no flaws." I watched Risa, who watched her hands. Double asterisk.

"What about the kids who survived the accident?

Some of them were injured pretty badly, I understand. Any of them whose parents you think might be willing to join you in this?"

Risa, as if relieved not to be talking about Billy Ansel any longer, rattled off the names of half a dozen families, including the Burnells, Mary and Sam, whose daughter Nichole was in the eighth grade, president of the class, queen of last fall's Harvest Festival Ball. "A potential Miss Essex County, or even a Miss New York," Risa said wistfully. "I'm serious." Nichole was in the hospital in Lake Placid with a broken back, still unconscious, as far as they knew. Her parents, they agreed, were poor but honest, churchgoers. Pillars of the community, Wendell noted sarcastically. Her father, Sam, was a plumber; her mother sang in the choir. Nichole had been everybody's favorite babysitter.

It was a promising start. I retrieved a contingency fee agreement form from my room, explained the terms and got the Walkers to sign it, and went out in search of a burger and beer, which I found at the Rendez-Vous, a tavern located practically across the road from the motel. Very convenient. I didn't even take the car; just strolled over. Turned out the burger wasn't bad.

There was no one in the place who looked local, other than the bartender and the waitress. I guess everyone was at home watching TV to see if they were on the news. But I wasn't the only customer. A couple of sharks in double-knit suits—Wendell was right: too old and too young, too eager—sat at the bar watching the Knicks clobber the Celtics, while a few guys whom I took to be reporters, in leather jackets and stone-washed jeans, trolled back and forth among the booths in back, talking shop and feeling superior to one another and to the town, practicing for the assignment that would bring them the Pulitzer. The reporters who cover these backcountry cases, even when they're stringers for the Plattsburgh *Press-Republican* or something, always try to look as if they work for *Rolling Stone* or *The Village Voice*.

No way I was going to sit with the sharks at the bar, though, in spite of the Knicks game, so I took a booth in a far corner, just beyond the reporters, and ate alone, working up my notes. I was off and running. Happy. More or less.

The next morning (I was right about the shower, by the way, and the bed was like a hammock made of wire, the room as cold as a fishing camp in Labrador), I drove over to the town of Keene Valley, ten miles to the southeast, where the bartender at the Rendez-Vous had told me there was a diner, the Noonmark, that served a decent breakfast and sold out-of-town newspapers. It was a pleasant drive. The snow-covered mountains loomed above the village, dwarfing it, making the buildings seem puny and temporary. Thin strands of wood smoke curled from the chimneys of the houses and disappeared into clean air. The sun was shining, the snow looked downy soft, the sky was a huge blue bowl, and according to the Lake Placid radio station, it was five degrees below zero. This place looks good in winter, but believe me, you want to observe it through the windshield of a warm car.

After a large country breakfast of pancakes and bacon among citizens who shook their heads sadly while they pored over the news accounts of the disaster in the village next door, I drove back to Sam Dent, where I found the Ottos at home—if you want to call it that. I couldn't tell if it was a DEW-line radar station or a house. They lived in a dome, definitely homemade, covered with wood shingles and half set into the side of a hill, with odd-shaped windows, diamonds and triangles, arranged in no pattern that I could discern from outside.

They didn't exactly welcome me in. Hartley Otto answered the door, and a huge black stupid-looking Newfoundland bounded past both of us and started barking ferociously at my car as if I were still inside it. The dog was enormous, but the car looked like it could handle itself. There are certain domestic animals, oversized and undersized dogs in particular, that ought to be granted extinction. Horses too, now that we have tractors.

Hartley Otto was a tall, scrawny man in his early forties with a patchy beard and long graying hair tied in a ponytail with a twisted pipe cleaner. In his union suit, baggy dungarees held up with old-fashioned galluses, and high-topped working shoes, he looked more like an Appalachian hillbilly than an aging hippie, but that was the desired effect, I suppose. It was political. His gaunt face was prematurely lined, and he had dark circles under intelligent blue eyes and clearly had not slept much, if at all, in the last two days. I wondered if he'd be willing to get a haircut for the trial.

I stood silently in bright snow-reflected sunlight on the steps at the doorway for a few seconds and let him look me over. I've learned not to rush these things. Then I said,

"Risa and Wendell Walker, they told me you might be willing to talk to me."

"Oh," he said. Just that, as if I'd told him it might soon snow. Though he was all sinew and bone, he looked fragile—as though a friendly clap on the shoulder would send him falling to the floor in a clattering heap.

"I apologize for coming over unannounced like this, Mr. Otto, but the Walkers said you would understand. I know it's a bad time, but it's important that we talk."

"Yes, well, all right," he said.

I took off my gloves, stuck my hand out, and said my name; he accepted my hand limply into his and let me shake the thing, as if it were an ear of corn. The guy's gone, I thought, he's off with his kid. I hoped his wife would turn out to be the angry one.

Usually, that's all you need. The angry partner carries the defeated partner, who hasn't the energy to argue against even the idea of a suit, let alone the actuality, which of course, once it's under way, provides its own momentum. You do need one of them fueled by anger, however, especially in the beginning; two defeated parties tend to reinforce each other's lassitude and make lousy litigants. The attorney often ends up fighting his own clients, especially near the end, when it gets down to dealing out the last cards, and the out-of-court settlement offers get made and refused. I wanted a mean lean team, a troop of vengeful parents willing to go the route with me and not come home without some serious trophies on our spears. Hartley Otto was lean, but he didn't seem very mean.

He made a feeble gesture, inviting me inside, and I

entered, bumped aside by the dog, who had apparently given up trying to scare my car. The place smelled like wood smoke and applesauce. There was no pattern to the windows from the inside, either, although I couldn't imagine how you'd fit symmetrical windows into the building without breaking up the structure altogether. It was that kind of design. The light fell from above in a soft and diffuse wave that was actually pleasant, if a little disorienting at first. Mostly what you saw out the windows were treetops and blue sky, like looking up out of a cistern. I guess they felt safe living in there. I would've felt trapped.

It took a few seconds to adjust to the hazy gloom of the interior, which, when you looked away from the windows, turned out to be more like the inside of an enormous tepee than a cistern. It was a large two-story space divided into several smaller chambers with sheets of brightly colored cloth—tie-dyes and Indian madras—that had been hung from wires. On a low brick platform in the center of the main chamber I made out a large steel wood stove; the dog had flopped next to it like a shot buffalo.

A few feet from the stove, sitting cross-legged on a huge overstuffed cushion like a Bedouin chieftain, was Wanda Otto, her face darkly intelligent, eyes narrowed with suspicion and intolerance. She was clearly ready to go to war. My kind of woman.

"What'd you say your name was?" Hartley asked me.

"Mitch Stephens." I drew out a card and gave it to him. He read it with deliberation and handed it to his wife, who swiftly passed her eyes over it and set it on the floor

next to her. I felt like Meriwether Lewis sent out from
Washington to treat with the Indians.

"The Walkers sent him by," Hartley said in a voice
that sounded the way a sheet of blank paper looks. He
moved around behind his wife and sat on what appeared to
be a stool but was in fact a cushioned tree stump with a
birch-stick back attached. Except for numerous large pillows
scattered around the room, all the furniture was made of
wood that still resembled trees, mostly birch, roughly cut
and unfinished, with the bark left on. Twig furniture, they
call it, made to look as if it grew in the woods in the
approximate shape of a chair or table or set of shelves, and
all you had to do was drag it home, strip off the leaves and
lop off a few branches here and there, and *voilà*. Some
people like that stuff, and they pay a lot of money for it.

"You want a cup of tea or something?" he asked me.

I said tea would be fine and took the liberty of shuck-
ing my topcoat. "All right if I sit down for a few moments,
Mrs. Otto? I want to talk with you. Same as I talked to the
Walkers last night." I was wearing a suit, tieless, still dressed
Manhattan style, which I regretted, but it was all I had
brought with me. I promised myself that when I came up to
Sam Dent a second time (and I was sure by now that I'd be
making a lot of trips up here), I'd stop at EMS first. Flannel
shirts, green wool pants, clodhoppers, down vest—the Adirondack look. By then, of course, it wouldn't much matter;
everyone would already know I was a New York lawyer.
When in Rome, however.

Wanda pointed at a nearby pillow, and I quickly took

it. The twig chairs and stumps didn't look very comfortable anyhow. Besides, I wanted to get down near the floor, where she was, and look her straight in the eye. Let Hartley hover overhead, out of it, making tea. We were going to deal, this lady and I, the Indian chief and the white man.

"I'm a lawyer," I said.

"I see that." She was large-breasted, square-shouldered, with long dark hair that hung in a thick braid down her back. She wore a floppy print blouse that emphasized her pregnant belly rather than hid it, and a long wool skirt and moccasins, and her volume seemed greater than her weight—she looked as though she was terrific on the dance floor and bossy in bed. A heavy turquoise and silver amulet hung on a thong at her throat. She had big strong-looking hands, nearly as large as mine, and thick wrists with half a dozen silver bracelets on each, and there were several heavily embossed rings on her fingers.

The woman was deeply into the Indian trip, more so now, no doubt, than usual, probably into chants and meditation, sweat lodges and omens. I figured she was Jewish, Great Neck, Long Island, NYU, class of '72, psych major, with a couple of years of social work and art classes at the New School, where she had met Hartley the Lutheran woodcarver, a draft evader from Wisconsin or someplace. They probably found this place on a camping trip. (Turned out I wasn't far off. I had Wanda pegged exactly, but Hartley had come from South Dakota; they bought this land with money borrowed from Wanda's father when they were crafts counselors at a nearby socialist summer camp and built the house the following year. I learned all this later, of course.)

"You know the Walkers, Risa and Wendell," I said.

"Yes."

"They speak highly of you."

"Good. Will they speak highly of you?"

"I think so. Especially when I have won their case for them."

"So they have hired you."

"Yes."

"I see. Their child has died, and they have gone out and hired a lawyer because of it."

"Yes. Although my task is to represent them only in their anger, not their grief."

"That's how you understand your job? To represent anger?"

"Yes. You are angry, are you not? Among so many other things."

She pursed her lips thoughtfully and remained silent for a moment. The dog had started to snore. Hartley had disappeared behind a curtain, and I could hear water running into a kettle, which surprised me—I'd imagined melting chunks of ice or maybe a hand pump, not a faucet and sink. They probably had a microwave oven and a food processor back there.

"Yes," she said, expelling her breath. "Oh, yes, we are angry. Among so many other things."

"That's why I'm here, Mrs. Otto. To give your anger a voice, to be a weapon for you."

"Against whom?"

"Against whoever caused that bus to go off the road into the sandpit."

"I see. You think someone, a *person*, caused the accident."

"There is no such thing as an accident."

"No. No, there isn't. You are right about that. But how will you know who caused this accident that took our son from us?"

"If everyone had done his job, your son would be alive this morning and safely in school. I will simply find out who did not do his job. Then, in your name and the Walkers' and the name of whoever else decides to join you, I will sue that person and the company or agency he works for, I will sue them for negligence."

"I want that person to go to prison for the rest of his life," she declared. "I want him to die there. I don't want his money."

"It's unlikely anyone will go to prison. He or his company will have to pay in other ways. But pay they will. And we must make them pay, Mrs. Otto, not to benefit you in a material way or to compensate you for the loss of your son, Bear, which can't be done, but to protect the child you're carrying inside you now. Understand, I'm not here to speak just for your anger. I'm here to speak for the future as well. What we're talking about here is our ongoing relation to time."

"I see." And I think she did. The Walkers had seemed more muddled in their motives. The money promised by the lawsuit meant a lot to them, of course, but in a greedy childish way, and certainly more than they were willing to admit to themselves or reveal openly to me. The Walkers were poor and in debt, and their poverty had bugged them for years, and it seemed even more unfair to them now, with their child gone, than before. But Wanda Otto, and her husband too, never struck me as having any selfish interest in the money; they cared only about its handy capacity to function as punishment and prohibition. They were too lost in their Zen Little Indians fantasy to be wholly believable, maybe, or as reliable as the Walkers were, but I admired them nonetheless.

Hartley had returned bearing a mug with a tea bag in it. "Let it steep a minute," he said. "You want milk?"

"No. A little sugar, though."

"We only have honey," he said.

"I'll take it straight."

"Well, Mr. New York Lawyer, what you've been saying makes sense," Wanda said to me. "Not much else in this world does." Then to Hartley, "We should hire this man to represent us. That way we won't have to deal with any of the others. He can advise us on how to talk to the reporters too. You'll do that?" she asked me.

"Yes. Certainly. For now, though, you should refuse all interviews. Say nothing to the press, nothing to any other lawyers. Refer everybody to me."

"Are you expensive?"

"No," I said. "If you agree to have me represent you in this suit, I will require no payment until after the suit is won, when I will require one third of the awarded amount. If there is no award made, then my services will have cost you nothing. It's a standard agreement."

"Do you have this agreement with you?"

"In my car," I said, and, not without difficulty, stood up, almost spilling my tea. I'm not used to sitting cross-legged on the floor. "I'll just be a minute. You should talk without me, anyhow, before you sign it," I added. Also, I needed a cigarette, and I hadn't noticed any ashtrays: the house was cluttered with small figurines and strange clay baskets that looked as if they were made to hold the spirits of ancestors rather than cigarette butts and ashes.

I stepped outside, coatless, still bearing my mug of tea, and the dog followed me and promptly pissed on the front tire of my car and took off down the road. I dumped the tea onto a snowbank, making my own mark. Then I got inside the car, where it was still warm, and lit a cigarette.

I felt terrific. My mind was off and running, switching options and tracking consequences like a first-class computer. Everyone has a specialty, and I guess this is mine. For twenty-five years now, and for three different firms, even after making partner, I've been the guy who handles these disaster negligence suits. I could pull away from tort cases and just handle the white-shoe stuff if I wanted—I've got the name and face for it—or I could quit the practice altogether, move permanently out to the house in East Hampton and maybe teach a course or two at Fordham; but I won't. Nothing else provides me with the rush that I get from cases like this. There is a brilliant hard-edged clarity that comes over me when I take on a suit for the Ottos and the Walkers of the world, an intensity and focus that makes me feel more alive then than at any other time.

It's almost like a drug. It's probably close to what professional soldiers feel, or bullfighters. The rest of the time, like most people, I muddle lonely through my days and nights feeling unsure, vaguely confused, conflicted, and aimless. Put me onto something like this school bus case, though, and zap! all those feelings disappear. Nothing else does it—not illicit sex, not cocaine, not driving fast late at night on the wrong lane of the highway, all of which I've tried. Nothing.

When I think about it, the only other event in my life that I can remember even coming close to giving me the same rush, the same hard hit of formalized intelligence, happened nearly twenty years ago, on the coast of North Carolina, when Zoe was two years old and we were renting a summer place way out on the Outer Banks. Klara and I were tight then, especially over Zoe; we still thought we had a future together, the three of us. Later, it would be only two of us with a future together, me and Zoe, or Klara and Zoe; then one of us, me alone, Klara alone, and who knows now about Zoe's future? Fission in the nuclear family. It's got a short half-life.

Klara had put Zoe down for her afternoon nap, and she and I were sitting out on the deck reading and watching the tide come in. I heard Zoe start to fuss and went in to check her; it was hot, North Carolina hot, and the house wasn't air-conditioned; I figured the heat had wakened her early. But when I saw her I was horrified—she was standing in the rented Portacrib, her red face sweating and swollen like a melon, with a pathetic froglike smile sliced across it. I touched her bare shoulder gingerly: she was feverish, her skin as hot as I'd ever felt it. I grabbed her up, rushed her out to the kitchen, and splashed water on her face, shouting for Klara to call the doctor, I think she's been bitten by an insect or something!

In that splendid isolation there was no doctor—or rather, there was only one, and he was off fishing in the Gulf Stream for yellowfin tuna. The nearest hospital was in Elizabeth City, forty miles inland, across the Great Dismal Swamp on a narrow, badly paved road. Zoe's face, arms, and legs continued to swell, although she seemed not to be in any pain or even discomfort. Klara took her in her arms and continued washing her body down with cold water, searching in vain for signs of a bite—snake or spider, I knew it mattered which—while I frantically dialed the hospital.

I finally got a doctor on the line; he sounded young, Southern, but cool. Instantly, he surmised that there was a nest of baby black widow spiders in the crib mattress. "They have to be little babies, or else with her body weight she'd be dead," he said. "You're way out there in Duck, eh? If Dr. Hopkins has gone fishin', then you'll just have to rush her here. I'm alone here and can't leave. There is a good chance you can get her to me before her throat closes, and then we can control the swelling with insulin," he said. But keep her calm, he told me, don't excite her. "Is she more relaxed with one of you than the other?"

"Yes," I said. "With me." Which was true enough, especially at that moment. Klara was wild-eyed with fear, and her fear was contagious. I was a better actor than she, that's all. Zoe loved us equally then. Just as she loathes us equally now.

"All right, then, you be the one to hold the child in your lap, Mr. Stephens, and let your wife drive the vehicle. And you better bring a small sharp knife along with you. Do you have one that's clean? You don't have time to sterilize it properly."

I said yes, my Swiss army knife. Clean and sharp. But what the hell for?

"Use the small blade," he said, and then he explained how to perform an emergency tracheotomy, told me how to cut into my daughter's throat and windpipe without causing her to bleed to death. "There will be a whole lot of blood, you understand. A whole lot."

"I don't think I can do that," I said, but I heard my voice go flat and toneless as I spoke, as if I were already doing it.

"If her throat closes up and stops her breathing, you'll have to, Mr. Stephens. You'll have a minute and a half, two minutes maybe, and she'll probably be unconscious when you do it. But listen, if you can keep her calm and relaxed, if you don't let her little heart beat real fast and spread that poison around, then you just might make it over here first. You get going now," he snapped, and hung up.

I relayed the bit about keeping her calm to Klara, but nothing about the knife, and without explanation said that she should drive while I held Zoe, which relieved her, I think. Then we took off down the long sandy beach road to the bridge and over the causeway to the mainland, speeding west through the swamp toward Elizabeth City. It was an unforgettable forty-five minutes. Throughout, I was neatly divided into two people—I was the sweetly easy daddy singing, "I've got sixpence, jolly, jolly sixpence, I've got sixpence to last me all my life," and I was the icy surgeon, one hand in his pocket holding the knife, blade open and ready, the decision to cut unquestioned now, irreversible, while I waited merely for the second that Zoe's breath stopped to make the first slice into her throat.

I can't tell you why I connect that terrifying drive to Elizabeth City over two decades ago to this case in Sam Dent now, where children actually died, fourteen of them, but there is a powerful equivalence. With my knife in my hand and my child lying in my lap, smiling up at me, trusting me utterly, with her face swelling like a painted balloon, progressively distorting her features into grotesque versions of themselves, I felt the same clearheaded power that I felt during those first days in Sam Dent, when the suit was taking off. I felt no ambivalence, did no second-guessing, had no mistrusted motives—I knew what I did and what I would do next and why, and Lord, it felt wonderful! It always feels that way. Which is why I go on doing it.

In the case of the drive to Elizabeth City, as in so many of the suits I've since undertaken, it turned out that I did not have to go as far as I was prepared to go. But this is only because I was indeed prepared to go all the way. I was at peace with myself and the world, and consequently Zoe, too, stayed calm and placid, her tiny heart beating slowly, normally, even after I ran out of songs and had to go back to the beginning of my repertoire, which usually irritated her; she almost fell asleep at one point.

Klara raced into the hospital lot, drew up at the emergency room entrance, and I stepped out of the car and calmly carried Zoe inside, where the doctor and two nurses with a gurney and an IV hookup awaited us. Five minutes later, her swelling had started to recede. By evening, the three of us were back at the beach, watching from the deck as the sun set behind the dunes and out near the eastern horizon the red sky streaked the sea in plum and cobalt blue. We had removed the mattress from the crib as soon as we got back from the hospital and, unsure of what to do with it, had tossed it into a patch of witchgrass beside the deck; but that night I built a driftwood fire on the beach and burned the thing, and Zoe slept with us.

Now in my dreams of her, and I dream of her frequently, Zoe is still that child in my lap, trusting me utterly—even though I am the man who secretly held in his hand the knife that he had decided to use to cut into her throat, and thus I am in no way the man she sees smiling down at her, singing ditties and rondelets and telling stories of owls and pussycats.

And sometimes when I wake, for a few moments I'm like Risa Walker and Hartley Otto and Billy Ansel and all those other parents whose children have died and who have been unable to react with rage—the dreamed child is the real one, the dead child simply does not exist. We waken and say, "I can't believe she's gone," when what we mean is "I don't believe she exists." It's the other child, the dreamed baby, the remembered one, that for a few lovely moments we think exists. For those few moments, the first child, the real baby, the dead one, is not gone; she simply never was.

After explaining to the Ottos the contingency fee agreement, which, like the Walkers, they quickly signed (once they realized it would cost them nothing up front), I returned to my car and drove along Bartlett Hill Road from their house back into town, following the route of the school bus, which took me past all the houses of the families who had entrusted their children to it. A morbid drive, but it gave me some insights and let me usefully imagine the event, despite the different weather and time of day. So that when I passed the town dump, pulled out onto the Marlowe road, and headed down from Wilmot Flats, I saw that wide snow-covered bowl open up before me and naturally picked up speed, as the driver of the bus must have, and my attention momentarily left the roadway altogether, as hers must have, and took in the marvelous view of valley and village, snowy mountains and deep blue sky, and I almost missed the place where the bus had gone over, where there remained all kinds of signs of the disaster—the broken and trampled roadside snowbank and the state police barriers still up, the tracks of trucks and ambulances, of snowmobiles and crowds of rescue workers on the embankment and the snow-covered ground around the water-filled sandpit below. The pit, although it had frozen solid again, was now an ice crater of sorts, with huge gray wedges and chunks sticking out of the new ice and lying along the bank like the walls of a building destroyed by a bomb.

I parked my car a ways beyond the scene and slowly walked back along the highway to it. No other vehicles in sight. The sun was bright, and a steady breeze was blowing out of the valley below, hissing in the trees and sending the powdery snow across the pavement in tiny fantails. It was definitely ghostly out there, but I've visited hundreds of scenes like this and can recreate the tragic event in my mind without being distracted by the atmosphere of the aftermath.

I saw where the bus had gone through the low three-cable guardrail and noted that it had been a relatively new rail, properly installed. On the other side of the highway, the posts were rusted near the base from the salty runoff; soon those rails, too, would have to be replaced. But, regretfully, Dolores Driscoll hadn't gone through over there; she'd snapped off the new poles here on this side, half a dozen of them, dragging the cables with her. From my point of view, the best thing you could say about the new guardrail was that it was utterly incapable of stopping or even diverting a fast-moving bus.

Beyond the broken guardrail, the embankment fell off precipitously, and the angle between the road and the line that ran from the road to the point where the bus had entered the sandpit below was twenty or twenty-five degrees. No way the bus could have cut that sharp an angle unless, when it left the road and broke through the guardrail, it was speeding, or damned near speeding. A hundred yards farther down the road, at a point directly opposite the sandpit, the drop was gradual. If the vehicle had gone off there, no matter how fast it had been going when it left the road, it wouldn't have traveled the several hundred feet down the slope to the sandpit: the impact of the guardrail and then the snowbank and the field of deep snow beyond would have stopped the vehicle first. Up above, though, all you had, after the guardrail and the snowbank, was free-fall.

It was inescapable—when the bus left the road, it had been moving pretty fast. And because of the drop-off, once through the guardrail, the bus was gone. There was no way for the driver to have kept it from going down the steep embankment and into the sandpit, even at that oblique an angle, without having immediately, deliberately, flipped it over on its side, which would have kept it out of the sandpit, at least. But what kind of driver could have pulled that off? Not the kind that's terrified of losing the lives of children, that's for sure. Not Dolores Driscoll.

I stepped over the rail opposite the sandpit and made my way down the trampled slope to examine the site up close. A chain-link fence surrounded the pit, most of it flattened now, smashed first by the plummeting bus and then by the rescuers. It had been a sturdy six-foot fence with a wide gate that no doubt had been padlocked. I thought, if one hot summer night some teenaged kids climbed over that fence to skinny-dip and one of them drowned there, the town would be negligent for not having drained it. That's a case I could win, despite the fence. But that, I had to note, was not the case I was chasing here. What I had here was fourteen kids on their way to school one winter morning dying in a sandpit a hundred yards off the road. They did not get there on their own. Concentrate on how they got there, I decided.

Which presented certain problems. Unless I could establish that the driver of the bus, this Dolores Driscoll, had been safely under the speed limit when she came down the highway that morning, there was no way I'd be able to blame the town or the school district or the state or anyone else with deep pockets for negligence. To nail them, I'd have to defend her. I'd have to defend her even if the brakes or some part of the steering had failed. No matter what the immediate cause of the crash, I'd still have to establish that at the time it left the road the bus was being driven in a proper way and at a safe speed for the conditions.

I damn sure did not want to go after Dolores Driscoll, and, for somewhat different reasons, neither did my clients. Never mind that her pockets weren't an inch deep; she was well-liked, sober, hardworking, from an old respected Sam Dent family, sole support of her crippled husband, and she'd been driving local kids to school safely for more than twenty years. Worse, the parents viewed her as having been victimized just as much as they were themselves, and a jury would agree with them. "Poor Dolores," Risa had said. "She must be destroyed by this."

My case would have to be built on the assumption that Dolores Driscoll was not at fault. The lawyers opposing me would simply hope to prove the opposite and go home early and type up their bills.

Two ways to establish the speed of the bus at the time it left the road, I figured: use the testimony of the driver and, more important, use the testimony of the sole witness, Billy Ansel. Which meant, of course, that he could not be one of my clients. Or anyone else's, for that matter. For him to testify that Dolores had been driving under the speed limit (and I couldn't even be sure of that yet), he could not be in a position to profit from his testimony. But with his impartiality established, I could then begin to hope that Ansel had in fact clocked the bus from behind with his truck and that neither of them had been traveling at more than fifty-five miles per hour. If he had not actually monitored the speed of the bus from behind, then I would have him testify as to his own safe driving habits—which, when challenged, I could support, if not verify. It would still be self-serving testimony, of course, but it would be enough for a jury that was inclined to believe him and did not want to blame Dolores Driscoll anyhow.

My first task, though, was to keep him impartial. Keep him clean. It would be easy to make him resist signing on with me, but I'd also have to help him resist the impulse to sign on with any of the double-knit sharks that were cruising these waters. I was sure he'd been contacted already, but my best guess so far was that he'd rebuffed them. Assuming that what I'd been told of him by the Walkers and the Ottos—that he had holed up in his house alone and was staying drunk—wasn't just village gossip. Drunks don't sue.

Originally, I'd decided that this guy, drunk or sober, was going to require some careful seduction. I myself had not planned to approach him until after the others had been turned down; let them seed the idea of a negligence suit, was my strategy, and then let me come along with my homework done and several of his more respected friends and neighbors in tow and all ready to file notices of claim, and the guy would sign on, I was sure.

Now, however, everything was different. Now I had to turn him *off* me, and in such a way that no other lawyer could get to him instead. This wasn't quite ethical, of course; maybe not even moral. Necessary, however—legal triage.

I'd planned to give Ansel another few days before making direct contact, but that seemed too risky now. Better hit on the guy soon, or better yet, talk to him this evening at his house, late, especially if he's into drinking. Give him a genteel nudge that pisses him off more afterwards than at the time of delivery, and he'll want to kill the next lawyer he talks to, I figured.

There was no point in contacting any additional parents until I'd first brought Ansel's testimony under my control and had answered the question of how fast the bus was moving when it went through the guardrail. So I went to work on the other aspects of the case—checked the state police in Marlowe, the county seat, to find out who had arrived at the scene first; stopped by the county mapping office for a look at the pitch and height of the highway and adjacent roads and lands; that sort of thing—gathering data, mainly, for later.

That night, after the blue-plate special at the Noonmark over in Keene Valley (ham and macaroni and cheese—kiddie food, but at least there weren't any lawyers or journalists eating there), I drove out to Ansel's house, which was up on Staples Mill Road. I passed the house by and parked a short ways beyond it with my lights out, thinking I'd reconnoiter a bit before approaching the man in person.

131

It was a lovely moonlit night, the snow a pale blue color under it, the trees black against the snow. And cold—I didn't even want to know the temperature.

I got out of the car and walked slowly back toward the house, a large well-maintained stone-faced colonial that looked recently renovated, with sharply cleared paths and driveway, two-car garage, breezeway—like a dentist's house in the suburbs. The only lights on were in the room adjacent to the breezeway, apparently the kitchen, and from the road where I stood, next to the mailbox, I could see him through the large picture window, seated at the table, alone.

Jesus, he looked sad. Tousled dark hair, shoulders slumped, elbows planted on the table, a single glass and a half-empty bottle in front of him—the picture of permanent depression. Gone to where he thought his kids had gone. If I'd wanted the guy for a client, I'd have been worried.

Suddenly, he stood up and turned and faced out the window, looking across the snow-covered front yard right at me. I froze and stared back at him. Nothing else to do. I remember that for several seconds we seemed to be gazing at one another, me in moonlight at the side of the road, him in the soft light of his kitchen a hundred feet away, neither of us moving a muscle. We were like mirror images of each other, but who knows if he saw me at all, or, if he saw me, what he thought he was looking at? Maybe all he could see was himself reflected off the window glass, a muscular bearded guy in his late thirties in a plaid flannel shirt and khakis; and saw nothing of the tall skinny fifty-five-year-old guy shivering outside in his camel-hair coat. It was a weird moment, though. As if we were long-lost brothers, separated early and passing by accident decades later, not quite recognizing each other, but then, for a second or two, something—something—clicks.

The moment passed. Ansel turned away from the window and poured himself another drink: it looked like straight whiskey. He sat heavily back down at the table, and I quickly walked back to my car. He's too drunk to talk to tonight, I thought; probably wouldn't even remember it in the morning. The aftereffect of what I had to say to him was more important to me than the immediate effect. I think I was rationalizing, though. Scared.

I decided to drive back to the motel by way of Ansel's garage in town, which was where they'd hauled the wrecked bus. I wanted some pictures of the vehicle while I could still get them, even if I had to take them at night with a flash. In a day or two, I knew, once I'd filed notices of claim, the bus was likely to disappear.

I pulled into the garage lot and drove around to the rear, where there were seven or eight different vehicles parked and stowed, including the school bus, which was pretty smashed up, although not as badly as I'd expected. Most of the windows toward the rear were gone, kicked in by the divers, probably, but the vehicle was basically intact, probably even salvageable—a repair job that I did not think Billy Ansel would be taking on.

I took maybe twenty pictures, from all sides and even a few through the windows, and had just got back into my car and started the motor, when I saw a pickup truck enter the lot. It was Ansel's. I kept the motor running but the lights off and watched, as he drew up behind the bus and after a few seconds stepped out of his truck. To my surprise, he walked steadily and didn't look especially drunk. A little crazy, maybe, which was okay; but not drunk. In the glare of his headlights I watched him walk over to the driver's side of the bus, where he stopped by the window and stood looking up at it for a long time, as if talking to someone inside.

Finally, he turned away from the bus and moved back toward his own vehicle. I decided to speak to him. I wasn't scared of him anymore. The timing and locale couldn't be better. It was invasive but not intrusive.

I got out of my car and crossed the lot toward him.

"You work for Ansel?" I asked him, as if I didn't know who he was.

"I am Ansel."

I moved closer and in a low voice said, "I'm sorry about your children, Mr. Ansel."

"You are, eh?" He was already combative.

"Yes."

We stared directly into each other's eyes. The old staredown.

He broke first and said, "I take you to be a lawyer," which let me counterpunch, which is how you control these things.

"Yes, I am an attorney. My name is—"

"Mister, I don't want to *know* your name."

True enough, but he was damn well going to learn it anyhow. "I understand," I said.

"No. No, you don't understand."

"I can help you."

"No, you can't help me. Not unless you can raise the dead," he declared, moving away from me and getting into his truck.

I quickly handed him a card. "Here. You may change your mind."

He read the card and then passed it back, looking me straight in the face, but distracted somehow, as if memorizing the card.

Fine by me. I stared him back.

"Mr. Mitchell Stephens, Esquire, would you be likely to sue me if right now I was to beat you with my hands and feet?" he growled. "Beat you so bad that you pissed blood and couldn't walk for a month? Because that is what I'm about to do, you understand. Whether you sue me or not."

Lawyers sue; he'd made the connection. And suing is bad; he'd taken his stand. In what I hoped was a slightly weary but kindly tone, because I did not want to sound in the slightest defensive, the way I knew those other lawyers would react when he started threatening them, I said, "No, Mr. Ansel. No, I wouldn't sue you. And I don't think there's anyone in this county who would even arrest you for it. But you're not about to beat me up, are you?"

He paused, reconsidering. "No, I'm not going to beat you up. Just don't talk to me again. Don't come around my garage, and don't come to my house or call me on the telephone."

The rest was finish work. "You may change your mind. I can help you," I said.

"Leave me alone, Stephens. Leave the people of this town alone. You can't help any of us. No one can."

"You can help each other. Several people have agreed to let me represent them in a negligence suit, and your case as an individual will be stronger if I'm allowed to represent you together as a group." This was no longer the hook I'd originally planned it to be; now it was merely a way for him to feel morally superior to his neighbors, which, of course, would keep him clean for me later on, when I put him in front of a jury.

"My 'case'? I have no case. None of us has a case."

"You're wrong about that. Very wrong. Your friends the Walkers have agreed, and Mr. and Mrs. Otto, and I'm talking with some other folks. It's important to initiate proceedings right away. Things get covered up fast. People lie. You know that. People lie about these things. We have to begin our own investigation quickly, before the evidence disappears. That's why I'm out here tonight." I showed him my camera.

He looked at it with disgust. "Our children aren't even buried yet," he said. "It's you—you're the liar. Risa and Wendell Walker, I know them, you're right, but they wouldn't hire a goddamned lawyer. And the Ottos, they wouldn't deal with *you*, for Christ's sake. You're lying to me about them, and probably to them about me. We're not fools, you know, country bumpkins you can put the big-city hustle on. You're just trying to use us. You want us to pull each other in," he announced, getting it nicely wrong.

Smiling at his minor triumph, he shut the door of his truck, backed the vehicle up and turned, then drove quickly from the lot. The truck fishtailed as it hit the road and turned left, heading toward the west end of town. Where the Bide-a-Wile Motel was located; and Risa Walker. I did not have too much trouble imagining the conversation that would take place between them there. Husband Wendell, I was certain, would not be a party to it. Poor sap. I liked Wendell. I did not like Billy Ansel.

Things moved pretty fast for a while then. A lot of it was strictly procedural, the kind of search-and-destroy that precedes filing a notice of claim, where you're essentially boxing off the defendants so that you can both narrow the terms and widen the areas of liability. I had some files and a fax machine shipped up from New York by UPS and set up a sort of office for myself in my room at the Bide-a-Wile. The Walkers seemed pleased by the arrangement, especially Risa; from their point of view, they now had a lawyer-in-residence. I wasn't exactly on retainer, but I did end up advising them, Risa in particular, on a few matters other than their negligence suit, which I was now attempting to aim at the State of New York, for not having installed sufficiently strong guardrails along that especially dangerous stretch of roadway, and at the town of Sam Dent, for not having drained the sandpit. And I was contemplating a suit against the school board, for having permitted Dolores Driscoll to service her school bus herself. I figured, cast as wide a net as possible and catch whatever fish you can in it.

As a defendant, the driver was out of bounds, of course, but I was now considering making even her a plaintiff, since, if she was not herself responsible for the accident, she might be shown to have a cause for action for emotional distress. What the hell, it was worth a try. It'd make an interesting precedent. Also, I might be able to run it backward: it would be that much harder for the state, town, and school lawyers to lay the responsibility for the accident on her if she was one of the parties suing them for negligence. In an important way, the whole case rose or fell on the question of Dolores Driscoll's liability, and it was a question I'd just as soon not get asked at all. At least not without a few roadblocks.

The funerals started the next day, all over town, going on for several days, for three or four children at a time, and naturally I planned on staying away. Out of decency, but strategy as well. It doesn't hurt to be the only lawyer in town who doesn't come off as a buzzard.

The town was beginning to formalize its response to the tragedy. There had appeared one morning fourteen tiny crosses out at the crash site, which turned out to be the work of schoolchildren, at the instigation of the school board. So much for separation of church and state. A memorial service for the victims, announced in the local weekly newspaper, was scheduled to be held the following week in the school auditorium, where the state representative from the district, the school principal, and half a dozen area clergymen would intone. Money was being collected, ostensibly for the families of the victims (although the exact purpose of the money was a little vague—funeral expenses for some, medical expenses for others, I supposed), in glass jars at all the local businesses, even at the Noonmark Diner over in Keene Valley. TV viewers from around the country were sending contributions—money, clothing, canned food, stuffed animals, crucifixes, and potted plants—all of which was being logged in and held at the school for eventual distribution. Even then I could see problems down the road with that, but it was none of my affair, so I just listened and nodded as Risa filled me in on the details. She was evidently quite touched by the generosity of strangers, and I saw no reason to disabuse her of it. Some people, when terrible things happen to them, take strength from believing that other people are better than in fact they are. Not me. I go in the opposite direction.

Actually, I knew that Risa's increasing confidentiality with me, her evident need to talk to me as frequently as possible, was her way of leading up to a conversation about how to divorce Wendell. I doubt she knew that herself then, but it was surely on the agenda. The death of her son had eliminated the one reason she was married to the boy's father.

I still hadn't taken the measure of Dolores Driscoll, however, so when Risa told me that the woman was showing up at all the funerals, sitting way in the back and then disappearing at the end of the service, only to reappear down the road at the next one, I decided to break my rule and take in a funeral myself, then head back to the city for a few days. I had several other cases that I'd left hanging and needed attention.

That morning at the motel, however, the phone in my room rang, and it was Zoe, out of the blue, after three months of silence, and it caught me completely by surprise, or I doubt I'd have handled it as badly as I did.

"Daddy, it's me!" she'd said. Her voice was full of the usual phony enthusiasm, but it was dead, dead as the kids in their caskets.

"Zoe! Jesus!" I'd been shaving, and I snapped off my electric razor and sat down on the bed. It was like getting a call from a ghost. Every time I think my period of mourning is over, she calls to remind me that I haven't really started yet.

"Hi! How're you doing? Where *are* you? Where's five one eight? I got this number off your phone machine."

"Yeah, well, I'm . . . I'm surprised to hear from you. I'm on a case, upstate, in the Adirondacks."

She said that was very interesting, and for a minute I gabbled on about the case, the motel, the town of Sam Dent, like we have these conversations, any conversation, all the time. Finally, I was able to stop myself, and I said, "Zoe, why are you calling me?"

"Why am I calling you? You're my father, for Christ's sake! I'm not supposed to call you?"

"Oh, Jesus, Zoe. Please, for once, let's talk straight."

"Fine. That would be terrific. I called Mom, and all she wanted to know was had I grown my hair back yet and what color was it, so I hung up. What do *you* want to know?"

"Well, to be perfectly honest, right now I want to know if you're high."

"You mean, Daddy, am I *stoned?* Do I have a *needle* dangling from my arm? Am I nodding in a phone booth? Did I *score* this morning, get whacked, Daddy, and call you for *money?*"

Trees, snow, mountains, ice. I could hear sirens, street traffic, a radio or TV newscaster in the background. I imagined some boyfriend behind her, sick and dying, smoking a cigarette, waiting for her to raise some money from her rich father. Who was I talking to? The living or the dead? How should I behave?

"God," she said. "I don't fucking *believe* it."

"I'm sorry. I just need to know, if that's possible. So I can know how to talk to you. So I can know how to act."

"Just act naturally, Daddy," she snapped.

The operator suddenly came on the line, instructing her to please deposit another two dollars and twenty cents for an additional three minutes.

"Where are you, Zoe? I'll call back."

"Shit!" she said. Then she hollered to someone, "What the fuck's the number of this phone? It's not here!"

"Zoe, just tell me where you are."

"It's this hotel, this . . . place. Where's the goddamned number? I can't find the fucking number." The operator's voice cut in again, repeating her instructions.

"Where are you, Zoe? Give me the name of the hotel; I'll get the number from Information. What's the address? You're in New York?"

"Shit! It's this pay phone. Yeah," she said, and then the line went dead.

What do you do when this sort of thing happens? I'll tell you what you do. You sit still and count slowly to ten, or a hundred, or a thousand, however long it takes for your heart to stop pounding, and then you resume doing whatever it was you were doing when the telephone first rang.

141

I had been standing in my socks and underwear at the bathroom sink, shaving. I went back to shaving. I was in the tiny village of Sam Dent, New York, in the middle of generating a terrific negligence suit. I went back to that. I'd planned to return to the city that day anyhow, and Zoe's phone call hadn't touched that. She was probably in a ratty, crack-infested single-room-occupancy hotel in back of Times Square, or had just been kicked out of one. And for all I could do about it, she might as well be in L.A. as New York.

I switched my mind onto the business at hand, which I could do something about. Breakfast at the Noonmark. Attending funerals. Dolores Driscoll. The need to sound her out before I got myself locked into this case.

There was only one funeral left, the service for the Catholic kids at St. Hubert's Church, a small white wood-frame structure out by the fairgrounds on the East Branch of the Ausable River, on Route 73, a few miles from town. The funeral was for the Bilodeau and Atwater kids, from Wilmot Flats, and there were five small open caskets up front, surrounded by flowers and miscellaneous plant life. There were maybe a hundred people attending, a sadly shabby crowd in their Sunday best, mostly somber young men with big Adam's apples and weeping overweight young women with rotten complexions, and bunches of kids and babies in hand-me-downs, with red runny noses and slobbering mouths. The kind of crowd the Pope likes.

I recognized several lawyers, easy to spot in their suits and topcoats, checking out the scene for potential clients, and a couple of journalists with cameras dangling from their necks and notebooks in their hands, waiting for visible signs of grief. Dolores I spotted immediately, thanks to Risa's description: late middle age, round face, frizzy red hair, a little on the plump side, and wearing a man's parka and heavy trousers and boots. "You'd think she was a lesbian or something, if you didn't know about her husband, Abbott, and her sons, who are all quite normal," Risa had explained. I noted that Risa herself seemed to prefer men's clothing, but said nothing. What the hell, it was probably just something between women, the way they compete with one another without having to acknowledge it.

I was standing by the door in a pack of late arrivals, still thinking about Zoe, I admit it, when I first saw Dolores. The tiny church was crowded, but she had half a pew at the back to herself, so I slid in next to her. Immediately four or five people followed and sat on my other side, filling the rest of the pew. It wasn't too hard to see what the difficulty was—these people liked Dolores, she was one of them, and they felt as profoundly sorry for her as for themselves; but they also could not help blaming her and wanting to cast her out. They would have preferred that she simply disappear from town for a while, go and stay with her son in Plattsburgh or at least hide behind the door of her house with her husband up there on Bartlett Hill. They wanted her to stash her pain and guilt where they didn't have to look at it.

But she wasn't having any of that. Silently, with her head bowed, Dolores was plunking herself down in the exact center of the town's grief and rage, compelling them by her presence at these funerals to define her. Was she a victim of this tragedy, or was she the cause of it? She had placed herself on the scales of their judgment, but they did not want to judge her. To them, she was both, of course, victim *and* cause; just as to herself she was both. Like every parent when something terrible happens to his child, Dolores was innocent, and she was guilty. We knew which, in the eyes of God and our fellowman, *we* were, despite the fact that most of the time we felt like both; but she did not. Denial was impossible for her, so she wanted us to come forward and do the job for her.

Toward the end of the service, when the short red-faced priest turned to the cross in the nave for a closing prayer and the pallbearers stepped forward from their front-row seats and took their posts by the caskets, Dolores suddenly stood and squeezed past me and the others in the pew. I followed her, excusing my knees as I worked my way to the aisle. From the foyer, I watched the woman hurry down the path to the road, then move rapidly past the hearses and the long line of parked cars. I broke into a run and caught up with her just as she reached a large dark blue van.

"Mrs. Driscoll!" I called. "Please!"

She turned and faced me, scared. "What do you want!"

"I can tell you, I can tell you whether you're guilty or not." I was out of breath; for her size, the woman moved pretty fast.

"Who are you? Who is it can do that? No one can do that."

"Yes, I can. Answer me one simple question, and I'll tell you if you are to blame."

"One question?"

"Yes. When the bus left the road, Mrs. Driscoll, how fast was it moving?"

"I don't know."

"Approximately."

"You said one question."

"It's the same question, Mrs. Driscoll. Approximately how fast?"

"The police already asked it."

"What did you tell them?"

"You said one question."

"Same question."

"Fifty, fifty-five at the most, is what I told them."

"Then you're not guilty," I said. "You're not to blame. Believe me."

"Why? Why should I believe you?"

"Listen to me, you poor woman. You didn't do anything wrong that morning. It wasn't your fault. I now know as much as anyone about what happened out there on the highway that morning, and believe me, it's not you who are at fault."

"Who, then?"

"Two or maybe three parties who were not there at the time," I said, and I listed them for her. I told her my name and explained that I was representing the Ottos and the Walkers, people who liked and admired her and who believed, with me, that she was in many ways as much a victim of this tragedy as they were. I said that I would like to represent her too.

"Me? Represent me? No," she said. "You can't. I only

145

said I was doing fifty, fifty-five. To the police; to Captain Wyatt Pitney, from the state police. Because that's how I remembered it. But the truth, mister, is that I might have been doing sixty miles an hour when the bus went over, or sixty-five. Not seventy, I'm sure. But sixty is possible. Sixty-five, even. And I would say that to a judge, if some smart lawyer like you, only working for the other side, took it into his head to ask it that way. And, mister," she said in a low voice, "let's face it, if I was over the limit, no matter how you tell it, I'm sure I'm to blame."

Yep. "But what if Billy Ansel insists that at the time of the alleged accident, you were going fifty-two miles an hour?"

"He knows that? Billy?"

"Yes. He does."

"Billy said that?"

"If he does not volunteer to say so in court, I will subpoena him and oblige him to testify to that effect—if you'll let me bring a suit in your name charging negligent infliction of emotional harm. It's clear to me and many other people that you have suffered significantly from this event. And then, Dolores Driscoll, your name, your very good name, will be cleared once and for all in this town. Everyone will know then that you, too, have suffered enormously, we'll have established it legally, and then you will not have to bear any of the blame."

"Well, I'm not to blame!" she said. "I'm not to blame." Her large round face crinkled suddenly, and she began to weep. I placed both hands on her shoulders and drew her toward me, and in a few seconds she was blubbering against my chest. Peering over her head, I watched the caskets come out of the church, one after the other. The pallbearers—uncles and older brothers and cousins of the kids inside the boxes—shoved the caskets into the hearses, and the somber black-suited guys from the funeral homes slammed the doors shut on them.

It was probably just as well that Dolores had her back to the scene. When the people coming out of the church saw us standing there, they stopped, many of them, and glared at us. And when they moved toward their cars and pickup trucks, they cut a wide swath around us, until finally we were standing there in the parking lot next to the church alone.

"Come out to the house," she said to me, wiping her red swollen face with her sleeve. "What I want, you can tell my husband, Abbott, what you've told me. Abbott's logical. Like you. But he's more interested than you in doing what's right. You'll see. If he says I should do this, go to court and all, like you say, so my name can be cleared and like that, then I will. But if he's against it, then I'm against it."

I hadn't planned on this, but I said fine, that made perfect sense to me, and agreed to follow her out to her house in my car. Yes, I suppose I had a few minor misgivings about having lied to her—I was a little worried that I wouldn't be able to get Billy Ansel to confirm that she had been driving under the speed limit. It was a gamble, a calculated risk, but the odds were maybe ten to one that no matter how fast they were going when the bus went over, Ansel, for several reasons, would say to a jury, just as she had told the cops, "Fifty, fifty-five." You have to gamble like this now and then.

"Would you say fifty-two miles per hour, Mr. Ansel?"

"Yeah. Fifty-two, I'd say."

"Would you say fifty-three miles per hour, Mr. Ansel?"

"Yeah. It might have been fifty-three. No more, though."

"At that time, Mr. Ansel, and under the weather conditions and road conditions that prevailed at that time, the time of the accident, and at that place on the road from Marlowe to the town of Sam Dent—a stretch of road that you, like Mrs. Driscoll, are extremely familiar with, are you not . . . ?"

"Yeah."

"Would fifty-three miles per hour have been a safe speed to be operating a school bus?"

"Objection! "

"Sustained."

"I withdraw the question. I have no further questions of the gentleman, Your Honor."

Piece of cake, on a plate.

Dolores and her husband, Abbott, lived near the top of Bartlett Hill Road in a large foursquare white house with a wide porch in front and a big unpainted barn in back, with nothing but dense woodlands beyond. From the porch you had a great one-hundred-eighty-degree view that included The Range, as they call it, from Mount Marcy to Wolf Jaw. A million-dollar view. For the area, it was an old house, and it had fallen on bad times. In the late 1800s, Dolores's grandfather had been a successful dairy farmer, she told me as we stood in the driveway before going inside. He'd built it himself from trees cleared off this land, and her father and then she herself had been raised in it. Back then, Dolores said, even in her father's day, these forested mountains were alpine meadowlands. "It was like Switzerland," she said, "although I can't say what Switzerland's like." Now, for miles, straight to the horizon, you saw nothing but trees— hardwoods, mostly, and hemlock and pine—and if it weren't for the occasional old stone wall sinking into the leafy ground, you'd think you were in the forest primeval.

Abbott Driscoll was a shriveled guy in a wheelchair; he'd had a stroke a few years before, and his whole right side had blinked out. He had long thinning white hair, bright blue eyes, and soft pink skin, and he drooled a little and sat canted to one side, like a baby in a high chair.

Although he seemed bright enough, his speech was seriously impaired, and I could make out only about half of what he said. Most of the other half Dolores translated, whether I wanted her to or not. He spoke in these odd cryptic sentences that didn't really mean a whole lot to me but to Dolores were like Delphic pronouncements. I guess she loved the hell out of the guy and heard what she wanted to hear.

I sat at the kitchen table opposite him, while Dolores took what appeared to be her customary position behind his wheelchair, where she rubbed his shoulders affectionately and now and then stroked his hair back.

It was a brief interview, mainly because I did a lot more talking myself than I normally do. I was still distracted by the business with Zoe. Essentially, I repeated what I had told Dolores outside the church, but said it at least three times, with a slight variation each time, as if I was cross-examining myself. I felt slightly out of control.

Abbott mostly gargled and sputtered, interrupting me occasionally with stuff like "Blame . . . creates . . . gabble-gabble . . . " and "Cluck-cluck-cluck . . . lives . . . longer . . . than . . . spe-lunk." Which Dolores, with modest downcast eyes and a small knowing smile, translated as "Blame creates comprehension" and "A person's name lives longer than her lifetime."

Yeah, sure, Dolores. Whatever you say. I merely nodded and continued talking, as if he'd said something I totally agreed with or had asked me to repeat myself. Yackety-yak: out of sync, out of character. Finally, I reached the end of my spiel one more time, and because this time he said nothing, no mysterious oracular pronouncements, just a drooling silence, I was able to stop, and for a few seconds all three of us were silent and apparently thoughtful.

There was a crackling fire in the kitchen wood stove, but that was the only sound. The house was warm and weathertight and smelled good, like baked bread. Most of the furniture was either homemade or yard sale stuff, twenty and thirty years old, repaired over and over with string, wire, and glue, but still sturdy, still serviceable. I waited. I wanted a cigarette, but it didn't look as if either of them smoked, especially him, so I just patted the pack in my shirt pocket for comfort.

Then Abbott spoke. He twisted his face around his mouth the best he could and pursed his lips on the left side as though he were sucking a straw and in a loud voice said something like "A down . . . gloobity-gear . . . and day old'll . . . find you . . . innocent . . . if a brudder . . . lands . . . gloobity first. . . ."

And so on and so forth. I was guessing, but it sounded like the old guy was ready for action. All I could read was his face, however, which was bright and open and smiling as he talked, not angry and vengeful, the way I like it. It was the longest speech he'd made so far, but to tell the truth, I hadn't the foggiest idea of what words, or even what language, he'd used for making it. Serbo-Croatian, maybe.

Dolores knew, though. She smiled and said to me, "You heard what Abbott said?"

"Yes, I heard. Can you make it exact for me, though? I think I missed some of it. You know, a word or two."

"Certainly. Glad to. What Abbott said was: The true jury of a person's peers is the people of her town. Only they, the people who have known her all her life, and not twelve strangers, can decide her guilt or innocence. And if Dolores—meaning me, of course—if she has committed a crime, then it's a crime against them, not the state, so they are the ones who must decide her punishment too. What Abbott is saying, Mr. Stephens, is forget the lawsuit. That's what he's saying."

"He is?"

"Yep."

"You're sure of that?"

"Yep. I told you he was logical," she declared. "He understands things better than most people. He understands me too."

"That right?"

"Oh, yes. Abbott's a genius."

A genius, eh? A gibbering fool, is what I thought. From what I could see and hear, Dolores was the ventriloquist and Abbott was the dummy. And you can't argue with the ventriloquist about what the dummy really said.

I got up from my chair, lit a cigarette, said my goodbyes, and I was gone. Not without a certain relief. It surprised me; I don't usually give up that easily. I guess I had my reasons: the Driscolls were too weird to bring into a negligence suit, but they were also too weird to sue, which did not displease me.

The guy Abbott Driscoll, though, he gave me the creeps. Whatever his wife claimed he said or meant to say, I was sure he knew things that neither of us knew and was just playing cat-and-mouse with us, using his affliction to make us say and do things we might not otherwise say or do, so that we would end up showing him who we really were. Which might have been okay for her—presumably, she *wanted* him to know who she really was, but I didn't. The guy would've made a hell of a lawyer if he could talk straight.

Well, you win some and you lose some, I said to myself. And this one was probably better off lost early than late. Down the hill and over to the west end of town I went, back to the Bide-a-Wile to pack. Halfway down the hill, I passed by the little handmade house in the pines where I'd been told Nichole Burnell lived with her mommy and daddy and two younger brothers and baby sister, and I thought for a second of stopping off there, just to put a scanner on the parents. But I was in a hurry to get back to the city now, and it was getting late in the day, so I let it go. I was sure I'd be back in a few days and could check them out then. The kid was going to be in the hospital for a long time anyhow. Apparently she was out of immediate danger, but they weren't allowing her any visitors yet, so I wasn't worried about the competition.

I pulled into the motel lot, and when I passed through the front office on my way to my room, Wendell stopped me.

"Phone message, Mitch," he said, and he handed me a pink slip of paper. "Came in a few minutes ago."

I remember it took me a few seconds to realize that I wasn't reading my secretary's name and number. It was Zoe, which Wendell had spelled *Zooey*, and there was a New York number, with the instruction to call back right away. Okay. Will do. I was on automatic pilot now. I knew she'd gone out and managed somehow to get high, swapping services for goods, no doubt, and, thus fortified, was ready to resume the enterprise she had begun earlier.

I went back to my room, sat down on the bed, and dialed. The phone rang only once, and she answered, apparently waiting beside it.

"H'lo?"

"Zoe? That you?"

"Oh, Dad, hi. Hey, listen, I'm sorry about this morning, I was really bumming, and this damn phone is all fucked up . . . ," blah blah blah, in a soft, accommodating voice that was all surface, a lid of sweetness and light over a caldron of rage and need.

I waited out the preliminaries, responding feebly but with caution, and in a few minutes we got around to the main event, as I knew we would, brought on by my asking a simple question, just as before. "Are you calling me for money, Zoe?" I asked.

She inhaled deeply, held her breath for a few seconds, then sighed. Real Sarah Bernhardt. "I'm calling," she said, "because I have some news for you. Daddy, I've got some big news for you."

"News," I said, suddenly fatigued beyond belief.

"You don't want to hear it?" I heard the lid on the pot start to wobble and jump.

"Yes, sure. Give me your news, Zoe."

"You always think you know what I'm going to say, don't you? You always think you're two steps ahead of me. The lawyer."

"No, Zoe, I don't always think that."

"Well, this time I'm two steps ahead of you!"

"Tell me your news, Zoe."

"Okay. Okay, then. You won't want to hear this, but I'm gonna say it anyhow. Dig it. I went to sell blood yesterday. That's how it is. I'm in fucking New York City, where my father is a hot shit lawyer, and I'm selling my blood for thirty-five bucks."

"This is not news, Zoe."

"No, but this is. They wouldn't take my blood." Long pause. "I tested HIV positive."

I said nothing; the blood, hers, surged past my throat into my face. I could hear the heavy slam of my heart. I was swimming in blood.

"You know what that means, Daddy? Do you? Does it register?"

"Yes."

"AIDS, Daddy."

"Yes."

"Welcome to hard times, Daddy."

"Yes, that's one way of saying it."

"Isn't that a kick, Daddy?"

"Oh, Lord," I said. "What do you want me to do, Zoe?"

"What do *I* want *you* to do?" She practically shrieked it. Then she laughed, a long high-pitched cackle, like an old madwoman, a witch on the heath.

"I'll do whatever you want, Zoe."

"Good. That's really good of you. I was hoping you'd say that. I really was." She laughed again, girlishly this time, a child who had tricked her grumpy old dad. "Money," she said. "I want money."

"What for?"

She laughed again. "You can't ask me that. Not anymore. You asked me what I wanted. Not what I wanted it for. I want money."

Suddenly, I was the man I had been twenty years earlier with the knife hidden in my hand, my child in my lap. "All right," I said. "Fine. I'll give you money. For whatever purpose." I was the calm easy daddy singing our favorite song. I've got sixpence, jolly jolly sixpence, I've got sixpence, to last me all my life.

"I'll come back down to the city this afternoon," I assured her, "and I'll give you as much money as you need."

"Want!"

"Yes, want."

We were both silent then.

"I can hear you breathing, Daddy," she said.

"Yes. I can hear you breathing too." I've got sixpence to spend, and sixpence to lend, and sixpence to take home to my wife, poor wife.

"I'll come to your apartment," she said. "Tonight. What time will you be there?"

"Oh, seven or eight, maybe sooner. It's about six hours' drive from here. I'll leave here today, as soon as possible. How much . . . how much money do you want, Zoe?"

"Oh, let's see. Give me a thousand bucks. For now."

"For now."

"That's all I've got, Daddy. All I've got is *now.* Remember? AIDS, Daddy."

"All right," I said. I almost smiled agreeably into the phone. "I'll meet you at my place, and we'll talk, won't we?"

"Yes. We'll talk. So long as you have the money. Otherwise, I'm out of there, Pops."

"Do you have the test? The blood test?"

"You don't believe me!" she shrieked. "I get it—you don't believe me, do you?"

"Yes. Yes, I do believe you. I thought, maybe, I thought I could get you to take another test. With a regular doctor, in case the first one was wrong."

"You don't believe me." She laughed. "I like it even better that way. It's better you don't believe me but have to act like you do."

"I do believe you, Zoe. You say you have *AIDS*, goddammit! I know what that means. Let me, for Christ's sake, be your father!"

She began to cry then, which didn't surprise me. And so did I. Or at least I sounded, to her and to me as well, as if I was crying. I was not, however; I was fingering the knife blade, testing its sharpness with my thumb.

"I love you, Daddy. Oh, God, I'm scared," she sobbed.

"I love you too. I'll be there soon, and I'll take care of you, Zoe. No matter what happens, I'll take care of you."

I felt incredibly powerful at that moment, as if I had been waiting for the moment for years.

We finally hung up, and I quickly packed my bag and put my room in order. Zoe was right, of course. I did not believe her. I did not disbelieve her, either. In that way, this call was like a thousand others. There was one important difference, however. Until this moment, I had for years been tied to the ground, helpless and enraged by my own inability to choose between belief and disbelief. That first task, to eliminate one or the other—to free one limb so as to untie the other—had until now been denied me; because I loved her. Oh yes, I loved my daughter. And because I loved her, I could not know the truth and then act accordingly. Now, for the first time in all those years, I was in a position to know the truth—and then to act. Out of desperation, Zoe had freed me from love. Whether she had AIDS or was lying to me, I would soon know. Either way, I was free. She'd played her final card with me; she could no longer keep me from being who I am. Mitchell Stephens, Esquire.

Nichole Burnell

T he mind is kind," Dr. Robeson told me, touching my forehead with his soft pink cool fingertips, which I couldn't move away from, so I just glared up at him.

I'm lucky, they all say, because I can't remember the accident. Lucky that it's like a door between rooms, and there was one room on the far side, and that room I remember fine, and another on the near side, and I remember it too. I'm still in it. But I don't have any memory of passing through, I don't remember the accident, and that's counted lucky by everyone.

"Don't even try to remember," Daddy said, and got up from his chair by the window and looked out at the hospital parking lot. I think it was snowing out. He was probably worried about the drive home.

Mom, seated in a chair next to the bed, kept patting the back of my hand and not looking at me and said, "You just think about getting well, Nichole, that's all."

By then I knew I was as well as I would ever be again, and Dr. Robeson had told me that just to stay like this I would have to work very hard. So shut up, Mom, go to hell. To live like a slug, I was going to have to work like someone trying to become an Olympic ski jumper. To feed myself, to go to the bathroom, to bathe, to get in and out of bed, to put my clothes on and take them off, to change channels on the TV or do schoolwork—for me to do these things as well as a three-year-old, I'd have to work out for years, maybe the rest of my life, in a room with pads on the floor and walls to keep my bones from breaking when I fell off the parallel bars or one of the shiny new exercise machines.

Anyhow, this was the room I woke up in after the accident, a hospital room, a weepy Mom and embarrassed distracted Daddy room, a doctor and nurse room, a room with a physical therapist who yells at you for your own good and another guy who's supposed to massage you, but I wouldn't let him, so they finally got a woman to do it. One room led into the next, but they were all the same. Even when I finally went home to my own room.

Daddy drove, with me in front next to him, and Mom and my new wheelchair, folded up beside her, in the back. It was spring already, late April, with only patches of snow left in the woods and on the mountains, a few old dry dirt-covered mounds along the sides of the road and at the edges of parking lots. No leaves on the trees yet, but you could see a light green haze and in some places a reddish glow over the branches where the buds were coming. At the edge of town, the fairgrounds was mostly under water and mud, but here and there in the field in front of the grandstand the snow melt had begun to recede, and yellow wet chunks of old dead grass had appeared. What happened to winter? I wondered. It was like I'd gone to Florida for the worst of it. Wouldn't that have been nice?

I was incredibly glad to be out of the hospital, though. I was sick of Dr. Robeson and had started calling him Dr. Frankenstein, even to his face, which of course he thought was cute. It wasn't cute; I did it because I felt like a monster and Dr. Robeson had created me out of all these different body parts. I couldn't walk as good as Frankenstein's monster, I couldn't walk at all, though I could talk fine; but I felt ugly like him and out of it, different from everyone else. I could really understand why the monster had turned on all the dumb villagers. Sometimes when one of the nurses came into the room and chirped like a birdie at me, "And how are *we* this morning?" I'd go, *"Argh-guh-guh!"* and cross my eyes and flop my head back and forth like a spastic.

The first thing I noticed, when Daddy opened the car door and pushed the wheelchair up next to it, was the ramp he'd built. It was made of wood and way too wide and sloped from the ground up to the front porch beside the regular people's steps. My very own entrance, like for a circus elephant. I pictured Daddy out there evenings after work, whistling like he does when he's got himself a new carpentry project, hammering and sawing in porchlight, feeling proud of himself—a good daddy.

"How do you like it, Babes?" he said.

"The ramp?" I swung myself out of the car seat and

lurched into the wheelchair. No way anybody was going to lift me up and set me down. Especially him.

"Yeah. Pretty slick, eh?" He got behind the chair and pushed me over to the bottom of the ramp and stopped so we could examine it more closely. Mom came along behind, lugging my suitcase and stuff. There was still a bunch more in the trunk, mostly presents from strangers but some from people in town and Mom's and Daddy's church friends and kids in school. The usual dumb things—handmade get-well cards, stuffed animals, and pictures of Jesus and other inspirational items.

"It's okay," I said. "Rudy and Skip can use it for skateboarding."

"They better not," Daddy said. "I made it for you."

"Thanks. Thanks a lot."

"I had to widen a few doors too. You'll see," he said proudly, and he pushed me up his ramp and into the living room, like I was a new piece of furniture. Then he didn't know what to do with me, where to park me. Put me by the window, I wanted to tell him, next to the plants. But I said nothing. He was confused, and I guess I felt sorry for him.

The phone rang, and Mom went off to the kitchen to answer it. Rudy and Skip came down from their bedroom and said hi and all, looking self-conscious and like they wished they weren't there, as if I was some old relative they had to be polite to. Jennie came along behind them, sucking her thumb as always, and she stared at the wheelchair for a minute and then decided it wouldn't explode or anything and came over and hugged me.

She's the one, she's the family to me, the whole family;

the rest of them, including Rudy and Skip, even though I love them the way you're supposed to, make me feel like I have to protect myself against them.

"You want to see your new room, Babes?" Daddy asked.

"My new room? What's wrong with the old one?" I knew what was wrong with it—it was upstairs, with all the other bedrooms and the big bathroom, and I couldn't get to it anymore. But it was mine, mine and Jennie's since she was a baby, and we were safe there, because there were two of us, and he never dared to come in there. Nothing bad had ever happened in that dark little room with the bunk beds and the clutter of all our clothes and her toys and my school stuff and pictures and posters on the walls. From that room we could hear the boys squabbling and playing late at night in their room next door, and we could hear Daddy and Mom on the other side and know to pretend we were asleep if they were arguing. There were places that weren't safe: the car at night with Daddy alone, the living room couch, the bathroom unless the door was locked, the toolshed out back—and, now, my new room?

Well, he said it was new, didn't he? And I was a wheelchair girl now, a cripple. Maybe everywhere was safe now. The whole house. Everywhere. A fresh start.

"Come along, come along," Daddy said. "I'll show you."

"You're lucky," Rudy said. "I still gotta sleep with *him*," he said, and he punched Skip on the shoulder, and Skip punched him back.

Mom came in from the kitchen, smiling like she'd just

eaten something sweet and light. "People are so kind," she said. "The phone's been ringing off the hook with people wanting to welcome you home. That was Edith Dillinger, the principal's wife. She sent her love."

"Show me my room, Daddy," I said, and he pushed me through the door and across the kitchen to where the sun porch was. We'd always used it in summers as a kind of playroom, setting up electric trains and Barbie doll villages and stuff that no one wanted to pick up and put away afterwards. But now it was a bedroom. My room. Daddy had walled most of it in and installed baseboard heating units, had even built a small closet in one corner, and had carpeted it nicely. One whole wall was still windows, and I could see the yard and the woods beyond. Mom had made white chintz curtains. There was a single bed and a new dresser and a worktable Daddy'd made from a door. My New Kids on the Block poster had been tacked on one wall, and a whole bunch of my other favorite things were there—pictures of kids from school, the cheerleaders' team photograph, with me front and center, looking grinny and dumb, my Albert Einstein picture, my books, and on the bed Fergus the Bear. There was a new picture of Jesus over the dresser that I knew Mom had put up; she'd no doubt left the old one upstairs to keep track of Jennie.

"And you've got your own private bathroom," Daddy said, swinging open the door of what used to be a washroom. He had enlarged it by cutting into the hallway and had installed a small tub with a shower and a sink with a big mirror above it. Hung too high, I noticed, but I didn't say anything.

It was all very nice. Like my own little apartment.

"You are really lucky," Rudy said again.

"Shut up, Rudy," I heard myself say.

"Yeah," Skip said, and he whacked Rudy on the back. That's all they do now, hit.

"You boys, get outside," Daddy said, and they left, happy to be relieved of duty.

"Can I come and visit you in your room?" Jennie asked.

"You better. And you can sleep in my new bed with me sometimes too. I'll get lonely way off here by myself," I said, and I grabbed her hand, and she moved in close to me. The phone rang again, and Mom went to answer it.

"So whaddaya think, Babes?"

"It's really very nice, Daddy," I said, and I meant it. But it was strange too. The room made me feel like I was suddenly a tenant, like I had been eased out of the family somehow. I wanted that, though. In a way, being a tenant was perfect. Except for Jennie, I didn't want to be a member of the same family as the rest of them, and I was glad that we could never go back to being the family we had been before the accident. Glad; not happy.

I wheeled my chair into the room and looked at the back of the door. "It needs a lock on the door," I said.

"It does. Sure it does. A girl needs her privacy and all, right? I'll fix that up now," he said briskly, and he left the room to get his tools and a lock from his shop in the basement.

"You got to keep the boys out," Jennie said. "I need a lock too. Mommy says I don't need one because I'm only six. But the boys're always barging in when I'm undressing and stuff."

"That's right. A girl needs her privacy," I said. "Don't worry, I'll get Daddy to do it for you," I said, and she grinned and pinched me on the cheek like she was the grownup and I was the baby.

Then Daddy was back with an awl and a hook and eye. He made a hole in the door with the awl and started screwing in the hook part, and I said, "That's too high. I'll never reach it."

"Oh, right, yes, of course," he said, all flustered. He studied the hole he'd made in his newly painted door. Now he'd have to fill it in and sand it and paint it over. Daddy's like that. "I better get some spackle," he said, and he left the room again. I saw him look at the bathroom mirror as he passed it and knew what he was thinking.

I heard Mom say goodbye on the phone, and then she talked in a low voice for a minute to Daddy. I couldn't hear what she was saying, but when they both came back I knew they had some kind of pronouncement to make. Mom sat down on the bed and crossed her legs at the ankles, like she does, and Daddy went to work filling the tiny hole in the door with spackle.

"So you like your new room?" Mom said brightly.

"Yeah, it's great." I wheeled over to the worktable and discovered that it was just the right height for my chair to slide under. That's when I saw the computer, a Mac. I guess I'd seen it before that, but the room at first had looked like a picture to me, a magazine photograph, and the new computer hadn't really registered or something. Slowly the whole thing was becoming real, though. "Wow. Is this mine? A Mac?" There was a printer and everything.

Mom said, "Yes, it is. It's yours. It's a present."

"Wow. Who from?" I turned to Daddy, but he was bent over at the door, still working on the lock, this time screwing it in at shoulder height for me, waist high for him. "You guys?"

"No," Mom said. "It came from Mr. Stephens. You don't really know him yet. As a matter of fact, that was him just now on the phone. He was calling to see how you were and all. Isn't that a coincidence?"

"Who's Mr. Stephens?"

"He's a lawyer," Daddy said. "He's our lawyer."

"You have a lawyer? You and Mom?"

"Well, yes, we all do. He's your lawyer too," Daddy said. He'd finished with the lock and closed the door and tested it. It worked, but the room seemed real small with the door closed and all these people in it, like a closet, except for the big window, and I was relieved when he unlocked and opened the door again.

"*My* lawyer? What do I need a lawyer for?"

Mom said, "Maybe we shouldn't be talking about this just now, with you barely home yet. Aren't you hungry, honey? Want me to fix you something?" She started to get up.

"No! What's this lawyer business? How come this Mr. Stephens gave me a computer?"

"He's a very kind man," Mom said. "And he knew you'd need one for doing schoolwork, and he knew you wouldn't be able to use the computers at school until next fall, when you go back. And naturally *we* couldn't afford one. . . ." She was picking invisible threads from the bedspread, not looking at me, but her legs were still crossed at the ankles, like she was on stage. I hate these kinds of conversations, like everyone but me knows the lines and has been rehearsing the scene without me.

Daddy sighed. "It's because of the accident," he said. "A lot of people in town whose kids were on the bus have got lawyers, because of the accident. Thank God we didn't lose you, but a lot of people . . . well, you know. People in town are very, very angry," he said. "Us included. There's been a lot of grief here. People lost their children, Babes."

"Yeah, but you didn't lose *me!*"

"No, honey," Mom said. "And we will thank the Lord for that every day and night for the rest of our lives. But you . . . you almost died, and you were badly injured, and you won't be . . . you can't . . ."

"I can't walk anymore." I said it for her.

"Well, that's . . . that's a terrible loss," Daddy said. "To you, especially," he said. "But to all of us."

I looked at him hard, and he said, "Because we love you so much. And because you're going to need special care for a long time to come, all that physical therapy and who knows what. For years, Babes. Spinal cord injuries don't just go away. It's not going to be easy. Not for you, not for any of us. And it's going to cost more money than we can imagine. For years."

"What about insurance? Doesn't insurance pay for these things?"

"Partly, yes, but it's still expensive. There's a lot the

insurance doesn't cover. That's one of the reasons we have a lawyer for you, to make sure the insurance gets paid and to help us pay for the rest."

"One of the reasons. What're the other reasons?"

Daddy said, "Well, Mr. Stephens is representing several families: the Ottos—you know them, of course—and Risa and Wendell Walker, and us, and I think a couple more. Mr. Stephens is suing the state and the town for negligence, because he is sure that the accident could have been avoided if the state and the town had done their jobs right."

"Suing! But it's not the *same* for us! The Ottos . . . I mean, they lost Bear in the accident, and maybe it's like that with the Walkers and poor little Sean, but . . ." I could feel myself starting to cry; I did not want to cry.

So I shut up. I did not remember the accident, maybe, but I definitely knew what had happened. I could read the newspapers, and of course I had asked people, and eventually people had told me, although they had not wanted to. Everyone had come to the hospital to visit and tell me how lucky I was, to touch me on the hands and shoulders and top of my head like I was some kind of rabbit's foot, so when I asked them about the other kids, what happened to the other kids who were on the bus that morning, at first no one was willing to tell me. Oh, now, Nichole, don't you trouble yourself about that. You just concentrate on getting better and coming back to school. That sort of stuff.

But what about the other kids? I really needed to know. What about Rudy and Skip, they were on the bus, were they okay? I had asked about them first, naturally, as soon as I learned what had happened to me. And what about the Lamstons, what about the Prescott kids, what about the Bilodeaus? What happened to Sean Walker, who had been sitting in my lap that morning because he didn't want to leave his mother? I could remember that much, Sean trying to catch a glimpse of his mother by the road. And what about Bear Otto? What about the Ansel twins? What happened to Dolores? Was she all right? How come I'm lying here in the hospital with tubes stuck in me and my body all numb. How come I'm not dead too? Someone, anyone, tell me where all the other children are!

Slowly people let me know. One by one. That's how I came to understand what they meant by lucky. Rudy and Skip, they were especially lucky; they had been up front in the bus and had been almost the first to be removed from it, with barely a scratch on either of them. Jennie had stayed home sick that day. There were a bunch like that. Close calls. Because I was regarded as one myself, people liked standing around in the hospital room talking to me and each other about all the close calls.

But so many of the other kids were dead, and no one wanted to talk about them. They told me with downcast eyes and sad slow shakes of the head and as few words as possible. The Lamstons were dead, all three of them. One of the Prescott kids was dead. Two of the Bilodeaus, who had been at the rear of the bus, had been trapped underwater. Sean Walker had been in front, like me, but when the bus flipped over he'd fractured his skull and died from it before they got him out of the bus, and I'd only broken my back. So I was lucky, right? And Bear and the Ansel twins and several other kids who'd been in the back, they were all dead. Dolores was okay, I learned. She'd been in shock for a while, people said, but now she was okay. So she was lucky too. I wondered if she had a lawyer, like me.

It just wasn't right—to be alive, to have had what people assured you was a close call, and then go out and hire a lawyer; it wasn't right. And even if you were the mother and father of one of the kids who had died, like the Ottos or the Walkers, what good would it do to hire a lawyer? To sue, because your child had died in an accident, and then collect a bunch of money from the state—it was understandable, yet it somehow didn't seem right, either. But to be the mother and father of one of the kids who had survived the accident, even a kid like me, who would spend the rest of her life a cripple, and then to sue—I didn't understand that at all, and I really knew it wasn't right. Not if I was, like they said, truly lucky.

There was no stopping Mom and Daddy, though. They had their minds made up. This Mr. Stephens had convinced them that they were going to get a million dollars from the State of New York and maybe another million from the town of Sam Dent. Daddy said they all have insurance for this sort of thing; it won't come out of anybody's pocket, he kept saying; but even so, it made me nervous. Since the accident, I had become superstitious, I think. Mom and Daddy are Christians, at least Mom is, and I sort of believe in God myself, so I did not want to appear ungrateful and end up losing what little luck I had.

"This Mr. Stephens, who bought me the computer— what does he want me to do? I don't have to be the one to sue anybody, do I? Can't you guys do it?"

Daddy was in the bathroom now, unscrewing the mirror. "Well, sure, but he's got to arrange for the other side's lawyers to take a statement from you, a deposition, it's called, and then we all go to court, and you'll be asked to testify and so forth—"

"About what?" I hollered. "I don't even *remember* the accident! It's like I wasn't even there!"

"Don't get excited, honey," Mom said, smooth as butter. God, I hate her sometimes.

Jennie was sucking her thumb. "Cut that out," I said to her. "You're too old for that," I said, and she started to cry. I'm such a rat. "I'm sorry, Babes," I said to her. I pulled her to me and hugged her. She stopped crying and didn't put her thumb back in her mouth, but now I was wishing she would.

Daddy said, "Mr. Stephens is really a very nice man, very gentle and understanding. He just wants you to describe in your own words what life was like before the accident, you know, with school and all, cheerleading, your plans for the future and all, that sort of thing. In your own words. He says it's much more effective if you tell it, instead of just us telling it."

"Yeah. I'll bet. Well, maybe I won't. I don't like even thinking about that stuff, and I sure don't want to talk about it to any lawyer or some judge in a courtroom. So maybe I'll just refuse to talk about it. They can't make me, can they?"

"C'mon, Babes, be reasonable," Daddy said, coming back into the bedroom.

"Let's talk about this later, okay?" Mom said. "She just

got home, Sam. Are you hungry, honey? You want me to fix you something, a sandwich or some soup? No more hospital food, honey, aren't you glad?" She had her cheery TV-mom voice working.

"Yeah," I said, and I suppose I was glad. I hate hospital food. "I am hungry. Maybe a sandwich and some soup would be good."

Mom got up and hustled out to the kitchen, and Daddy slowly gathered his tools and followed. I rolled over to the door and shut it and put the new hook in place. "It works," I said to Jennie.

"Cool," she said, imitating me.

"I'm sorry I yelled at you."

"That's okay. Can you make the computer work?" she asked. "Can you show me how to use it?"

I said sure and wheeled back to the table and switched on the computer. "Cool," I said, and winked at her and laughed. Quickly, she came up next to my chair and put her arm around my shoulder, and we started fooling around with Mr. Stephens's computer, writing our names and silly messages on the screen.

I was home again, and lots of things were the same as before. But a few things, important things, were different. And not just my room, either. Before the accident, I was ashamed all the time and afraid. Because of Daddy. Sometimes I even wanted to kill myself. But now I was mostly angry and never wanted to die.

Back then, though, with Jennie sound asleep in the bunk above me, I used to lie awake at night thinking up ways to kill myself. Dying was the only way I could imagine the end of what I was doing with Daddy, although sometimes I imagined that he had suddenly decided to leave me alone, because weeks would go by, whole months, when he did leave me alone, when he just acted regular, and I thought then that maybe he had decided that what he was making me do with him was wrong, really wrong, and he was sorry and wouldn't come to me anymore when we were alone in the house or in the car and touch me and make me touch him.

Those times when he left me alone, I thought maybe I had dreamed the whole thing up, dreams are like that, or had imagined it, because even when I was a little kid like Jennie, before Daddy started touching me that way, I had imagined some things that had made me ashamed, sexual things, sort of. Everybody does that. So maybe I had imagined this too. A few weeks would pass, and I'd start to forget that it had actually happened, and then I'd feel guilty for having been so upset and confused.

But late one night he would pick me up from baby-sitting at the Ansels' or somebody else's, and in the darkness of the car he'd slide his hand across the seat to me and put it on my leg and pull me toward him and keep sliding his hand up my leg, under my skirt, and I knew his pants were undone and he wanted me to put my hand on him there again, and so I would, and then we would do things to each other, like he had taught me, things like I knew my girlfriends did with their boyfriends after school dances and in cars with older boys but that I would never do with a boy and pretended to be disgusted about when they told me.

When we got home I would run into the house from

the car and go straight to my room upstairs with my heart pounding and a roaring sound in my ears. It was awful. I lay in bed in the darkness with my clothes still on and listened to him lock up below and walk slowly up the stairs and go into his and Mom's room and shut the door. I could hear the bedsprings squeak as he got into bed next to Mom, and soon I heard him snoring. For hours I stayed there, still as a log, until finally the roaring in my ears stopped and I dared to get out of the bed and take off my clothes in the darkened room and put on my nightgown and go down the hall to the bathroom and come back to bed, where I lay awake trying to think up ways to kill myself that wouldn't upset Jennie too much. Usually, I decided on sleeping pills and Daddy's vodka in the kitchen cupboard. Like Marilyn Monroe. But I didn't know how to get hold of any sleeping pills, so the next day I always gave it up and instead tried to make what had happened in the car coming home from the Ansels' seem like I only dreamed it.

I didn't have to try very hard, because Daddy, except when he wanted to do those things with me, the rest of the time treated me normally, like nothing wrong had happened. Always, the next morning at breakfast he was just the same old Daddy, grumpy and distracted, bossing the boys and me and Jennie around, ignoring Mom the way he does, while she fussed in the kitchen, shoving food at the rest of us and as usual worrying over her diet. She never eats anything in front of anybody but keeps getting fatter and fatter all the time. She's not a blimp, but she is fat.

"Look at Nichole," Daddy always said to Mom. "Look at me. We never diet, we just eat three squares a day, and we're not fat. What you got to do, Mary, is stop all the in-between-meal snacking," he'd say.

"Nichole's *fourteen*," Mom would answer. "And you, everyone in your family is skinny as a rail. And I *don't* snack; it's my metabolism." Then she'd pout and try to change the subject. "Rudy, you keep your hat on today; you're coming down with a cold," she'd say, and start hurrying us from the table so we wouldn't miss the bus.

Normal life at the Burnell house.

What *used* to be normal life anyhow. Because after the accident, things changed. For one thing, when the other kids went off to school in the mornings, I stayed home. Mr. Dillinger, the principal, came over one day and brought a bunch of assignments from my teachers so I could catch up with the rest of my class and pass into the ninth grade with them. He's a huge gawk who wears a bow tie and always has dandruff on his suits, and he sat in the living room with me and Mom, all hearty and cheerful, talking real loud, like being in the wheelchair had made me deaf, and together they tried to convince me to come back to school and attend classes with everyone else. He said the school board had authorized a special van to bring me back and forth. "Isn't that *terrific!*" he said, like I was supposed to jump up and give a cheer for the school board.

"No way," I said. "I'm never going back to that school," I said, and I noticed he didn't argue very hard. Mom didn't, either, but she never argues hard when an official man is around. She just takes her cues from him and agrees. Later on, Daddy tells her what she should have said.

Anyhow, I don't think Mr. Dillinger wanted me

wheeling around the school reminding everyone of the accident and the kids who had died in it. They'd hired some woman from Plattsburgh, I heard, and arranged all these special group therapy meetings and assemblies for the kids after the accident, and things had more or less returned to normal now. Besides, Mr. Dillinger knew I could do all the work at home and still be ahead of most of the kids in my class, except for the real brainy ones. And next year my class would all be going on to high school in Lake Placid, and then I'd be somebody else's problem.

I didn't want to stay home alone with Mom all day, that's for sure, but I really did not need to see any of the kids from school. I didn't want to watch them strolling around in the hallways and the cafeteria, sneaking into the lav between classes to put on lipstick and share a cigarette, going off to cheerleading practice and hanging out after school in the parking lot together. I didn't want them to stop what they were doing or saying when I rolled up in my wheelchair, "Hi, guys, what's up?" I knew what I'd look like to them, how they'd all go silent for a minute when the dweeb arrived and then change the subject not to embarrass her or make her feel bad because they were talking about something she couldn't do, like dancing or sports or just hanging out. Poor Nichole, the cripple. That's the best I'd get from them—pity. And no matter how many of those group therapy sessions they'd been to, everyone would see me and instantly think of the kids who weren't there anymore, the kids who had not been lucky like me, and maybe they would hate me for it. And I wouldn't blame them.

At the hospital, lots of kids from school, even the little

kids from the Sunday school class I taught, had come to visit me, like official delegations at first, in groups of three and four at a time, but it was always self-conscious and embarrassing, especially with the kids my age, my friends, so called, and I knew they could hardly wait to leave, and I was glad myself when they did. Then only my best friend, Jody Plante, and one or two others, when they could get someone to drive them over, came to visit, and that was okay. But by the time I left the hospital to come home, I had pretty much run out of things to talk about with them. We were living in different worlds now, and they couldn't know about mine, and I didn't want to know about theirs anymore.

For a while after I got home, Jody called me on the phone and even came over once or twice, and she yacked brightly about school and cheerleading gossip and boys, the usual stuff. But she was forcing it, I knew, and I never seemed to have the desire to call her, and of course I couldn't visit, so pretty soon she didn't call me anymore and never came to visit, either.

I stayed in my new room, with the door closed and locked, except when I came out to eat or use the bathroom. For supper, I had to sit at the table with the rest of the family, but breakfast and lunch I usually ate alone. One Saturday morning Mom and Daddy moved everything in the cupboards—dishes, glasses, food, everything—down to the lower cabinets, so I could reach them from my wheelchair. It was Daddy's idea. I think Mom would have preferred to have me go on asking her for help every time I wanted a sandwich or a bowl of cereal. But since Jennie was in school now, Mom was gone a lot of the time herself, working part time over to the Grand Union in Marlowe, so she had to go along with my taking care of myself in the kitchen.

During the days, I pretty much had the whole house to myself, but I still stayed in my room. One night Daddy brought home a portable black-and-white TV for me that he had bought used in Ausable Forks, and he tied it into the regular cable, so I was able to watch TV then without leaving my room. Soaps and game shows, mostly, which were fine by me. And music videos. And Oprah and Donahue and Geraldo. After a month of that stuff you feel like it's all one show, ads and everything, and you've been watching it for years. But I had Mr. Stephens's computer to play with, and plenty of schoolwork to do, and books that Mrs. Twichell, the school librarian, brought over for me, mostly sappy young-adult novels about race relations and divorce, which I don't like but will read anyhow because the writers seem so intent on having you read them that you feel it's impolite not to.

Things with Daddy were different now too. I had become a wheelchair girl, and I think that scared him, like it does most people. You see them on the street staring at you and then looking away, as if you were a freak. To Daddy, it was like I was made of spun glass and he was afraid he would break me if he touched me. Probably I wasn't pretty to him anymore, either, and he couldn't pretend that I was like some beautiful movie star, the way he used to. Miss America, he always called me. "How's my Miss America today?" But not anymore. Which was fine by me. If he did touch me, by accident or because he couldn't avoid it, like the time he had to carry me up the stairs at the courthouse in Marlowe when I had to make my deposition for Mr. Stephens and the other lawyers, he backed away from me right away and wouldn't look at me.

I looked at him, though. I looked right into him. I had changed since the accident, and not just in my body, and he knew it. His secret was mine now; I owned it. It used to be like I shared it with him, but no more. Before, everything had been fluid and changing and confused, with me not knowing for sure what had happened or who was to blame. But now I saw him as a thief, just a sneaky little thief in the night who had robbed his own daughter of what was supposed to be permanently hers—like he had robbed me of my soul or something, whatever it was that Jennie still had and I didn't. And then the accident robbed me of my body.

So I didn't own much anymore. My new room, maybe, and Mr. Stephens's computer, which weren't really mine and weren't worth much anyhow. No, the only truly valuable thing that I owned now happened to be Daddy's worst secret, and I meant to hold on to it. It was like I carried it in a locked box on my lap, with the key held tightly in my hand, and it made him afraid of me. Every time he saw me looking at him hard, he trembled.

I remember the first time Mr. Stephens came over to the house, how strained and nervous Daddy was when he wheeled me out into the living room and introduced me. It was like Mr. Stephens was a police officer or something, probably because he's such a big shot lawyer and all, and Daddy was afraid I'd say something to make him suspicious.

Of course, he was also afraid that I would refuse to go along with their lawsuit. I still hadn't agreed to do it, not in so many words, but in my mind I had decided to go ahead and say what they wanted me to say, which they insisted was only to answer Mr. Stephens's and the other lawyers' questions truthfully. That couldn't hurt anything, I figured, because the truth was, I didn't really remember anything about the actual accident, so nothing I said could be used to blame anybody for it. It was an accident, that's all. Accidents happen.

Mr. Stephens was this tall skinny guy with a big puffy head of gray hair that made him look like a dandelion gone to seed and a gust of wind would blow all his hair away and leave him bald. I liked him, though. He had a small pointy face and red lips and a nice smile, and he looked right into my eyes when he talked to me, which is something that most people can't do with me. Also, he reached down and shook my hand when Daddy introduced us, which I liked. Adults almost never do that, especially with girls. And with wheelchair girls, I've noticed, they actually take a step backward and put their hands on their hips or in their pockets, like you've got something they don't want to catch. Mr. Stephens, though, after he shook my hand and Daddy went to stand edgily by the porch door, pulled a kitchen chair up next to my wheelchair and sat right down and got his head the same level as mine, and I felt like he could see that I was really a normal person.

He talked funny, fast and like he had already thought out ahead of time what he wanted to say, the way city people or maybe just lawyers do, but I liked it, because once you trust a person like that, you can have a real good conversation with him. You can concentrate on what the words mean and not have to worry all the time about what the other person is thinking.

"Well, Nichole," he began, "I've been wanting to meet you for a long time now, and not just because I've heard so many good things about you all over town, but because, as you know, I'm the guy representing you and your mom and dad and some other folks here in town," he said, diving right in. "We're trying to generate some compensation, however meager, for what you all have suffered and at the same time see that an accident like this one never happens again. And you, Nichole Burnell, you're pretty near central to the case I'm trying to build," he said. "But you would probably just as soon let the whole thing lie, I'll bet, so you can get on with your life as quickly and smoothly as possible, right?"

I said yes, as a matter of fact I would. He waited for me to go on, so I did. I said that I didn't like thinking about the accident, which I couldn't remember anyhow, and I really hated talking with people about it, because I didn't even know what the accident meant, and since it was obvious to me that anyone who wasn't there couldn't possibly know what it meant, why bother at all? Besides, I said, it just made people feel sorry for me, and I hated that.

From his perch by the door, Daddy said, "What she

means, Mitch—" and Mr. Stephens shushed him with a wave of his hand.

"Why do you hate it when people feel sorry for you?" he asked me. "Do you mind if I smoke?"

Mom jumped up from the couch and said, "I'll get an ashtray, Mr. Stephens. I'm sorry, we don't smoke, and I just didn't think—"

"Actually, I mind," I said. If I wasn't allowed to smoke in this Christian house, why should he? And it was me he had asked, not her.

"No problem," Mr. Stephens said, and he smiled broadly at me, like he was a teacher and I'd just aced a test, and said to Mom, "Please, Mary, that's fine. No ashtray. I can wait." Then to me, "Go ahead, Nichole, tell me why you hate it when people feel sorry for you. Because they can't help it, you know. They really can't. When they see you in this wheelchair, especially if they know what your life was like just six months ago, people are going to feel sorry for you. No way around it. I'll be honest: we just met, and already I admire you—who wouldn't? You're a brave tough smart kid, and that's obvious right away. And I didn't know you or know how exciting and promising your life was before the accident. But listen, even *I* feel sorry for you. Do you hate that?"

Yes, I said, certainly I did, because all it did was remind me that I wasn't normal anymore. "You can feel lucky that you didn't die for only so long," I said. "And then you start to feel unlucky."

"That you didn't die, you mean. Like the other children."

"Yes!" I said. "Like Bear and the Ansel twins and Sean and all the other kids on the bus who died out there that morning!"

"Nichole!" Mom said.

"It's the *truth!*" I said.

"It is the truth," Mr. Stephens said in a calm sure voice, like he was correcting her on what time it was, and I knew that he understood what I was feeling and Mom didn't have the foggiest. I think Daddy understood, but he couldn't say it, not to me. I wouldn't let him.

"It would be strange," Mr. Stephens said to me, "if you *didn't* feel that way about the other kids."

Then he got me talking about last year at school, how I had tried out for cheerleading in the seventh grade and had made the team easily, which is unusual for a seventh grader, and how last fall I was captain, and that's a big deal in Sam Dent, because the boys' football and basketball teams are so important to the town. I was Queen of the Harvest Ball too, and I went with Bucky Waters, the captain of the football team, even though he wasn't my boyfriend.

I never actually *had* a boyfriend, no one steady, I told Mr. Stephens, but Bucky was okay to go to the dance with, because he was sort of famous at school as a playboy who wouldn't go steady with anybody, and I was famous for being churchy and stuck-up, or so some kids thought. Bucky was chosen King of the Harvest Ball, naturally, and for a while everybody thought we were a couple, but we knew we weren't. I didn't say this to Mr. Stephens, but after the dance, Bucky tried really hard to make out with me at Jody Plante's party, and I wouldn't let him, so he got mad and went off with some of the other football players to drink beer in Gilbert Jacques's older brother's car, I heard later.

We stayed friends, though, Bucky and I, and let people think what they wanted. It suited him that kids thought I was his girlfriend, at least during football and basketball season, and it suited me too, because then no one else bothered me, since he was such a big shot and all. Boys are so immature, I said to Mr. Stephens. At least the boys in Sam Dent are.

"Have you seen Bucky since the accident?" Mr. Stephens asked. Mom was in the kitchen making tea, and Daddy had left the room to go to the bathroom, I think.

"No."

"Not once?"

"Nope."

"What about the other kids, your girlfriends?"

"I saw them some at the hospital. But not lately," I said.

"No one?"

I knew I was going to cry and sound stupid if we didn't change the subject, so I said, "Tell me what I have to do for the lawsuit."

That got him talking about depositions and lawyers for the state and the town, and by the time Daddy came back from the bathroom and Mom came in with her tea and cookies, which I knew she'd already eaten a bunch of in the kitchen, Mr. Stephens was going on about how tough it would be for me to answer some of the questions those other lawyers would ask. "They work for the people we're trying to sue, you understand, and their job is to try to minimize the damages. Our job, Nichole, is to try to maximize the damages," he explained. "If you think of it that way, as people doing their jobs, no good guys and no bad guys, just our side and the other side, then it'll go easier for you."

No one was interested in the truth, was what he was saying. Because the truth was that it was an accident, that's all, and no one was to blame. "I won't lie," I told him.

"Some of the questions will seem pretty personal to you, Nichole. I just want to warn you up front."

"No matter what they ask me," I said, "I'll tell the truth," and I looked straight at Daddy, who had taken a seat next to Mom on the sofa. He studied his tea when I said that, as if he had seen a fly in it. I knew what he was thinking, and he knew what I was thinking too.

"Fine, fine, I don't want you to lie," Mr. Stephens said. "I want you to be absolutely truthful. Absolutely. No matter what I or the other lawyers ask you. They'll have a laundry list of questions, but I'll be right there to advise and help you. And there'll be a court stenographer there to make a record of it, and that's what'll go to the judge, before the trial is set. It'll be the same for everybody. They'll be deposing the Ottos and the Walkers, the bus driver, and even your mom and dad, but I'll make sure you go last, Nichole, so you can keep on getting well before you have to go in and do this. It'll all take place over the summer," he said to Mom and Daddy. "And the trial will be set for sometime this fall, probably."

"When do they award the damages?" Daddy asked,

and he and Mom leaned forward for the answer.

"Depends," Mr. Stephens said. "If they appeal, and they probably will, this could drag on for quite a while. But we'll be there at the end, Sam, don't you worry," he said. He put his cup on the coffee table and stood up, thinking about a cigarette, I bet. He said his goodbyes, and Daddy saw him out to his car, where they talked together for a while.

I went back to my room and closed the door and locked it. Let them discuss their lawsuit without me, if they wanted; I had done my part for now, and I didn't want to speak about it again until I had to.

The whole thing, even though I liked Mr. Stephens and trusted him, made me feel greedy and dishonest. I looked at my picture of Einstein. What would he have done, if he'd been in an accident and been lucky like me?

I hitched myself out of the wheelchair and when I swung onto the bed, my skirt got hitched up, and I sat there for a minute, looking at my dumb worthless legs reflected in the window glass. They looked like they belonged to someone else. How much had they been worth a year ago, I wondered, or last fall, at the Keene Valley game and the Harvest Ball afterwards, when Bucky Waters and I, with crowns on our heads, danced in the gym in front of the whole school? And to *whom*? That was the real question. To me, my legs were worth everything then and nothing now. But to Mom and Daddy, nothing then and a couple of million dollars now.

After that night, I remember, a long time passed when it seemed no one talked about the lawsuit, at least not to me, and I didn't hear anything more about Mr. Stephens, either. Which was fine. I sure didn't want to bring it up, and I guess Mom and Daddy, for different reasons, didn't want to, so it was as if it had never happened. Like I had dreamed it, the way I used to about me and Daddy; and just as before, I felt guilty for having so much emotion about the subject. When you live with people like my mother, who thinks Jesus takes care of everything except your weight, and my father, who goes around whistling and hammering and sawing all the time, you tend to feel guilty for your emotions. At least I did.

Then one night we were having supper together; it was in June, I remember, because Mom and Daddy were trying to get me to attend my graduation ceremonies with the other kids. I had come out second in my class, and Mr. Dillinger had told Mom and Daddy that everyone thought it would be great if I would give the salutatorian's speech from my wheelchair in front of the whole town.

I thought it was a terrible idea, and I said so. I had written a research paper for English on Sam Dent, the man the town was named after, and had received an A + for it, and Mr. Dillinger and Mrs. Crosby, the English teacher, said that with a little revising it would make a perfect salutatorian's speech. The way they wanted me to revise it, I knew without their even saying, was to turn Sam Dent into an example for the kids who were graduating, which meant that I'd have to cut out all the bad things he'd done, like cheating the Indians out of their land and buying his way out of the Civil War things that lots of people did in those days but that were just as bad then as they would be now.

"C'mon, Babes," Dad said. "You'll be the star of the show."

"Some star," I said. "What you mean is, you and Mom'll be the stars of the show!" That was the main reason I didn't want to do it. Of course, they thought I was just ashamed of being in a wheelchair, which was partly true, but I was slowly getting over that by then. Twice a week, since I'd come home from the hospital, Mom had been carting me over to Lake Placid for physical therapy at the Olympic Center, where there were lots of kids and young people who were even worse off than I was, and some of them had made friends with me, so I was beginning to see myself in the world a little clearer by then. I didn't feel so abnormal anymore, and I didn't worry so much about whether I was lucky or unlucky. I was both, like most people.

No, the reason I was dead set on avoiding the graduation ceremonies was because Mom and Daddy were so dead set on getting me to do it and because they wanted it for themselves, not me. They didn't realize that, of course, but I did. Sometimes I almost felt sorry for them, the way they desperately needed me to be a star, and that's why in the past, before the accident, I had always given in to them. But no more. Now I only did what *I* wanted to do, for *my* reasons. For my reasons, I didn't go to church with them anymore, I didn't teach Sunday school, I didn't baby-sit for anyone in town (although no one had asked me to), I didn't go to the movies or to restaurants with the family. Instead, I stayed home, behind the door of my new room, and that I did for my reasons too. No one else's.

Anyhow, in the middle of our arguing about this, the phone rang, and Mom got up to answer it. Daddy hates talking on the phone and never answers it himself, even if he's standing beside it when it rings. He walks away and lets one of us do the job for him. I never minded, and I used to rush to the phone when it rang, hoping it was for me; but no more, of course.

A minute later, Mom came back to the table, looking worried. "That was Billy Ansel," she said to Daddy. "He wants to come over. To talk to us, he said."

"He say what about?" Daddy asked, sounding suspicious, although as far as I knew then, he liked Billy Ansel well enough. Everyone did. In fact, Billy Ansel was more of a local hero than Sam Dent was. If they wanted a graduation speech about a role model, they ought to get someone to make it about him.

"No," Mom said.

"Was he drinking, could you tell?"

"I can't tell about those things, Sam, you know that."

I just listened. This was new, Billy Ansel drinking and Mom and Daddy worried about his coming over to talk with them.

Rudy asked to be excused, and then Skip did, and Daddy said sure, and they took off to watch TV in the living room, with Jennie following along behind. Usually, that's when I disappeared from the table too, heading for my room, but this time I stayed.

"Is he coming over now? Right away?" Daddy asked.

Mom got up and started clearing the table. "That's what he said."

Daddy turned to me and said, "What're you up to tonight, Babes?" Trying to get rid of me.

"Nothing."

"No homework?"

"Done. Besides, it's Friday."

"Nothing good on your TV?"

"Nope. Thought I'd wait around and see Billy Ansel," I said, but as soon as I said it, I realized that I didn't want to see him at all. Because of the accident. Maybe that's why Mom and Daddy were so nervous about his coming over.

In the last couple of years, after Billy's wife died, I had become his kids' regular baby-sitter, and now they were gone too. Maybe I was stuck in a wheelchair and all, but I sure wasn't dead, like his twins, so the idea of him seeing me made me cringe with shame. I didn't want to be seen by *anyone* whose kids had been killed in the accident, but especially not Billy Ansel.

"Actually," I said, "now that I think about it, I'd just as soon stay in my room when he comes."

"Fine," Daddy said, obviously relieved, as I shoved my chair away from the table and rolled across the kitchen toward my room.

"Daddy, when he comes . . . ," I said, trying to think of what I wanted him to say for me to Billy Ansel, remembering all the times I had tucked Jessica and Mason into bed, remembering how they loved to have me read their Babar the Elephant books to them before they went to sleep, remembering their faces, their bright trusting motherless faces; and I had to give it up—there was nothing I could say to Billy, except I'm sorry. I'm sorry that your children died when my parents' children didn't.

"Just tell him I'm sleeping," I said, and wheeled into my room.

In a little while, I heard his pickup truck drive up and crunch across the gravel of the driveway. He knocked on the door, and Daddy greeted him in his fake-surprise way. "Hey, Billy! What brings you out on a night like this? C'mon in, c'mon in, take a load off."

I shut off the TV sound and with Fergus the Bear in my lap rolled my chair over next to the door so I could hear them better. Mom was washing dishes at the sink; I heard Billy and Daddy scrape their chairs on the floor as they sat down at the kitchen table. Billy still hadn't said anything. I wondered what he was like when he was drinking. He used to go out a lot at night, which is why I baby-sat so often for him, and most times when he left the house he said he'd be having a few beers with the boys down at the Rendez-Vous or the Spread Eagle, in case of an emergency or something, but when he came home he never seemed drunk or anything. Just sad, as usual. Because of his wife, I assumed. That and Vietnam. He was a well-known Vietnam vet, and those guys are always a little sad.

"Would you like a cup of tea, Billy?" Mom said. "There's a piece of cake left, if you want."

"No. No, thanks, Mary," he said in a flat voice.

"So," Daddy said. "What brings you out tonight?"

"Well, Sam, I might's well tell you the truth. It's this

lawsuit you've gotten yourself all taken up with," he said. "I want you to drop the damned thing."

"I don't see how that concerns you, Billy," Daddy said. I could tell from his voice that he was smiling but was seriously mad. That's what he does when he's mad, keeps on smiling but shifts his voice down a notch. It's scarier that way.

"It does concern me."

Daddy said, "I don't know why it should. There's a whole lot of people in town that's involved with lawsuits. We're hardly unique here, Billy. I mean, I can understand how you feel, it's depressing, sure, but it's reality. You can't just turn this off because you happen to think it's a bad idea. Half the town is suing somebody or other, or getting ready to."

"Well, I'm one who's not suing anybody. And I don't want a damned thing to do with it, either."

"Okay, so fine. So stay out of it, then."

"That's exactly what I've *tried* to do. I've really tried to stay the hell out of it. But it turns out that's not so easy, Sam. You've gone and got yourself some hotshot New York City lawyer, this Mitchell Stephens—you and Risa and Wendell Walker and the Ottos."

"Yeah, so? Lots of folks have got lawyers."

"But yours is the one who's gonna subpoena me, Sam. Force me to testify in court. He came by the garage this afternoon, real smooth and friendly."

"Why would he do that?" Mom said. "You didn't have anything to do with the accident." She's so out of it. Even I knew that Billy had been driving behind the bus that day, so he could wave at his kids, like he always did. That made him the only person not on the bus who'd actually witnessed the accident, which meant that he'd be the one to tell if Dolores had been driving safely. They naturally couldn't sue anybody if Dolores was driving recklessly, and only Billy knew the truth about that.

"And if the bastard does subpoena me," Billy said, ignoring Mom, "then all these other lawyers are gonna line up behind him and try to do the same thing."

"No, that won't happen, Billy. Mitch Stephens's case is small, compared to some of these guys, and very focused. The way he told me, all he needs is for you to say what you saw that day, driving along behind the bus. I know it's a painful thing to have to do, testifying and all, but it'll only take a few minutes of your time, and that'll be the end of it."

"Wrong," Billy said. "That's purely wrong. The other shysters'll copy him, or do a version of whatever he's doing, and there'll be all kinds of appeals, and I'll be tangled up in this mess for the next five years. And believe me, you and Mary will too," he said. "This thing is never going to go away, Sam."

"C'mon," Daddy said. "You know that won't—"

"Do *you* know," Billy interrupted him, "that we got lawyers suing lawyers, because some people were stupid enough to sign up with more than one of the bastards? And we got people switching lawyers, because these sonsof-bitches are bribing them, making deals and dickering over percentages." I hoped Mom and Daddy hadn't done that, switched lawyers, because of Mr. Stephens's computer.

Billy said, "A couple of local folks I won't bother to name—but you know them, Sam, they're friends of yours—they've even started a suit against the school board, because they're not happy with the way they decided to use the money that got collected around town last winter and the junk that people sent in from all over. There's one group in town that agrees with the school board and wants to spend the money for a memorial playground and donate the junk to the Lake Placid Hospital, and another that wants the money to go against this year's town tax bills and maybe have a tag sale or something to get rid of the stuff." He laughed, but he wasn't amused. I knew Mom and Daddy were in the second group, but I guess Billy didn't.

"Yesterday," he said, "I heard somebody wants to sue the rescue squad, for Christ's sake. The *rescue* squad. Because they supposedly didn't act fast enough.

"This whole town," Billy said in a suddenly dead voice, "the town has gone completely crazy. I used to like this town, I used to really care about what happened here, but now . . . now I think I'll sell my house and the garage and move the fuck away."

That got Mom upset—the word "fuck," not the idea of Billy's moving. "Billy, please," she said. "The children." Like they could hear him over the television. It was her own ears she was trying to protect, not theirs. "I can't have you talking that way in this house," she said. Right, this Christian house.

He said he was sorry, and the three of them were silent for a minute. "I was thinking, if you two dropped the

195

case," Billy said in a low voice, "then maybe the others would slowly come to their senses and follow. You're good sensible people, you and Mary. People respect you."

"No, Billy. We can't drop the lawsuit," Daddy said. "I shouldn't have to tell you, because I run a pretty good tab at your garage, but we need the money, Billy. For hospital bills and suchlike. Just for living."

"Christ, I'll pay Nichole's hospital bills, if that's what you're talking about. The Walkers, they'd drop out if you did. And the Ottos, I don't think they want to be doing this, either. Then your lawyer wouldn't have any reason to pursue the case. I bet he'd pack it in, cut his losses, and go home."

"None of us wants to be doing this, Billy."

"If you two could make a smart shyster like Stephens pull out, then maybe the other people in town would start to see the light, and people could get their mourning done properly and get on with their lives. This has become a hateful place to live, Sam. Hateful."

"Not for us," Daddy said.

"No, not for us," Mom chimed in.

What a dumb thing for them to say. It shocked even me. I heard Billy's chair bump against the floor as he stood up.

"Not for you. Right," he said, "not for you." He must have thought they were the stupidest people he'd ever met. Then, naturally, because of what they'd said, he thought of me. "How's Nichole? She around?"

Mom jumped in. "She's resting, in her room."

"Yeah. Well, that's too bad. I haven't seen her, you

know. Since the accident. I guess no one has. Tell her hello for me," he said in a low sad flat way that made my chest tighten, and I wanted to fly out into the kitchen and hug him.

But I didn't. I stayed there by the door, patting Fergus the Bear and listening, and suddenly I was aware that I was shaking all over.

At that moment, I hated my parents more than I ever had. I hated them for all that had gone before—Daddy for what he knew and had done, and Mom for what she didn't know and hadn't done—but I also hated them for this new thing, this awful lawsuit. The lawsuit was wrong. Purely and in God's eyes, as Mom especially should know, it was wrong; but also it was making Billy Ansel sadder than life had already done on its own, and that seemed stupid and cruel; and now it looked like half the people in town were doing it too, making everyone around them crazy with pain, the same as Mom and Daddy were doing to Billy, so they didn't have to face their own pain and get over it.

Why couldn't they see that? Why couldn't they just stand up like good people and say to Mr. Stephens, "No, forget the lawsuit. We'll get by somehow on our own. It's too harmful to too many people. Goodbye, Mr. Stephens. Take your law practice back to New York City, where people *like* to sue each other."

I heard the door close behind Billy, and then Mom and Daddy went up to their bedroom, probably to discuss things in private, which they were doing more and more now, talking alone in their bedroom. We were becoming a strange family, divided between parents and children, and even among the children we were divided, with me and

Jennie on one side and the boys on the other. No one in the family trusted anyone else in the family.

It had started back when Daddy began touching me and making me keep his secret, but he and I were the only ones who knew about that, so we had all gone on afterwards as if we were still a normal family, with everyone needing and trusting one another, just like you're supposed to. But now it was like everyone, not just me and Daddy, had secrets. Mom and Daddy had their secrets, and Jennie and I had ours, and Rudy and Skip had theirs, and we each had our own lonely secrets that we shared with no one.

I knew it was all directly connected to what had happened between me and Daddy before the accident, and through that to the accident itself, which had changed me and my view of everyone else, and now from the accident to this lawsuit—which had set Mom and Daddy against me, although they didn't know that yet, and me against everyone.

Maybe my realizing this, after Billy left the house, is what let me start to evolve a plan in my mind that I couldn't share with anyone, certainly not Mom or Daddy, and not Jennie, who would never understand, and not the boys, who would have ratted on me. If our family was going to be all fragmented like this, I figured, then I might as well take advantage of it and, for once, act completely on my own.

The first glimpse of it had come to me in a flash, as I sat there by the door with my sweet old teddy bear, Fergus, in my lap. I suddenly realized that I myself—and not Daddy and Mom or the Walkers or the Ottos—could force Mr. Stephens to drop the lawsuit. I could force their big shot lawyer to walk away from the case. And Daddy would know that I did it. Which would give me a good laugh. And because of what I knew about him, he wouldn't be able to do a thing about it afterwards. It wouldn't really matter, but maybe then we could become a regular family again. Husband and wife, parents and children, brothers and sisters, all of us trusting one another, with no secrets.

Except the big one, of course. Which would always be there, no matter what I did, like a huge purple birthmark on my face, something that he alone could see whenever he looked at me, and I, whenever I looked in the mirror.

Graduation came and went, and, yes, I did stay home, and the school board mailed me my diploma, along with official notification that I would be attending ninth grade next year at Lake Placid High School and there would be a special van to transport me. At the last minute, Mom and Daddy almost went to the graduation ceremonies without me, just the two of them, all dressed up, but I talked them out of it. It was a stupid idea, but typical of them. They couldn't bear being kept out of the limelight.

"It's not the same as going to church every Sunday without me," I explained, "where people feel sorry for me and proud of you. People at school will just think you're dumb and will feel sorry for *you* instead of me," I said.

"Don't talk to your mother that way," Daddy said. They were all sitting in the living room watching television together, like a good American family—it was *The Simp-*

sons, probably, which was the one show the whole bunch of them thought was funny. Even Jennie. Me, I can't stand that show; it's insulting.

"Actually, Daddy," I said, "I'm talking to you both," and I backed my wheelchair out of the room, turned, and went into my own room. I wasn't afraid of him anymore, and he knew it, but he couldn't do anything about it.

With summer here and school out, the kids were at home more, and because Mom was working at the Grand Union full time now, I had to baby-sit. That was all right by me, since I didn't have anyplace else to go, except physical therapy in Lake Placid two afternoons a week, which Grand Union let Mom take off, so she could drive me to the Olympic Center. Most days, Rudy and Skip ran wild, off in the woods and fishing or swimming in the Ausable River or riding their bikes all the way into town to goof around at the playground with their friends. I just let them go, as long as they got home before Mom did, and lied for them when Mom asked where they'd been all day, since they were supposed to stay around the house.

Jennie stuck close to me and was easy enough to amuse, especially if I let her play in my room with her Barbie dolls, which I did most of the time. We talked a lot that summer, almost as if she were a few years older than her real age and I were a few years younger, and it was one of the nicest things I can remember about our family. It was like I was ten years old again, and in the company of a sister who was also ten, because Jennie met me halfway. Sometimes I almost forgot about all the bad things that had happened to me, and I felt safe again and whole, untouched and innocent.

We both played Barbie dolls and read the same books and talked about things like witches and ghosts and whether we believed in them or not, and we wrote funny poems about people we didn't like or thought were stupid and ridiculous, like Mr. Dillinger and Eden Schraft, the postmistress. Silly nonsensical stuff.

> There once was a man named Dillinger,
> Whose brain had only one cylinder.
> His wife's had none, but she called him "Hon,"
> Now he's convinced he's thrilling her.
>
> Eden Schraft was slightly daft
> And learned the alphabet late.
> She sorted the mail in a plastic pail,
> And licked her stamps from a silver plate.

Those summer mornings and afternoons alone in the house with Jennie were, in a way, the last days of my childhood; that's how it felt, even at the time it was happening to me.

Then one night Daddy knocked on the door of my room and said, "Nichole, are you there? Can I come in a minute?"

"Yes, Daddy," I said, "I'm here." Where did he think I was? I rolled over to the door and unlatched it, and he walked in. I reached over to the television and shut off the sound; I knew he had an announcement to make. He never came into my room alone now, unless he had to. In fact, he almost never talked directly to me anymore, probably because he couldn't be sure of what I would say in response. He knew I hated him.

He sat down on the bed and put his hands on his knees and studied them. He has big hands. To me, they look like animals, thick and hairy. To him, I suppose, they're just hands.

"Nichole," he said, and he cleared his throat. "Tomorrow, Nichole, tomorrow Mr. Stephens wants you to make your deposition over to the courthouse in Marlowe. I thought, even though it's a weekday, I'd stay home from work so I can take you over, and Mom can stay with the kids, if that's all right."

"Sure," I said. "Whatever."

"Whatever. You sure are . . ."

"What? I'm what?"

"I don't know. Well, distant, I guess. Distant. Hard to talk to."

"Daddy," I said, looking right at him. "We don't have much to talk about. Do we?"

"What?"

"*Do* we?"

He inhaled and sighed heavily, as if he felt suddenly sorry for himself. "Well, then, it's okay? I'll take you over about nine-thirty in the morning? That's okay with you?"

"Sure," I said. "Whatever."

"I wish you wouldn't always say that."

"Say what?"

"Whatever."

"Why?"

"It's just . . . it sounds like you'll do whatever I want, like you think you're in my power or something. Only sarcastic. That's the part I don't like, the sarcasm."

I looked at him and didn't say anything. Sometimes I don't know who's more out of it, him or Mom. Slowly he got up and went out to the living room, and I heard him and Mom go upstairs to their room.

The next morning, he drove me over to Marlowe. We rode the whole way without saying anything, although once or twice Daddy started whistling a little tune and then after a few seconds trailed off into silence. It was a balmy clear day, with small white puffs of cloud sailing over the mountains from Sam Dent. Daddy parked the car in the lot and wheeled me around to the main entrance of the red-brick building, which looks more like a mental hospital than a courthouse, and it gave me the willies. Unexpectedly, I was very nervous and dry-mouthed, scared of what I was about to do.

Daddy huffed and puffed carrying me up the long stairs, because I kept my body stiff and wouldn't hold on to him, and I must have felt heavier to him than I really was. Like he was lugging a hundred and ten pounds of cinder blocks. After he set me into a regular chair and went back down for my wheelchair, I looked around me and saw that I was in a nice large book-lined room with a huge table in the middle and these big leather-covered chairs pulled up to it.

Mr. Stephens was there, wearing a dark pin-striped lawyer suit, and he shook my hand with obvious pleasure.

He was glad to see me, I could tell, and this relaxed me some. When I first met him at our house, he had worn his regular clothes, a plaid shirt and wool pants, and had seemed even friendlier and gentler then. I had liked him, but he wasn't what you'd call impressive, probably because of his hairdo. Now he looked important and smart, and I was glad my lawyer was him and not one of the other guys he introduced me to there, a Mr. Garay and a Mr. Schwartz. They were all suited up too, like him, but their suits looked like K Mart compared to his, and they were both short and baldish, and one of them, Mr. Garay, had real bad breath that he was trying to kill with Feen-a-Mints. Good luck.

Mr. Schwartz stood at the far end of the table and shuffled a messy pile of papers over and over, as if he was looking for a lost document. Every few seconds, Mr. Garay walked down to Mr. Schwartz's end of the table and watched over his shoulder and waited, then came back and stood nervously near me and Mr. Stephens.

"Well, Nichole, are you all ready for this?" Mr. Stephens asked me, and he smiled and winked. We're on the same side, and we're smarter than these other guys, was what he was communicating to me.

"I'm ready," I said. And I was.

Daddy came back then with the wheelchair and opened it out for me, and when I had hitched myself into it, Mr. Stephens rolled me up to the table and took the seat beside me on the right. He asked Mr. Schwartz where the stenographer was, and Mr. Schwartz looked up from his papers, blinked, said to Mr. Garay, "Dave, you can tell Frank we're ready. We're ready, right?"

"Yes, indeed," Mr. Stephens said. Daddy dragged one of the leather chairs from the table over by the wall next to the door, where he sat down and crossed his legs and tried to look casual, like he does this all the time.

Mr. Garay went out and a few seconds later came back followed by a short dark man I recognized from Mom and Daddy's church—which is how I thought of it by that time. It wasn't my church anymore, that's for sure. The man carried a tape recorder and some papers, and he nodded and smiled at Daddy as he passed him, and Daddy nodded back. I realized then that this was probably the third or fourth time Daddy had been in this room, so maybe he did have a reason to look casual. He was getting used to this legal business.

"This is Frank Onishenko, he's the stenographer, and he'll be taking down everything we say," Mr. Stephens said to me. "This is called an examination before trial, Nichole," he explained, "and these gentlemen will ask you some questions, and I may make a few comments about the questions or your answers. Then Mr. Onishenko will make a transcript of the whole thing, which we'll sign, and we'll all have notarized copies, so there won't be any surprises. Right, gentlemen?"

Mr. Schwartz looked up from his papers. "What?"

"Just explaining to Nichole what's going on here," Mr. Stephens said. "Are you ready?"

"Yeah, sure," Mr. Schwartz said, as if he'd really rather be doing something else. Mr. Garay didn't seem too interested in what was happening, either. I guess I was Mr. Stephens's choice witness, Exhibit A or something, and they figured there wasn't much they could ask me that would help their case. They knew the facts already, and I was obviously exactly what I looked like, a poor teenaged kid in a wheelchair, a victim—and that served only Mr. Stephens's purpose, and of course Mom's and Daddy's purpose, and the Walkers' and the Ottos'. But not Mr. Schwartz's or Mr. Garay's.

Mr. Stephens made some legal talk then. Stuff like "Pursuant to the order of Judge Florio" and "all parties to appear today for the court-ordered deposition, blah blah blah." He talked like that for quite a while. "Prior to this date . . . numerous discovery and inspection . . . furnished to my office . . . the defendant, the State of New York . . . the codefendant, the Town of Sam Dent, Essex County, State of New York . . ." Et cetera, et cetera. It was pretty impressive, though, and if he hadn't been my lawyer, here to protect me, I would've been seriously scared of him.

He went on growling and barking like that for a while, and the other lawyers cut in and out a couple of times and made legal speeches of their own. After each speech, they would all three fall into a conversation among them that they said was off the record, so Mr. Onishenko would stop the tape and look at me and smile a little, like we were actors in a play rehearsal forced to stand by while the director consulted with one of the other actors.

Finally, it looked like the lawyers had got all their technical difficulties ironed out, and Mr. Onishenko asked me to swear to tell the truth the whole truth and nothing but the truth so help me God.

I said I would, and then Mr. Schwartz looked straight

at me, smiled, and gazed into my eyes like the next words I heard were going to make us lifelong friends. "Nichole," he said, "good morning."

"Good morning."

"Nichole, I'm going to ask you a series of questions about this case. If at any time you do not understand the question or would like me to rephrase or repeat it, please just ask me and I will do so. Is that agreed?"

"Yes."

"Good. Could you tell me your full name?"

"Nichole Smythe Burnell." I didn't mention it, of course, since he didn't ask, but Smythe is Mom's maiden name. At school in the fall I was planning to start calling myself Smythe Burnell. No more Nichole. No more Nickie, Nike, Nickle, Nicolodeon. From now on, Smythe.

"Where do you presently reside?"

"Box 54, Bartlett Hill Road, Sam Dent, New York 12950."

"How long have you resided at that address?"

"All my life. Since December 4, 1975." I figured I'd throw that in, so he wouldn't have to ask my age.

"Fine. And with whom do you presently reside at that address?"

"With my parents, Samuel and Mary Burnell, and my two brothers, Rudolph and Richard, aged eleven and ten, and my sister, Jennifer, aged six."

For a long time, that's how it went—Mr. Schwartz asking these boring questions, like he was filling out a job application for me, and me answering with the basic facts of my life so far. But I liked it. I liked the way it was so factual and impersonal, almost as if we were talking about someone else, a girl who wasn't even in the room.

After a while, though, he started asking more personal things, like about my health and my daily activities. I realized that he had done some research already, because it was obvious from the questions that he already knew the answers to most of them. It was like that TV game show *Jeopardy*, where the MC gives the answers and the contestant has to come up with the questions. Except that here the contestant, Mr. Schwartz, seemed more in charge than the MC, me.

At one point, he asked me questions about how I spent my days now. He wanted me to tell about my new room on the first floor and how I stayed there almost all the time and hadn't gone to school and so forth. When he asked about graduation, I told him I hadn't attended it, and I thought he would ask why not, but he didn't. He was trying to make me look pampered and spoiled, I knew, but even so, I was glad he didn't go any further into my home life or school stuff than he did. Instead, he wanted to know about the physical therapy I was getting, and I told him; and then he asked me if I was in any pain now, suddenly, just like that.

I said, "Well, no, not really."

"You're not in pain?"

"Actually, I don't know."

"What do you mean, Nichole, that you don't know?"

"Well, I mean, it's like I can't feel it. I don't have any feelings. In my legs, I mean. From my waist down. That's why I'm in a wheelchair, Mr. Schwartz," I said. "It's not like

I'm paralyzed or anything. I just can't *feel* anything down there, so I can't move anything down there. That's what the physical therapy is for, to keep the muscles from atrophying from disuse. Because even though they're basically okay, the muscles and bones and all, it's actually like they're dead."

I looked over at Mr. Stephens, and I saw him tighten his mouth against a smile. He said, for Mr. Onishenko's record, that he would be introducing a set of medical reports along with depositions from Dr. Robeson and the other doctors at Lake Placid Hospital who had taken care of me, and I saw Mr. Garay make a few notes on a yellow lined pad. "And unless the medical records are allowed to go into evidence," Mr. Stephens added, "I will of course object to this line of questioning."

After that, Mr. Schwartz wanted me to tell them about my social life.

"Now or then?" I asked.

"Then."

Mistake. He would not enjoy what I was about to tell him. I started with cheerleading and talked about how big a deal that is to the kids at school, and then I told him about the Harvest Ball and Bucky Waters, even, and Mr. Schwartz started looking flustered. I was telling him the truth, though. More or less. It was Q and A, not multiple choice. On paper or like this, in a deposition, I probably came out looking like Miss Teenaged America or something. I'm talking about before the accident.

I knew, of course, that was where he would eventually have to lead me, to the accident itself, and sure enough, pretty soon he was asking me about what happened that morning.

"Now, on January 27, 1990, did there come a time, Nichole, when you left your parents' house on Bartlett Hill Road?"

"Yes."

He asked a bunch of small questions for a while, nailing down details, like what time of day was it, where did the bus pick us up, who was at the stop with me, and so forth. "I was with my brothers," I said. "Rudy and Skip. Jennie was sick and stayed home that day."

"Was there anything unusual about the driver, Dolores Driscoll, or the bus this morning?"

"Like what? I mean, I don't remember a lot."

Mr. Stephens jumped in. "I object to the form of the question. Note that."

"Was the bus on time?" Mr. Schwartz asked.

"Yes."

"And where did you sit that morning?"

"My usual place, on the right side, the first seat."

"But according to your recollection, there was nothing unusual about the drive that morning," he said.

"Until the accident?"

"Yes."

"No. Yes, there was. It was when Sean Walker got on, because he was crying and didn't want to leave his mother. So I sat him next to me and quieted him down, and Dolores and Sean's mother talked for a second. Then, when Dolores started up again, a car came around the corner there by the

Rendez-Vous and almost hit Sean's mother. She was okay, but it really scared Sean, because he saw it out the window."

After that, he didn't want to ask about individual stops anymore, which was fine by me, because except for when we picked up Sean, the rest of the route was like every other day and I couldn't be sure if I was remembering something from the actual day of the accident or just making it up from my usual experiences.

"Can you remember what the weather was like that morning?" he asked me.

"I think it was snowing. Not hard, not at first. It wasn't snowing at all when we left the house, but it was snowing a little by the time we stopped at Billy Ansel's."

Mr. Stephens interrupted again. "Unless the report from the National Weather Bureau for the town of Sam Dent of January 27, 1990, goes into the record, I will object to that question."

"I will offer that report," Mr. Schwartz said. Then he asked me if I saw Billy Ansel that morning.

I said yes, he was driving behind the bus in his pickup, like he did every morning, following the bus in. I was exact and said I saw Billy's pickup truck, not Billy himself. "I sit in front; it's the kids in the back who always watch and wave at Billy."

"Who were they?"

"In the back? I don't know: Billy's kids, of course, and Bear Otto, and a couple of others."

"Objection," Mr. Stephens said. "Note my objection. She said, 'I don't know.'"

Mr. Schwartz slipped a quick smile past me, his old friend. "Did there come a time when all the children had been picked up?"

"Yes."

"You remember that much," he said. Like, How interesting.

"Yes. As I'm talking, I'm remembering more about it." And I really was, which surprised me probably as much as it was surprising the lawyers.

Mr. Stephens looked worried. "Note my objection. She said, 'As I'm talking.' "

"Do you remember, did there come a time when the bus turned off Staples Mill Road onto the Marlowe road at what's called Wilmot Flats?"

"Yes," I said. "There was this big brown dog that ran across the road up there, right by the dump, and Dolores slowed down so's not to hit him, and he ran into the woods. And then Dolores drove on and turned onto the Marlowe road, as usual. I remember that. I'm remembering it pretty clearly."

"You are?" Mr. Schwartz said, eyebrows raised.

"Yes."

"Note that she said 'pretty clearly.' Not 'clearly,' " Mr. Stephens put in.

Then Mr. Schwartz asked me some more questions about Billy Ansel, like, After we turned onto the Marlowe road, how far behind the bus was his truck?

"I don't know," I said. "It was snowing pretty hard by then. Dolores had the windshield wipers on."

"She did?"

"Yes."

Mr. Stephens said, "You remember that?"

"Yes."

Mr. Schwartz went on, "Well, then, what else did you observe at that time? Before the actual accident, I mean."

"I was scared."

"You were scared? Of what? This is *before* the accident, I'm asking. Do you understand what I'm asking, Nichole?"

"Yes, I understand. Dolores was driving too fast, and it scared me."

"Mrs. Driscoll was driving too fast? What made you think that, Nichole?"

"The speedometer. And it was downhill there."

"You could see the speedometer?"

"Yes. I looked, because it was snowing so hard. And because it seemed to me that we were going very fast coming down the hill there. I was scared." Mr. Stephens, I noticed, had gone silent.

"All right, then, Nichole, how fast would you say she was going? To the best of your recollection."

"Seventy-two miles an hour."

"Really? Seventy-two miles an hour. You're sure of this?"

"Yes." I had my back to Mr. Stephens now and couldn't see him, but I imagined him slumped in his chair, looking at his fingernails.

"You believe that the bus driven by Mrs. Driscoll was going about seventy miles an hour at that time?" Mr. Schwartz asked.

"No," I said. "I know she was going seventy-two. The

213

speedometer is large and easy to see from where I was. I was in the first seat, right beside it, practically."

"I see. Did you say anything to her about this?"

"No."

"Why not?"

"Well, I guess I was scared. And there wasn't time."

"There wasn't time?"

"No. Because then the bus went off the road. And crashed."

"You remember this?"

"Yes," I said. "I do now. Now that I'm telling about it."

"She said, 'Now that I'm telling about it.' Note that," Mr. Stephens said in a weary voice.

"What do you recall of the accident itself? Exactly."

"I remember the bus swerved, it just suddenly swerved to the right, and it hit the guardrail and the snow-bank on the side of the road, and then it went over the embankment there, and everyone was screaming and every-thing. And that's all. I guess I was unconscious after that. That's all. Then I was in the hospital."

Mr. Schwartz smiled and made some notes on his pad. Mr. Garay was furiously doing the same. "Do you have any questions, Mr. Stephens?" Mr. Schwartz said without look-ing up.

I made like I was straightening my skirt across my knees, but I could see off to the side that Mr. Stephens was staring at me, and for a long time he didn't say a word. He just breathed hard through his nose. Of course, he didn't know if I had told the truth or not, but he was leery of pressing me too hard to find out, or he might end up asking questions that Mr. Schwartz and Mr. Garay would love to hear me answer.

I glanced up at Daddy, who was leaning forward in his chair, his mouth half open, as if he wanted to say something but he didn't dare.

"I have no questions," Mr. Stephens said quietly.

Mr. Schwartz said, "I have no further questions. Mr. Garay?"

"No questions," Mr. Garay said.

"Thank you, Nichole. You can go now," Mr. Stephens said. He didn't get up from his seat; he sat there, sliding some papers into his briefcase. Glancing along the table, I saw Mr. Schwartz and Mr. Garay doing the same, only quicker. Mr. Onishenko had shut off the tape recorder and was writing on a self-stick label. I pushed myself away from the table and turned my wheelchair toward Daddy, who was standing now but looking kind of wobbly.

As I passed by him, Mr. Stephens, in a voice so low only I could hear, said to me, "You'd make a great poker player, kid."

I said, "Thanks," and quickly moved away from him. Daddy was in shock, I could tell, white-faced and slouched, like someone had punched him in the stomach. Probably, the meaning of what I had told Mr. Schwartz was just now registering in his mind, over and over, and he hadn't begun to react yet.

I rolled my chair up beside him, and to further delay his reaction, and maybe because I didn't want him to embarrass himself in front of the lawyers, for he was, after all, my father, I said, "Let's go, Daddy. We have to get home now."

Like a kind of numb servant, he nodded okay and lifted me out of the wheelchair and carried me down the stairs. This time I wrapped my arms around his neck and shoulders and held on tight, making it easier for him to lift my weight and carry me to the car.

While he was setting me into the front seat, I saw Mr. Schwartz and Mr. Garay get into a fancy gray car parked on Court Street and drive quickly away. They were loosening their neckties and smiling and in general looking very pleased with themselves.

Daddy hurried back to retrieve my wheelchair from the courthouse, but I knew he'd be longer than necessary, because he and Mr. Stephens would want to have a few words up there in private. Mr. Stephens would probably be incredibly mad at Daddy for not having warned him that I had remembered so much about the accident, and Daddy would be insisting that he hadn't expected it, either.

Daddy would have concluded by now that I had lied, however, and he would try to tell that to Mr. Stephens. She lied, Mitch, she doesn't remember anything about the accident, she has no idea how fast Dolores was going. And Mr. Stephens would have to point out to him that, Sam, it doesn't matter whether she was lying or not, the lawsuit is dead, *everyone's* lawsuit is dead. Forget it. Tell the others to forget it. It's over. Right now, Sam, the thing you got to worry about is *why* she lied. A kid who'd do that to her own father is not normal, Sam.

But Daddy knew why I had lied. He knew who was normal and who wasn't. Mr. Stephens couldn't ever know the truth, but Daddy always would. He put my wheelchair into the trunk of the car and came around to the driver's side and got in and sat there for a minute with the key in his hand, looking at it as if he didn't quite understand its purpose. He said nothing for a long time.

Finally, he reached forward and put the key into the ignition, and speaking slowly, he said in a strange half-dead voice, "Well, Nichole, what do you say we stop at Stewart's for an ice cream? We haven't done that for a long time," he added.

"That sounds fine, Daddy. I'd really like it."

He started the car up then and drove across the road to Stewart's and bought each of us a huge pistachio cone, which is the kind we both like best but that no one else in the family likes.

When we had left Marlowe and were coming along the East Branch toward Sam Dent, with Daddy's cone dripping and me handing him napkins, we passed the fairgrounds at the edge of town, and I noticed that they were setting up a midway. I hadn't realized that it was so late in the summer. Winter and spring and now summer had passed by, and it was like I had been in some other land, traveling.

"Is it time for the fair already?" I asked. It looked beautiful, and sad somehow. The white grandstand and the covered stage facing it had been freshly painted, and the field of mown grass inside the oval racetrack in front of the stand was bright green and shiny under the huge blue sky. When I was Jennie's age, the grandstand had seemed enormous to me and frightening, especially when we went at night and it was filled with a huge noisy crowd of strangers.

Now the structure seemed tiny and almost sweet, and it would no longer be filled with strangers; I would know the faces and even the names of almost everyone up there on those board seats, and they would wave at me and say, Come on over, Nichole, and sit here with us. The track that looped around the field and passed between the stage and the grandstand had been raked smooth and watered until it looked like it was made of chocolate frosting. Scattered among the pine trees behind the grandstand were the low livestock barns and pens and the exhibit halls, where over the years I had won ribbons for my 4-H projects—my angora rabbits, Tweedle Dee and Tweedle Dum; and my plaster-of-paris relief map of Sam Dent in 1886 with balsa wood houses and lichen woods and painted fields; and my Just Say No to Drugs poster. They had all won blue ribbons, which Daddy had framed and hung on the living room wall and which were still hanging there, although I had not looked at them in a long time. The skeleton of a Ferris wheel and the long arms of the octopus ride were already in place, and the game booths and tents were being assembled by a gang of tanned shirtless young men and boys with tattoos on their arms and cigarettes in their mouths, probably the same out-of-town men and boys who last year had flirted and called to me and Jody and the other local girls as we strolled along the midway and tried to ignore them but always found an excuse to turn around at the end of the row of booths and walk back, more slowly this time, looking at each other and rolling our eyes as the boys asked us to come on over and try our luck.

"Would you like to go to the fair this year, Nichole?"

Daddy asked. He had slowed the car and had been looking at the fairgrounds with me, probably thinking some of the same thoughts.

"When is it? When does it start?"

"Starts tomorrow, runs all week, right through the weekend."

"I don't know, Daddy. Maybe, though. Let me think about it, okay?"

He said sure, and we drove on into town.

We had one more conversation before we got home, which I think was responsible somehow for my deciding to go to the fair, although it's not really connected. As we pulled into the yard, I said to Daddy, "Nothing will happen to Dolores, will it?"

He shut off the engine, and we sat there for a moment in silence, listening to the dashboard clock tick. Finally, he said, "No. Nobody wants to sue Dolores. She's one of us."

"Will the police do anything to her now?"

"It's too late for that. Dolores can't drive the school bus anymore, anyhow; the school board saw to that right off. I doubt she even wants to. Everyone knows she's suffered plenty."

"But everyone will blame her now, won't they?"

"Most will, yes. Those that don't know the truth will blame Dolores. People have got to have somebody to blame, Nichole."

"But we know the truth," I said. "Don't we?"

"Yes," he said, and for the first time since before the accident, he looked me straight in the face. "We know the truth, Nichole. You and I." His large blue eyes had filled with sorrowful tears, and his whole face seemed to beg for forgiveness.

I made a small thin smile for him, but he couldn't smile back. Suddenly, I saw that he would never be able to smile again. Never. And then I realized that I had finally gotten exactly what I had wanted.

"Well," I said, "it's over now."

He turned away from me and got out of the car, and when he came around to my side with the wheelchair and opened my door, I said to him, "Daddy, I think I do want to go to the fair."

He concentrated on unfolding the chair and said nothing.

"Let's go Sunday afternoon and see everything," I said. "The last day is always the best. Everyone in town goes then, and we can sit in the grandstand, and everyone will see us together. We can look at the livestock too, and the rides, the midway, the games, everything. All of us together, the whole family."

He nodded somberly and lifted me out of the car and set me into my wheelchair. Then he pushed me up the ramp and into the house.

Dolores Driscoll

Every August since we were married, and before that, separately, since childhood, Abbott and I have attended the Sam Dent County Fair, which by rights should be held over in Marlowe, since that's the county seat. Instead, it's held here in Sam Dent, where there is a fine old fairgrounds out along the East Branch of the Ausable River. Abbott loves the fair, especially the demolition derby; weeks in advance, he gets himself worked up to a fever pitch, practically, almost like a child.

Except for the pleasure I get from his excitement, I myself can take the fair or leave it, it's just one of the stops that a person makes in the course of a year, but I do confess to enjoying the livestock exhibitions. I like to wander through the dairy barns more than any of the other exhibits, probably because of my childhood experiences, what with my father having been a dairy farmer. The dim warm stalls and the smell of wood chips and hay and fresh cow manure, the slow and gentle movements of cattle and their large moist eyes—those things cut straight through all my troubles to my heart and bring me practically to tears as I pass along the long low barns and stop here and there to admire and maybe even speak to an especially fine Jersey or a pretty black and white Holstein, which is the type of cow my father raised.

It's not the same for Abbott. He's more at ease in the flash and bustle and noise of the midway and, as I said, the demolition derby, which he prefers to watch from high in the grandstand. "You . . . need . . . perspective . . . to . . . experience . . . it," he explains. That's a problem, of course, with his being confined to a wheelchair in recent years. Normally, what happens is that a couple of men from town spot us before we even get to the grandstand and meet us at the bottom of the steps and, one on each side, latch on and carry Abbott in his wheelchair to the top level, where he can set his brake and watch the whole thing to his heart's delight, to the very end. Afterwards, usually the same fellows from town show up and carry him back down to the ground, where I take over and wheel him to the parking lot.

This year, though, things were different. I probably should have expected it, but it caught me by surprise. Although I don't think it surprised Abbott one bit—there's very little surprises that man. But without having said anything to him, without our actually discussing it, I figured that enough time had passed for people to have gone through their first tangled reactions to the accident and come out on the other side, just as I more or less had myself;

I had pretty well stayed out of sight and, I hoped, mind, all these lonesome months, which was only proper; by now, I thought, people would have put their dark conflicted feelings about me behind them and would once again be free to act toward me and Abbott like the dear friends and neighbors they had always been. Sam Dent was our permanent lifelong community. We belonged to this town, we always had, and they to us; nothing could change that, I thought. It was like a true family. Certainly, terrible things happen in every family, death and disease, divorce and blood feuds, just as they had in my own; but those things always have an end to them and they pass away, and the family endures, just as ours had. The same must hold for a town, I thought. But I'm a sanguine person, as Abbott says. Too sanguine, I guess.

It was early Sunday evening when we got there, the last day of the fair, and I had to park the van at the farthest end of the parking lot, a long bumpy haul from the grandstand. There had been a thunderstorm earlier, one of those late August storms that move quickly and heavily through the mountains like a freight train from Canada, and we had waited at home for it to pass over into Vermont, which it did around six o'clock, leaving the sky cloudless and tinted a stony shade of blue and the air moist and scrubbed and cool. For the first time that summer, you could smell fall coming on.

Because of the storm, though, we were late and didn't have time to visit the livestock barns, which grieved me some, or linger along the midway like Abbott enjoys. They start the demolition derby right at sundown, for it is definitely more exciting to sit up high in the old wooden stands and watch the cars down below smash against each other under spotlights than to do it in broad daylight, when the whole event might seem a foolish thing for a normal person to view. At least I would find it somewhat embarrassing in daylight, although I doubt that would matter much to Abbott. He's not as self-conscious as most people, due to his stroke, no doubt, and what he's learned from it.

From the parking lot, we made our way through the gate and along the far side of the field in front of the grandstand, which wasn't easy, as the lane was rutted and wet, the grass trampled by the crowds of the last week. We were cheerful, though, Abbott and I; it was our first time out in public together since last winter. After the accident, I had attended the funerals, but alone, without even Abbott to accompany me; it was a way of bearing witness, I guess you could call it. I kept to myself, spoke to no one, and left immediately after the services. It was just something I had to do, something crucial between me and the children. I don't think people, the adults, quite wanted me there among them, which was understandable, but I had to do it—for the children, who, if they could have spoken for themselves, would surely have asked me to attend their funerals and say a prayer for each of their dear departed souls. And I did. They would have thought me cowardly if I had stayed home instead.

That done, though, I kept myself away from all town functions, church affairs, meetings, bake sales, and so forth, and more or less oriented myself west and south, faced our life toward Lake Placid, where I had to take Abbott twice a week for his physical therapy anyhow. Naturally, I no longer drove the school bus; two weeks after the accident, the school board mailed me a certified letter saying my services were no longer required, but I had already made that decision for myself, thank you. And since Eden Schraft never called me, the way she usually did, about carrying mail in the summer months, I gave that up too; a bit more reluctantly, however, than I gave up the bus, for I had no terrible associations with that particular job. Now, whenever I saw one of those big yellow International school buses on the road, I simply had to look away or else concentrate on a single detail, like the sum of the numbers on the number plate or the poker hand the numbers made, until the thing was gone from view.

I did all our grocery shopping at the Grand Union in Lake Placid, and even started reading the Lake Placid newspaper, which is how I got my job driving for the hotels. We needed money—since Abbott's stroke, I have been the sole breadwinner in the family. I started with the Manor House, who'd advertised for a part-time driver with a van to carry guests in from the Saranac airport. They did not connect my name to the well-known accident in Sam Dent, and naturally I did not give the school board as a reference. Then on my own initiative I added a few more hotels and got me one of those belt beepers and a CB, until soon I was on call twenty-four hours a day and in Lake Placid five and six full days a week, lugging folks back and forth from the airport, cruising in and out of the downtown shopping area with a load of Canadian souvenir hunters and off to view the local sights—Whiteface, the Olympic ski jumps, the John Brown house, and Kate Smith's grave. Lake Placid can be an interesting town when you see it from a tourist's perspective.

Sometimes, out of the goodness of his heart, because he's easily bored and would have preferred staying home with his radio and books and magazines, Abbott came along, and that cheered me somewhat. I was very lonely in those days, still in a kind of shock from the accident, I think, and Abbott was the only person I could communicate with. But soon winter passed over, and spring appeared and rolled on a few weeks later, and then it was summer, and now in late summer I had begun to feel more like my old self—although I knew, of course, that I would never be the same person again. You can't raise the dead. I knew that.

Anyhow, it seemed like an appropriate time and way for me to reenter the life of my town—coming out here to the fairgrounds with my husband and joining the crowd and not making anything large of it, just saying howdy to those folks who seemed willing to speak with me, and enjoying ourselves for a few hours, like normal people, and then going home. Tired but happy, as they say.

Was I nervous or scared? Yes, of course I was. My son Reginald had warned me off it. "Ma, forget it, forget that damned town. C'mon up here, you and Dad, sell the house, for God's sake, and move up here to Plattsburgh with me. I can build you an apartment upstairs or renovate the basement or something, and I'll look after you both." As if we were a helpless pair of elderlies. I think he had his own motives, now that he and Tracy were separated and he was living alone in their house. Reginald has always been something of a mama's boy and secretly ashamed of it; and while

he'd never move back to Sam Dent just to be near me and
his father, he was not above trying to talk us into moving
near him.

The large oval field in front of the grandstand is
ringed by a dirt track that's generally used for racing trot-
ters. Tonight, though, the racetrack, along with the field
itself, was entirely covered by old banged-up cars hand-
painted in garish colors, slapped-on shades of pink and aqua
and yellow, with slogans, mottoes, girls' names, and huge
numbers on the doors, hoods, and roofs. Parked around the
cars in no evident pattern or order I saw flatbed trailers and
tow trucks, pickups, and even some fancy new Z cars here
and there, with what looked like a couple hundred people
lounging around the vehicles, all drinking beer and having
a fine time together. They were mostly young men and
women and teenaged boys and girls, all of whom love cars
and machinery. The boys and men, and many of the females
too, moved and mingled among the tow trucks and pickups
and Z cars and the old painted-up clunkers familiarly, as if
the vehicles were beloved and admired animals that they
had raised themselves. It was a whole pack of muscular
good-looking youths in excellent health showing off to one
another, with the boys' sleeves rolled practically over their
shoulders so as to expose their tanned arm muscles and new
tattoos and the girls in tight shorts or jeans and halters, their
hair all moussed and swirled and curled in the newest styles
from the TV singers and soaps. They had tape decks set out,
blasting rock 'n' roll and country and western songs from
the hoods of their vehicles, and coolers of iced beer all
around, and here and there a couple was dancing together.

It was almost dark now. Huge spotlights in front of the grandstand had been turned on to illuminate a short section of rain-soaked track that had been blocked off between the stands and the raised open stage facing it. From the field, the pale glow of the spotlights and the flashing lights from the midway and the rides—strips and circles of red, yellow, purple, and green—passed like firelight from a huge bonfire across the faces of the young people hanging out in the field. I cut between a pair of beat-up sedans right onto the field among them and pushed Abbott's wheelchair over the grass between pickups and flatbeds and knots of kids clutching beer cans. In the distance, I heard the announcer start to call out the order of the upcoming heats.

Abbott swung his head around and said to me, "Can't . . . be . . . late." I started to hurry, but while I wheeled him through the vast conglomeration of cars, trailers, and trucks toward the stands, I kept peering around in search of my old station wagon, Boomer, which I had good reason to hope would be entered in the derby tonight, resurrected and driven by Jimbo Gagne. It would have been difficult to recognize it—they take out all the window glass and lights, and you can barely tell what brand or model car it was originally, except by the shape of its fenders and grille and so on. Forget telling who owned the car originally.

All the way across the field to the stands, I kept an eye out, but I never caught sight of anything that resembled Boomer more than superficially. Boomer was, of course, the name my boys and I had given to that old Dodge wagon, which had served back in the 1970s as my very first bus and which, after 168,000 miles, had finally thrown a rod and generally collapsed. I'd pushed it out behind the barn and stashed it on blocks, in case Abbott or I or one of the boys ever needed parts from it, which need never arose, as my boys were by then obsessed with off-road vehicles and four-by-fours and I was driving first the GMC and then the International. And then Abbott had his stroke. The old Dodge got more or less forgotten over the years that it sat back there, and in time meadow grass and tall weeds and berry bushes grew around it. Until one day in June of this year, when Jimbo Gagne came out to the house unannounced and asked to buy it. He said he liked its power-to-weight ratio, it had plenty of both, and he would like to get it running again and enter it in the demolition derby at the fair.

I said, "What the heck, Jimbo, just take it. Haul it out of here and keep it," I said, and on the spot wrote him a bill of sale for one dollar. He was the first person from town who had come out to the house in a normal way and on his own since the accident, and I was so grateful to him for that, I'd probably have given him my almost new Voyager van for a dollar, if he'd asked me for it. Jimbo is one of Billy Ansel's Vietnam vets, the one who's been working at the garage the longest, nine or ten years now, and though he still lives over in Ausable Forks in a trailer with his wife and a dozen sled dogs that he houses in oil drums spread around the yard, he's practically a local person now, because of his association with Billy Ansel's garage. People talk against the way he uses oil drums for doghouses, but I can't see how they're any worse for dogs than house trailers are for people. Jimbo is a lanky brown-eyed man with stringy black hair who wears one of those long Fu Manchu mustaches and a gold earring and looks downright evil. But he's actually a very shy and sensitive man, a respectful soft-spoken gentleman, underneath that pirate's costume, and when he came with Billy's wrecker to haul old Boomer away, he treated me with courtesy and kindness. He knew that I would take one look at that tow truck and remember the last time I'd seen it, when it had slowly drawn the bus out of the water-filled sandpit that snowy morning last January, and so he telephoned before coming out and in a joking way said he was calling ahead in case I didn't want to be there when he took old Boomer away.

"I know how sentimental you are about that junker, Dolores. It's like I am about some of my dogs. But I ain't going to put your car down. In fact, I'm going to give the old boy a second life. Maybe you should think of it that way," he suggested.

I did, but I also made sure not to be home when he arrived with the big blue wrecker. In fact, that night Abbott and I drove into Placid for supper at the Ponderosa restaurant, where they serve good beefsteaks cheap and have a long salad bar that Abbott particularly likes to partake of, because he can reach everything from his wheelchair. He always returns for seconds and even goes after salad for me. "Sit . . . now . . . and . . . I'll . . . serve," he says. "Everyone . . . must . . . serve . . . sometimes," he says.

I'm not inclined to notice, but now and then poor Abbott must feel a wave of guilt because of the way I've taken care of him in these last years of our life together, and the few occasions when he can perform some little physical task for me are no doubt of greater importance to him than they are to me. I try to keep alert to such opportunities and to make myself available to them, but they rarely come along, due to his condition. To me, it never matters, because it's his mind that takes care of me, not his body. In the old days, before his stroke, he took wonderful care of me with his body, which I will say was always a creamy white and tender delight to me, providing me with all the necessary and loving services a woman could imagine, and consequently I did not pay sufficient attention to his mind, which from the beginning was superior to mine, more logical and just. Now Abbott and I live together like the perfect brother and sister, and I do not think I would have been intelligent enough to do that back before he had his stroke.

When we reached the edge of the field, we had to cross the track behind one of the fire engines to get to the right-hand corner of the grandstand, and I saw a few folks there that I recognized, volunteer firemen from Sam Dent, and I know they saw and recognized me—I'm pretty easy to recognize, even in twilight dark: I'm big and have red hair, and here I am pushing this small man in a wheelchair. Not wanting to put myself in a needy position, though, I merely nodded a short hello, which I was glad of right after, as not a one of those boys acknowledged me and Abbott when we passed by the fire engine and crossed the track.

We came up on the gate, where I paid, and passed through to the bottom of the grandstand. The thing was nearly filled already, with lots of folks standing around at ground level by the rail. I knew many of them, naturally— most of the town of Sam Dent comes out for the demolition derby—and saw them glance at us and then look quickly back toward the track and stage in front or nudge the person next to them, who would then take his turn casting a quick expressionless glance at us. No one said a word to me and Abbott or even acknowledged our presence. I knew it was not Abbott they were snubbing; it was me. But he was with me, so they ignored him too. That made me mad.

Several times I started to say hello, to force the issue, but before I could open my mouth, the person had turned his back to me.

I studied the stairs for a second; they looked steep and long. Down here in front, I might be able to see some of the action over and around the crowd of people at the rail; but not Abbott. "Hold on tight, honey," I said to him. "I believe I can get you up there a ways."

He has the good use of his left hand and arm, although his right is gone, of course; consequently, when he grabbed the left armrest tightly, he had to flop his whole body against that side of the chair for leverage, which put the chair all out of balance. Still, it was the only way to do it. I backed him around and drew the chair up backward to the first step, thinking I'd try to lug him up one step at a time, thinking also that maybe someone kind would see me struggling and would come to my aid. It'd probably have to be a stranger. A tourist, even. I grunted and yanked, and the chair came along with a thump, and we were up one step. Then another. Then a third, until soon we had made the first landing.

Out of breath, with my back and legs hot and wobbly

from the effort, I had to stop for a breather, when, all of a sudden, of all the people I did *not* want to see, there was Billy Ansel standing right next to me, with a woman I didn't know bouncing up the stairs behind him.

He grinned widely, which was not exactly a characteristic expression, and said, "H'lo there, Dolores! Come out to see the demolition derby, eh? Attagirl, Dolores!" he said in a loud voice, and for a second I thought he was making cruel fun of me. His grin made his teeth show through his beard, like he was clenching them. He was dressed up, in his usual way, khakis and white shirt and loafers, but I saw he was carrying a small paper bag with a bottle in it, and then I realized he was drunk.

I took a look at the woman with him. She was maybe thirty-five trying to look twenty—barefoot, in tight cutoff shorts and a tee shirt with the words "Shit Happens" printed across the front. Taller than Billy and skinny as a stick, she was dark-haired and had a small head made to look even smaller by one of those pixie haircuts that used to be so popular with teenagers. Her thin lips she had painted over and around with bright red lipstick, trying to make her lips look full; it only worked from a distance, though. Not the sort of woman you'd expect to see in Billy Ansel's company. She was drunk too.

"Goddamn, Dolores, you look like you an' ol' Abbott here could use a hand," Billy said, and he passed his brown bag to his friend. "Oh, sorry, this here's Stacey," he said. "Stacey Gale Morrison, from Ausable Forks. Stacey Gale, like you t'meet Dolores an' Abbott Driscoll, old friends from Sam Dent. Salt of the earth, both of 'em," he declared.

"Pleased to meetcha," Stacey Gale said. She didn't put her hand out to shake, and neither did I.

"Where you headed, Dolores? All the way to the top? Lemme give a hand here."

"No, that's okay," I said. "I can manage."

"The hell you can. Here, you get on one side, an' I'll grab hold the other, an' we'll scoot ol' Abbott right to the top, just like that. What's a neighbor for, right? We got to lend each other a helping hand, right, Abbott? Neighbors got to help each other out. Am I right?"

Abbott swung his head around and looked straight into Billy's bearded face, probably seeing grim things there that no one else could. "You . . . help . . . Dolores . . . help . . . me . . . ," Abbott said to him. "Give . . . thanks . . . then . . . all . . . around," he added.

"How's that, Abbott? I didn't quite getcha. What'd he say, Dolores?" Billy asked. "No offense, Abbott."

I told him, although I doubt he really got it.

"Damned straight. Let's go, Dolores," he said, and he grabbed onto one side of the chair, and I grabbed the other, and we lifted Abbott and his wheelchair together and crab-walked our way sideways up the stairs. Stacey Gale came along a few stairs behind us, looking slightly put out by the whole thing.

At the top, we put the wheelchair down, and I set the brake and parked it there on the landing. The folks who were seated along the last row silently moved in a bit on the long bench and made room for Stacey Gale and then Billy Ansel and, finally, me. I noticed a few familiar faces down along the row—a couple of the Hamiltons and Prescotts, some Atwaters from up to Wilmot Flats, a bunch more from town—but everybody kept themselves face-forward, like they hadn't noticed our arrival.

I sat down on the end seat, with Abbott on my left and Billy Ansel on my right, and dropped my head and put my face in my hands. Oh, this was hard on me. Much harder than I'd imagined. My heart was pounding lickety-split, and my ears were hot. I was truly sorry that we had come.

"Hey, Dolores," Billy said, and he flopped a heavy arm over my shoulder. "You just got to have a good time, Dolores, that's all. Whenever you can, you just go out there an' you have yourself a good goddamn time. The hell with the rest, that's what I say. The hell with 'em."

He extended his bottle toward me. For a second, I was tempted, but I shook my head no, and he took a slug himself. "What about Abbott?" he asked in a low voice and wiped his mouth with the back of his hand. "He up for it?"

"No. Abbott doesn't drink."

Billy apologized, although I don't know why, and passed the bottle to Stacey Gale. She took a long pull that she tried to make look like a sip, and Billy smiled approvingly and put his hand on her bare knee.

I didn't know what to think of how Billy had changed since the accident. He scared me; but mostly he made me sad. He had been a noble man; and now he was ruined. The accident had ruined a lot of lives. Or, to be exact, it had busted apart the structures on which those lives had depended—depended, I guess, to a greater degree than we had originally believed. A town needs its children for a lot more than it thinks.

I reflected on the Walkers, Wendell and Risa, and how they were separated now, getting divorced, with their motel up for sale. A week before, I'd run into poor fat Wendell sitting on a stool rewinding rental videos at the Video Den in Ausable Forks, which is where I'd been going for movies these days, and he told me Risa was selling chili dogs at the Stewart's in Keene. It was a short conversation; I think we were both uncomfortable to see each other there.

And the Lamstons, gone up to Plattsburgh and living on welfare in an old rooming house by the lake. Kyle Lamston had been committed for a spell to the mental hospital to dry out, and afterwards, as I later learned, he'd gone straight back to drinking, but with a vengeance this time, and had done himself some permanent brain damage and would never work again.

There had been trouble up on the Flats all spring and summer, bad enough to get into the papers, with Bilodeaus and Atwaters dealing in small quantities of drugs, cocaine and marijuana that they were sneaking across from Canada. Three or four Bilodeaus and as many Atwaters, the young ones, who a year ago had been parents, heads of households, you might say, were now locked up in prison over to Ray Brook.

All over town there were empty houses and trailers for sale that last winter had been homes with families in them. A town needs its children, just as much and in the same ways as a family does. It comes undone without them, turns a community into a windblown scattering of isolated individuals. Take the Ottos. With Bear gone, it was hard to imagine the two of them together. Significant pain isolates you anyhow, but under certain circumstances, it may be all you've got, and after great loss, you must use whatever's left, even if it isolates you from everyone else. The Ottos were lucky, though—in addition to their pain, they had that new baby. Otherwise, I'm sure, their lives, too, would have come undone.

I wondered if my own children, Reginald and William, had accomplished that for me and Abbott, if their presence in our lives had held us peacefully together all those years. When Abbott and I were young, we were so obsessed with each other, so enthralled by what we thought were our striking similarities, that if I hadn't twice gotten accidentally pregnant, we might have lost touch with everything and everyone else and maybe never would have grown up ourselves. Our obsession with each other was like the isolation that comes with great pain; it was like extreme sadness. Without our children, we might never have discovered our differences, which is what has made our abiding love for each other possible. We would have been like a pair of infatuated teenagers, drowning in each other's view of ourselves, so self-absorbed that we'd never have been able to help each other over the years the way we have.

I looked across to Billy Ansel and realized that what frightened and saddened me most about him was that he no longer loved anybody. All the man had was himself. And you can't love only yourself.

About that time I noticed a buzz going on down front, over at the grandstand gate directly opposite to the one we had come in. People were knotted up there, a whole bunch of folks who all looked to be from Sam Dent, making a fuss over something or someone by the gate, and the rest of the crowd was looking that way now, hooking and craning their heads to see what was going on down there.

Then, in the center of the group by the gate, I saw the tall figure of Sam Burnell, and behind him his wife, Mary, and three of their children, the younger ones, Jennie, Skip, and Rudy. A second later, several of the people in the crowd stepped back, and I saw that Sam was pushing a wheelchair, and seated in it was his daughter Nichole. It was an amazing sight. Everyone was smiling, and the folks nearest to Nichole were reaching out as if to touch her. A few people had started to clap their hands, and more and more of them were picking it up, as Sam and his family, with Nichole in the lead, made their way from the gate straight to the bottom of the stairs at the far side of the grandstand. Nichole had a lovely sweet smile on her face—she's a beautiful girl anyhow, a fourteen-year-old blessed with movie star looks, practically—and she waved one hand back and forth slowly, like a saint in a religious procession or something, while the people applauded and backed out of the way of her wheelchair.

Billy nudged me with an elbow and in a low voice said, "What we got here, Dolores, is the local hero," and he chuckled in a knowing way that I couldn't interpret.

I turned and said to Abbott, "Billy says Nichole is the town hero."

"No . . . surprise . . . there."

Several men, three or four of them, gathered around her wheelchair and lifted it, like it was a throne, and with her father, Sam, and the rest of her family falling in behind, they carried Nichole up the stairs in a stately way, while the applause grew, a steady respectful clapping, with even strangers, people who must have been tourists, who couldn't possibly have known who she was or what had happened to her and to our town, joining in the applause.

"What's the big deal with the kid?" Stacey Gale asked. Even she had her hands out, ready to clap.

It was a hard question to answer. Part of it, I knew, was that Nichole Burnell had survived the accident and had suffered terrible loss, loss made visible by the wheelchair, and now for the first time, after many months away from us, she was at last returning to us, returning in a kind of triumph. Part of it was that she was a beautiful young girl purified by her injury. I remembered how I used to regard some of the Vietnam vets who worked for Billy Ansel. And part of it, I also knew, was me, Dolores Driscoll, the fact of my presence here tonight and the way people felt compelled to treat me. If they could not forgive me, they could at least celebrate Nichole, and then maybe they would not feel so bad that I, too, was one of them.

If she'd been capable of understanding it, that's how I would have answered Stacey Gale's question. But then Billy Ansel said to her, "That kid has saved this town from a hundred lawsuits. She's kept us all out of court, when it looked like half the damned town wanted nothing else but to *go* to court."

Abbott swung his head around and peered inquisitively at Billy, who saw him and suddenly looked embarrassed.

"You heard about that, didn't you?" Billy said.

"No," Abbott said firmly.

"I figured you knew all about that legal crap."

Abbott and I both shook our heads.

"Oh. Well, I guess it's not really all that important," he said, and he took a quick swig from his bottle and kept looking at it while he talked. "I mean, it's not old news, actually. But any kind of news travels fast in this town, so I thought you knew. But I guess you folks've been out of touch."

"Pretty much," I said, still waiting.

"Yeah. Well, what it is, Nichole Burnell was s'posed to help this big-time New York lawyer sue the town and the state for negligence. She was like a witness." He paused for a second. "I thought you knew all about this."

We shook our heads again.

"Yeah, well, when she refused to help him, when she wouldn't tell the judge or whoever what they expected, this lawyer, a guy that Sam and Mary and the Ottos and who knows how many other people in town had hired, he had to drop the case. And then everyone else who was going to sue, they've been dropping out too. The Ottos went first. I don't think they were ever that serious and were probably happy for the excuse. It just got too . . . it got too complicated, I guess. People just said the hell with it, the Burnells are off the case, the Ottos are gone, it's a big mess, so the hell with it, let's just get on with our lives. You know."

I told him that a lawyer had come out to the house and had tried to get us to sue too, but I didn't remember the man's name. "Tall guy. Drove a big Mercedes-Benz sedan. Abbott sent him packing, though. Probably the same lawyer as you're speaking of," I said.

"Yeah. Probably was."

The men who had carried Nichole up the stairs to the top of the grandstand had set her down in the aisle there, in the same manner that Billy and I had situated Abbott over here, and the Burnell family had found seats for themselves at the farther end of the same topmost bench. The derby was about to start, and people had turned their attention back to the track now, where a batch of old cars were lining up in single file, making a big racket as they positioned themselves to enter the derby area for the first heat.

Abbott said, "What . . . did . . . Nichole . . . witness?"

"How's that?"

"Abbott asked what did Nichole witness."

"Oh." Billy was watching the cars now. Out in the shadowy track beyond the fire trucks, the half-wrecked cars shuddered and rocked on their wheels, their engines hammering like kettledrums. That's part of the fun of it—the huge uncontrolled noise of it. All sixteen drivers in the heat sit out there and race their motors as loudly as they can, and clouds of exhaust and sparks fly out, and everyone cheers wildly with excitement. The announcer, a short balding fellow in a green satin jacket, stood on the stage facing the grandstand, and you could barely hear him, despite the excellent loudspeaker system, as he singled out individual drivers to comment on and make fun of, since most of the drivers are local and there are inside jokes that everyone knows.

Then down on the track one of the green-jacketed referees waved a small yellow flag, and one after the other, four of the gaudy battered old junkers came roaring into the derby area, which is more like an arena, a large rectangular muddy pit, than the finish-line section of a racetrack. The four crossed in front of us, spinning wheels and cutting reckless half circles, lurching forward and then suddenly stopping, until all four of them were lined up at the right, side by side and facing away from the direction they'd come. At a signal, a second line of four cars sped into the arena, digging up the dirt with their tires as they abruptly stopped, turned around, and backed up to the first set, rear bumpers, or what was left of them, against rear bumpers. A third row of cars charged out and slapped on their brakes, and as soon as their front grilles faced the grilles of the second bunch, the last set roared in, swiftly spun and whipped around, reversing direction, and backed their rear bumpers up against the rear bumpers of the previous four. And then they were ready—four rows with four cars in each row, all squared off like sixteen gladiators, armored and breathing fire and exhaling smoke, snarling and growling into each other's faces. The helmeted drivers were young men and boys, most of them grinning fiercely and punching the air with fists or waving out the windshield opening at the cheering crowd. It was a thrilling spectacle, even to me.

I glanced off to my left, to see how Abbott was

enjoying his favorite aspect of the fair, but to my surprise, he was ignoring the cars altogether. Instead, he looked intently past me and straight at Billy Ansel, and I realized that he was waiting for an answer to his question. What did Nichole witness?

I didn't know whether to say anything or not, which is unusual for me, as I'm rarely undecided. I hate that state, so I made a decision not to say a word. Leave it to the men to settle, was my decision. I was aware that somehow I was at the center of this, my honor, perhaps, but I was not sure how. I just trusted my husband to know.

Billy was hunched over, pretending to be engrossed in the scene down below, but I could tell that he knew Abbott was watching him. The girl, Stacey Gale, was off on her own planet.

Finally, Billy chanced a self-conscious glance at Abbott and got caught at it. "Pretty good, eh, Abbott?" he said. "The ol' demolition derby."

Abbott didn't say anything. When he chooses, his gaze alone makes a powerful statement. Without a word, just by sitting there and putting on a hard look, he can set me or Reginald or William to jabbering elaborate apologies and explanations, until finally he smiles and we can stop. Sometimes I think that's why Reginald moved to Plattsburgh and William joined the army, just to get away from their father's gaze. For privacy. Me, of course, I never really thought I needed that kind of privacy.

Billy said, "You're still wondering about that Nichole Burnell business, I suppose. Well, I don't know what to tell you. There's not much more to it than what I already said.

Their lawyer, this guy Mitchell Stephens, he couldn't get Nichole to testify the way he wanted her to, that's all. And then I guess he didn't feel he had a strong negligence case anymore, so he went home. Since then, other folks have heard about it, and they've started having second thoughts themselves, and their lawyers, too, have started dropping out, one by one. So now it looks like we won't be seeing any lawsuits, after all. Which is fast bringing this town back together," he said. "The girl has done us all, every single person in town, a valuable service. Even you, Abbott. Even you, Dolores, believe it or not."

Abbott said, "Why . . . us?" Billy looked like he understood him fine, so I didn't translate.

What he did, though, was stammer a bit and then say something to the effect that what was good for the town was good for everyone in it, which, by my lights, seemed to evade the question somewhat. Also, he still hadn't answered Abbott's earlier question, What did Nichole witness? Down below, the first heat was well under way, and the cars were slamming against one another, making an incredible noise as they roared back and forth in the mud and struggled to smash each other into submission. There were only about half the original sixteen still moving, crawling like huge wounded beasts in the mud to get away or, if they could, lining up to get one more good bash in before giving out themselves. Stacey Gale was hollering along with everyone else in the crowd, shrieking every time one of the remaining cars got in a good loud hit and the car it hit got stopped and couldn't move again, eliminated.

Billy put his bottle down on the bench next to him

and started wringing his hands, and I felt a wave of sympathy for the man. I already knew what he would say next, and Abbott surely did too. Billy was the messenger bringing bad news, and no one wants that job. In a low, uncertain voice, Billy said, "You ought to know, I guess. Somebody's got to tell you."

I nodded my head yes, but Abbott didn't even blink.

"What Nichole said she witnessed," he said, "was the accident. She was sitting in the bus up front next to you, Dolores. I guess I was the only other witness, but I was driving a ways behind you, and not paying much attention, either. So what Nichole had to say counted a whole lot. Because they subpoenaed me, Mitchell Stephens did, and when they did that, I told him and the other lawyers that I frankly couldn't say for sure how fast you were driving that bus that morning. When it went over. Which is the gospel truth. All I knew was the speed that I myself *usually* drive up there. Fifty-five to sixty, is what I told them. Nichole, though, she was very certain. She said she remembered it clearly—she knew how fast you were going when the bus went off the road. That's what she told them."

He paused and looked back down at the track, where the winner of the first heat had been determined: car number 43, a pink beetle-shaped Hudson with "Death to the APA" painted across the roof, "Tatum" on the hood, and "The Bone Rules" along the sides. That was the driver's name for himself, I guess—The Bone. In reality, it was Richie Green, a good kid, not really a bone. Tatum is Tatum Atwater. Wreckers and pickups with winches were rapidly hauling the smoking carcasses of the losers off the track and onto the field, and a second group of sixteen cars was lining up to enter the arena.

"How fast did the child say I was going?" I asked him. To save Abbott the trouble, I suppose.

"Seventy-two miles an hour is what she told them." He wouldn't look at me when he said it, but he said it. I have to hand Billy that.

"She told them I was driving seventy-two miles an hour?"

"Yes. Dolores, I thought you knew."

"How would I know?"

"No way, I guess. I just figured you knew, like everybody else. I'm sorry, Dolores," he said.

"No, don't be sorry to me, Billy. Not as long as you know the *truth*."

"Well, yeah, I know the truth."

"That's two of us, then," I said. There were three of us, of course, counting Nichole. Well, four, actually, counting Abbott. But Abbott knew the truth because he happened to believe me, and I only assumed that. Abbott hadn't been there with me that January morning, out on the Marlowe road with the snow coming down and the sight of the mountains and the valley so lovely that when you see it your legs go all watery and you have to hold your breath or you'll say something foolish, with the children all easy and at play in the school bus, and me in charge of picking them up on time at their homes scattered across the town and carrying them over those narrow winding roads for miles, until we came to the big road and began our descent to the school in the valley below. Abbott wasn't with me then; I was alone.

Now, in addition to the truth, I knew what nearly everyone else in town knew and believed, and if they didn't, they were learning and coming to believe it this very minute, probably, from the person standing or sitting next to them here at the fair—they were learning that Dolores Driscoll, the driver of the school bus, was to blame for the terrible Sam Dent school bus accident last January. They were learning that Dolores had been speeding, that she had been driving recklessly, driving the bus in a snowstorm at nearly twenty miles an hour over the limit, that Nichole Burnell, the beautiful teenaged girl who'd come out to the fair in her wheelchair, a child who herself had almost died in the accident, had sat next to the driver, that Nichole had seen how fast the vehicle was moving, that she had told it to a court. Dolores Driscoll was the reason why the bus had gone off the road and tumbled down the embankment and into the icy water-filled sandpit. Dolores Driscoll was the reason why the children of Sam Dent had died.

What did I feel then? I remember feeling relieved, but that's a weak word for it. Right away, without thinking once about it, I felt as if a great weight that I had been lugging around for eight or nine months, since the day of the accident, had been lifted from me. A huge stone or an albatross or a yoke. One minute it was there, and because it had been there for so long, I had grown used to it; and the next minute it was gone, flown away, disappeared, and I was suddenly able to recognize what a terrible weight I had been carrying all these months. That's strange, isn't it? You'd expect me to feel angry, maybe, unjustly accused and all that. But I didn't. Not at all. I felt relieved. And, therefore, grateful. Grateful to Billy Ansel, for revealing what Nichole had done, and grateful to Nichole for having done it.

And for once, possibly for the first time in our life together, I did not know what Abbott was thinking or feeling. Even more peculiar, I didn't care, either. He might be angry, he might be resentful, he might even think I had lied to him. I didn't care; it didn't matter what Abbott thought. I felt myself singled out in a way that had not happened to me before, and although I have never experienced such a solitude as that, I have also never felt quite so strong.

I looked over at Abbott; he had no idea what I was feeling, and it actually pleased me that he didn't.

As soon as Billy had ceased speaking, Abbott had swung his attention back to the derby. The second heat was now almost over. Billy was concentrating on his bottle, and when he wasn't drinking, he appeared to be studying his feet. Stacey Gale was like Abbott, all caught up, apparently, in the smoke and the furious sound and sight of the cars smashing one another to bits.

I said nothing. I just sat there and contemplated my strange new feelings, letting them wash over me—relief, gratitude, aloneness—naming them to myself as they came, one hard upon the other, in a series, or a cycle would be a better word, for each wave of feeling seemed to be the direct and sole cause of the next. Down below, the single surviving car, a mangled old Impala with a front fender crumpled and dangling off it, was pronounced the winner, and the tow trucks rushed into the arena and hauled the losers off, and the cars in the third heat came roaring in.

Suddenly, Abbott raised his left arm, his good one, and pointed. I followed his finger down to the arena and saw what he saw, old Boomer, my Dodge station wagon. Number 57, it was. Jimbo Gagne had painted the car black and had written the number and his first name and a peace symbol across the hood in big yellow letters. Along the side was the name of the sponsor, not-quite-free advertising for Billy Ansel's Sunoco station. And on the top of the wagon, in huge letters, he had painted the word BOOMER. I might not have recognized it otherwise. All the window glass was gone, of course, and the trim and hubcaps, and with no muffler it was blatting like the others, but I could identify its beat, and it sounded pretty good to me: Jimbo had not just got it running again, after it had sat dead on cinder blocks for years, but got it running smoothly. It looked good too—glossy black all over, with no chrome, no gaudy decorations; like a ghost car, it was dark and unadorned and all business. The car was positioned in the middle of the pack, not an advantageous spot in a demolition derby, but it was bigger than most of the others in the heat, and like Jimbo had said, it had a good power-to-weight ratio— plenty of both.

What happened then surprised me at the time but seems natural now. The flag was dropped, and the cars commenced to smash into one another, ramming each other from behind, the stronger cars quickly driving the weaker against the heavy steel railing in front of the stage and grandstand, shoving them sideways and backward through the mud, with wheels spinning and tires smoking and clods of dirt flying through the air. And every time Boomer got hit, no matter who hit it, the crowd roared with sheer pleasure. A car with the words "Forever Wild Development Corp." painted over the hood slammed Boomer from the side, driving it into another car, the Cherokee Trail Condominium car, and everyone in the stands stood up and cheered. I could see Jimbo wrestling with the wheel, frantically trying to regain control, shoving the gearshift forward and back, rocking Boomer until it was freed from the Cherokee Trail car, when another car hit it from the front and sent it up against the rail, pinning it there, and everyone cheered happily to see it. But somehow, before the referees were able to slap it with one of their flags and pronounce it out, Jimbo got it moving again, and Boomer charged back into the pack in the middle. Seven or eight of the cars were dead by now, stalled, trapped against the rail or boxed in between two other dead cars and unable to move. But Boomer was still alive.

My heart was pounding furiously. I was standing now, everyone was standing, and if he hadn't been positioned at the top of the stairs, Abbott wouldn't have been able to see. I hoped that Nichole, at the other side of the grandstand, could see this. Everyone wanted to see Boomer get hit, and again and again they got their wish, as Jimbo seemed unable to get free of the pack long enough to do any of the hitting himself. The other drivers were ganging up on Boomer, going around one another, abandoning good clear shots at nearby cars for a glancing shot at

Boomer. Its front bumper had been torn off, and the right front fender dangled like a broken limb. Jimbo kept working, though, and the old engine wouldn't let go, and every time one of the other cars slapped Boomer from the side or rear and sent it into the guardrail or against one of the stilled cars piled up in the middle, Boomer would come to life and chug back for more.

Until finally there were only three cars left that could still move, and they were moving slowly, like prizefighters with all the fight gone out of them, coming forward on instinct now, bashing one another blindly, stupidly, straight ahead, again and again. There was a torn-up Ford Galaxie four-door from Chick Lawrence's garage in Keene, with Tom Smith driving, and I recognized JoAnn Bruce's old brown Eagle, sponsored by Ethel's Dew Drop Inn in Willsboro and driven by JoAnn's cousin Marsden. All the other cars were smoldering in dented and bent heaps, permanently stopped and eliminated. The Galaxie was at the left of Boomer, and the Eagle was at the right, and at last it looked like certain elimination for Boomer and Jimbo Gagne.

The crowd started to applaud then, clapping hands the way they had when Nichole Burnell had first arrived. They didn't cheer; they just applauded. The drivers in the Galaxie and the Eagle revved their motors and spun their wheels and lurched toward Boomer, stuck in the middle, and suddenly it seemed like everyone in the stands stopped clapping at once and the grandstand went silent, as the two cars crossed the space between them, on a line toward the black station wagon sitting at the center of that space. Boomer was held by the mud, with its rear wheels blurred and tires sending up dark gray smoke and chunks of dirt. Jimbo wrestled with the gearshift but couldn't seem to shift and rock the car free. It was a terrifying moment—in my memory, it takes place in utter silence, and everyone is watching with great seriousness, as if a matter of terrible importance is being settled before them, instead of this dumb small-town demolition derby.

And then it happened. Boomer backed slowly away, a few inches, a foot, three feet—just enough to miss the charge first of the Galaxie and then, a split second later, of the Eagle—and unable to swerve away in time, the two cars hit each other instead of Boomer, and when Jimbo saw that, he shifted into first gear and shot straight ahead, right against the two of them, spinning them away and half around again. The crowd erupted joyously, filling the night air with wild shouts and cries, and when Jimbo had Boomer lined up on the Eagle, with the rear bumper headed straight toward the right front end of the other car, the people hollered for him to do it! Do it! *Do it!* and when he smashed into the fender and wheel and tore the steering rods of the Eagle, stopping it dead where it stood, and the official smacked it with the flag, the crowd jumped up and down and yelled with delighted approval and slapped each other on the shoulders and backs.

Then Jimbo went after the Galaxie, which was struggling in the mud to turn and protect its front end. Boomer was moving smoothly now; Jimbo had control of it. He spun the steering wheel, got Boomer backed away from the wreckage of the Eagle, and turned and aimed its rear end, which still had the bumper attached, toward the Galaxie. The black station wagon came on slowly, chugging and slogging across the open ground between them, while the Galaxie tried to turn, to take the blow from behind. People were calling out Boomer's name now, almost chanting it: Boo-mer! Boo-mer! Boo-mer! At that instant Jimbo squeezed a last burst of speed out of the old station wagon, and it slammed into the Galaxie cleanly, catching it on the rear door, just behind the driver, driving it sideways through the mud into the heap of cars beyond it, where it ended jammed tightly against them, unable to move. The official scrambled across the arena and whacked the Galaxie on the hood, and Boomer had won.

Everyone in the place was happy. Even Abbott had a grin on his face. I myself was neither happy nor disappointed. I remember having decided beforehand that as soon as this heat was over, regardless of how it ended, we must leave this place. Or I must, and Abbott would have to leave with me. Naturally, I was glad when it turned out that my old car had emerged victorious over the others. Glad for Jimbo Gagne, glad for the town of Sam Dent, glad, I suppose, for Billy Ansel's Sunoco station too. But that's a trivial kind of pleasure. Not what I'd call happiness.

To tell the truth, up there in the stands, after Billy had revealed to me what everyone in town now regarded as the truth, in the passage of but a few moments' time I had come to feel utterly and permanently separated from the town of Sam Dent and all its people. There was no reason for me to want to stand up there alongside them in the grandstand, to help them cheer first to see a car once owned and driven by Dolores Driscoll get destroyed by a bunch of other cars and then join in when the very same people cheered to see it turn and destroy the others. This demolition derby was a thing that held meaning for other people, but not for me.

I do not believe that Nichole Burnell could have joined them, either; nor would any of the other children who had been on the bus with me that morning. All of us—Nichole, I, the children who survived the accident, and the children who did not—it was as if we were the citizens of a wholly different town now, as if we were a town of solitaries living in a sweet hereafter, and no matter how the people of Sam Dent treated us, whether they memorialized us or despised us, whether they cheered for our destruction or applauded our victory over adversity, they did it to meet their needs, not ours. Which, since it could be no other way, was exactly as it should be.

Nichole Burnell, Bear Otto, the Lamston kids, Sean Walker, Jessica and Mason Ansel, the Atwater and the Bilodeau kids, all the children who had been on the bus and had died and had not died, and I, Dolores Driscoll—we were absolutely alone, each of us, and even our shared aloneness did not modify the simple fact of it. And even if we weren't dead, in an important way which no longer puzzled or frightened me and which I therefore no longer resisted, we were as good as dead.

"Abbott," I said, "let's go now. It's time for us to leave."

Without waiting for an answer, I stepped behind his wheelchair, released the brake, and tipped it toward me on its rear wheels, preparing to thump it down the stairs, one step at a time. It would be a bumpy ride for him, but I knew he could take it. He's not as fragile as he looks.

But as I rolled him to the edge of the landing, a young fellow seated in the row in front of me stood up and, to my surprise, turned to help. I recognized him but did not know him personally. He was from Sam Dent, one of Carl Bigelow's sons, I think, a bearded potbellied young man wearing a John Deere duck-billed cap, a squinty-eyed fellow who looked like he did a lot of beer drinking down to the Rendez-Vous, one of a hundred young men in town just like him. He wanted to give me a hand. Another man suddenly appeared on my other side, an older man who looked like a summer person, gray-haired, trim, in sandals and Bermuda shorts and blue dress shirt. Then a third and a fourth man moved into place, and before I could say a word, they had lifted Abbott's chair and were carrying him smoothly down the stairs.

I followed along behind. The crowd had gone silent now, and it seemed that everyone had decided to watch us descend the stairs. I held my head up and tried to look like I didn't notice. When I reached the ground, I said thanks to the four men, and took over Abbott's wheelchair, and pushed him quickly through the gate. As I myself exited the grandstand, I glanced back and saw that the fourth heat of the derby had begun, and the crowd had gotten itself attentive and noisy all over again. Even Billy Ansel. Life goes on, I might have said, if there had been anyone to hear me. Nichole Burnell I could not see from there.

The sky was a pale sheet of light sent up from the fairgrounds, but the field was dark as we crossed it toward the parking lot, passing the hulks of wrecked cars, idling pickups, and tow trucks. The grass was wet with dew. Except for a couple of drivers seated or snoozing in their vehicles, everyone was over by the stage and the railing, watching the derby, and the sound of the cars as they roared back and forth and collided with one another was dulled and dimmed, softened, like background noises in a bad dream. Over by the midway, the Ferris wheel spun slowly, rising and falling in the distance like a gigantic clock. The faint music of the merry-go-round mingling with the gravel-voiced calls and come-ons of the midway barkers was strangely sad to me; it was like the sound of child-hood—mine, Nichole's, everyone's. Even Abbott's. Our childhoods that were gone forever but still calling mourn-fully back to us.

There's not much more to tell. I got Abbott to the van, situated him by the side door and lowered the lift for him, raised him up and locked the wheelchair into place next to the driver's seat. Then I came around and got in myself and started driving. We departed quickly from the parking lot, which was pretty much filled, with no more cars arriving this late and no one but us leaving this early, and soon we were on the road, headed home.

When the fairgrounds and all its illumination were sufficiently behind us, the sky darkened nicely, and the stars seemed to come out all at once, a wide swath of them spreading like sparkling seeds overhead. It was a clear night, fresh and cool, and I knew that autumn was going to come on fast now, the way it does up here.

Over to my left, the East Branch of the Ausable ran

through the darkness, and a dark spruce woods hove up on my right. At the edge of the road, low and close to the ground, first on one side, and then on the other, I began to see the eyes of animals suddenly flash and glitter as I passed along the way, reflecting my headlights back at me and then as quickly flaring out. For a brief second, though, their eyes were pure white and flat, like dry, coldly glowing disks, and it was as if the animals had all come to the edge of the forest, and there by the side of the road they had waited and watched for me, until I had passed them by and the safe familiar darkness had returned.

BAN   Banks, Russell,
              1940-

           The sweet hereafter.

$20.00

		DATE	12/96